Reviews for the PRECIOUS GEMS series
By EM Lynley

Rarer Than Rubies (Book 1)

Recommended Read at Guilty Pleasures

"…the story line moves fast and is filled with wonderful descriptions of food and culture in Bangkok and the surrounding countryside….. filled with mystery, lost treasure, gangster bad guys, an intriguing hottie who keeps popping up, and a romance writer who's stronger than he knows. This book is part travelogue, romance, and hot sex between two sexy men! If any of these appeal to you, this book's for you!"

Joyfully Jay—4.25 stars

"*Rarer than Rubies* is a fantastic beginning to EM Lynley's *Precious Gems* series. Treasure hunting, action and adventure, unlikely love, and mystery are only a few of the main elements in this story. The action scenes were fantastic – suspenseful and dangerous. The love-making was hot and dirty as well as sweet and tender." —Crissy

Mrs. Condit's Reviews – 4 Sweet Peas

"…an action-packed, suspenseful love story… we are treated to some vivid descriptions of the land and the food. Ms. Lynley went into a lot of description and I felt like I was there on the streets enjoying the amazing food. The story does have a great HEA but I could see more adventures for these two." —Lady McNeill

Reviews for the PRECIOUS GEMS series
By EM Lynley

Italian Ice (Book 2)

Mrs. Condit's Reviews—4.5 Sweet Peas

"Overall a great blend of action, adventure and romance! … one thing I've loved about both books in the series is the amount of details when it comes to the setting. After finishing *Italian Ice* I really want to go visit Italy, see Sicily and the volcano Stromboli. Ms. Lynley does an amazing job describing the sites that I could see the houses, the islands, the ferries, the artifacts." —Lady McNeill

Literary Nymphs—4.5 Nymphs

"The chemistry between the two still exists however, and the passion they display really heats up the pages." —Critter Nymph

Night Owl Reviews—4 Stars

"Trent and Reed make for an interesting storyline to keep readers going. In the first book the attraction and suspense of their relationship had just started and with *Italian Ice* it just got better. The humor also added to the spice of the romance and suspense. I highly recommend this one for the suspense and humor as well as continuing the storyline from *Rarer than Rubies*. You have a very good read here." —Sandra

THE DELECTABLE SERIES

Brand New Flavor by EM Lynley
An Intoxicating Crush by EM Lynley
Lighting the Way Home by EM Lynley & Shira Anthony

PRECIOUS GEMS BY EM LYNLEY

Rarer Than Rubies
Italian Ice
Jaded

ALSO BY EM LYNLEY

Disguises
Hostile Takeover

Published by DREAMSPINNER PRESS
http://www.dreamspinnerpress.com

Jaded

EM LYNLEY

Published by
Dreamspinner Press
5032 Capital Circle SW
Suite 2, PMB# 279
Tallahassee, FL 32305-7886
USA
http://www.dreamspinnerpress.com/

ISBN: 978-1-62798-202-3
Digital ISBN: 978-1-62798-017-3

Printed in the United States of America
First Edition
November 2013

With gratitude to all the wonderful people I met and worked with during the five years I spent in Japan. Your kindness and hospitality has stayed with me in the years since I left, and I cherish the memories I made with you.

I hope I've managed to convey the crazy mix of old, new, wild, and wonderful that comprises modern Japan.

Special thanks to the real people who inspired Motofuji, Shindo, and Kobayashi.

AUTHOR'S NOTE

AS SOME of my readers know, I have set the Precious Gems series in countries where I have spent extended periods of time. One of my goals has been to share the excitement, wonder, and respect that accompany an in-depth knowledge of a place and a love for the people who live there.

Japan is no exception.

I lived and worked in Japan for five years during the late 1990s. I held a variety of jobs, for a variety of reasons, but for most of the time I worked in the international banking world as a financial markets economist. I dreamed of working in Japan since my freshmen year at the University of Michigan and my very first Japanese language class, and the day I landed in Japan was one of the most exciting of my life.

Life for a foreigner in Japan is quite different than for a Japanese, and foreign women have a whole other existence than Japanese women. That may be changing now, but it defined my time in the country, even though I spoke fluent Japanese during the time I lived in the country and had many Japanese friends. For that reason, the observations about Japan and Japanese culture here are very much from a foreigner's perspective, and completely my own.

Trent Copeland might have been me during the first confusing weeks I spent in the country, though thankfully I was never arrested. But I experienced many of the same surprises and wonder at the myriad paradoxes found in modern Japan. Over the years I traveled to cities outside of Tokyo and was lucky to experience many aspects of the traditions from a more Japanese perspective, thanks to my many Japanese friends.

I loved the five years I spent there, and it took me a long time to get used to living in California when I moved back. For years, my main group of friends included others who had lived in Japan, because we shared so many memories, even if we had just met.

I hope my readers will take away an understanding of my fascination with the country and culture and be inspired to someday visit Japan.

I owe a debt of gratitude to Thea Nishimori, who set me straight where my memory was hazy and provided details of how the country has changed in the years since I left. Not to mention providing a wealth of information on Japanese jails and prisons. Just in case I run into trouble on my next trip.

PROLOGUE

THIS ALL started with a knock at the door, Trent thought as he paced back and forth on the tatami mats covering the floor of the small cell. An innocent knock on the door and his desire to try something new, to push himself past his usual limits. He hadn't expected it to turn out like this. Should he have brought Reed? Reed would never have said Trent wasn't ready for something like this, but he suspected that's what Reed really thought.

No. Reed was wrong. Trent was ready, had been ready for a while, and it was just what he needed. It wasn't his fault it had turned out like this.

A knock sounded on the door and a tray of food appeared through a slot in the door. He took the tray and muttered thanks.

More rice and vegetables, and a piece of fish. And some tea. A far cry from the sumptuous feast he'd enjoyed a few nights earlier.

He grabbed the teacup and gulped it down. He couldn't stand to eat another mouthful of rice, but his stomach growled. It could be worse. It could be a hell of a lot worse. He picked up the bowl and the pair of flimsy chopsticks he couldn't control very well. He scooped gobs of rice and vegetables out of the bowl and pushed them into his mouth. It only took a couple of minutes to finish the portions. Too small for someone his size. He hoped the nice guard was working tonight, the one who'd get him another bowl later on if he asked. Even another bowl of rice was fine when you were hungry.

It wasn't the food, or the cell, or even that he didn't understand most of what was said to him. The worst was not knowing what would happen to him.

Reed had been through this, only he hadn't been in a clean cell with a sink and regular meals. Thinking how much worse Reed's experience in Myanmar had been only served to depress Trent further. His stomach roiled, but it wasn't from hunger.

He leaned down to put the bowl back on the tray, and then he noticed the note. A folded-up piece of paper with handwritten Japanese on the top.

He picked up the paper and lay back down on his cot. Then he unfolded it.

1

TRENT PILED out of the SUV with the others in his group. They dropped low, holding their weapons and moving as silently as possible. He kept close to the man in front of him, and they took their positions as the leader determined the best approach. There were two men inside—according to the intel—and the group was to apprehend them.

Trent kept his eyes on the leader, watching for the hand signals giving silent orders. He was to cover the leader as he approached the door, while other members of the team fanned out around the rustic shack. They thought there were drugs in there with the men, but they had to be ready for any surprises.

The group leader glanced back at Trent and locked gazes before he moved toward the door, crouching low so no one inside could see them. Trent used the suspects' car for cover. He had a good view of the door as well as through the front window—two men sitting inside at a table in dirty white T-shirts.

The leader stood and shouted a warning. The men inside jumped in surprise. One headed for the back of the shack while the other came out of the front door.

"Hands on your head!" the leader shouted.

The man obeyed and Trent moved close, keeping an eye on the suspect while the leader trained his weapon on him and forced him to his knees. When Trent was five feet from them, the suspect leapt up and grabbed the leader's weapon from him. Trent pointed his own weapon at the man, but less than a split second passed before the suspect turned the leader's gun on him and the leader fell to the ground.

Trent aimed, but before he could squeeze off a shot, the suspect's shirt erupted in a splatter of blue.

They used paint, not bullets, in these exercises, but the suddenness of the shot still shocked Trent and threw him off. He fired, but his own shot went wide. Now he heard gunfire from the other side of the house. He couldn't worry about what was happening there—his role was covering the front door, and his partner, but he'd botched that up royally. Had this been a real suspect with real ammo, his partner would have been dead. Maybe Trent too.

The suspect dropped the weapon, and Trent's leader stood up—as if from the dead—and turned toward him. "Copeland, what happened?"

Trent froze, uneasy in the man's powerful glare. He shook his head. "I didn't shoot fast enough." It hadn't been the first time. He'd let all but one of his partners die in these training exercises.

"What's holding you back?" This question came from the suspect—in reality one of the FBI's firearms and tactics instructors. By now the rest of the men and women in the training unit had come around to the front of the house. They were at Hogan's Alley, the make-believe town where the FBI held training sessions in order to give agents a taste of real fieldwork.

"I don't know." Trent looked at the rest of the team. None of them had paint on their clothes—none of them had been shot or "killed." Only the other "suspect"—another instructor—had been hit. Everyone else on the team had done their jobs correctly. "I didn't want to shoot until I knew he was gonna shoot."

"He grabbed the leader's weapon…."

"I know. I just couldn't believe that. How Marlow let his weapon get taken. It threw me off."

The others looked at their feet as the instructors dissected the errors in the exercise. No one had gotten a perfect score, though no one else had let another man die. "Copeland, this exercise scenario was designed for the suspect to attempt to disarm one agent. The point was for the second—that's you—to spot the danger and neutralize him before he took down an agent."

"I didn't know that." Trent frowned.

"You're not supposed to know what's going to happen, Trent. Real life doesn't have a script. The agents in the back of the shack faced the same scenario, but the second took appropriate action."

Trent wanted to remind them he was just a writer, not a real law enforcement officer. But he'd signed up for this training with the understanding he wouldn't ask for or receive special treatment. "I'll do better next time."

"I know you will, Copeland." The instructor slapped Trent on the back as the team climbed into the SUV and headed back to the main FBI Academy campus for more tactical sessions.

Trent was the worst in the group when it came to these exercises. He didn't belong here. Today had proved that to him, as well as to everyone else in the course. Why had he thought he could do this?

He knew the tactics, and he was surprisingly good on the firing range—surprising to everyone else—but he couldn't stomach shooting someone face-to-face, even with a paint gun. Because most FBI agents used their guns in this kind of close-range combat, the FBI had redesigned the entire firearms training program in recent years to ensure agents had the skills and determination for the situations they would most likely face on the job.

"Tomorrow's the final run in TEVOC," Randi Boorman said as she let her dark curls loose from the tight ponytail she'd worn for the training. She punched Trent on the knee as they rode back from Hogan's Alley. "You ready for that?"

"Yeah. I'm pretty good at it." It was Trent's favorite part of the training that Reed and his boss Tom White had suggested after their return from Italy six months earlier. Reed wanted to make sure Trent could at least protect himself, even if he wasn't ready to lead a raid on a shack of suspected drug dealers.

THE FOLLOWING day the trainees—most in one form of law enforcement or another, many of whom had been in administrative roles and had let their field skills deteriorate—suited up at the start of the two-mile driving obstacle course for what would be their final exam on this portion of the training.

The goal of TEVOC—the Tactical and Emergency Vehicle Operations Center—was teaching evasive and pursuit driving tactics. Nowhere else could you race around a track, skidding and spinning, without getting hurt or into trouble. Trent had surprised himself that he had a real aptitude for these maneuvers. He never much liked driving in LA, but on the course he handled sharp turns with ease and didn't back away from close pursuit. Helmets and race-car versions of seatbelts made him feel safe enough. And there was no LA traffic to contend with.

"Here's the order of drivers: Chen, Boorman, Copeland, Fielder, Chavez…." The instructor shouted the full roster of names, then posted the list on a board near the edge of the track. He wore the ubiquitous dark FBI baseball cap and carried a stopwatch, binoculars, and a clipboard. Two cars stood at the head of the track, both American made and both pretty banged up. Trent wondered how often they replaced them.

"Who's playing the suspect today?" Chen asked. During training, one instructor drove the getaway car and the other coached the trainees, giving tips and evaluating their performance, but both their usual instructors were on the track with them. Today they had brought in someone else to drive, someone whose tactics they were unfamiliar with.

"No idea." Randi Boorman put a hand up to shield her eyes from the sun's glare and stared at the front car—the one the trainees would be chasing. "Can't see a thing. He's wearing a helmet."

"It's probably a really hot chick, and you guys will be embarrassed when you can't catch her." Rita Chavez laughed as she explained her theory.

"You know, if one of us guys said that, we'd get a write-up for sexual harassment," Bob Fielder said, and the other guys—including Trent—nodded in agreement.

"Well, if I were in the getaway car, you'd be eating my dust!" Chavez taunted. She was the best driver in the group.

Trent watched as Chen drove off after the suspect's car. Despite some impressive moves, he never caught up, and at one point it looked like Chen might go right off the course. The training cars were modified so they wouldn't roll over, which disappointed Chavez, who didn't stop trying to tip one anyway. Trent was glad he never broke the law, because knowing Rita Chavez, an LAPD officer, was out on the streets of LA scared the crap out of him.

Boorman drove second, and Trent studied the getaway driver's tactics during these first two rounds, but didn't spot any pattern to his maneuvers. He'd be difficult to catch. Trent went over which tactics he'd use in each situation if he were driving. It made his head spin, but it kept the jitters at bay as he waited his turn. He had to do well here, since he'd fucked up all the tactical portions. He wasn't being evaluated like the others, but he still wanted a passing score. He just might manage that if he got a good score on the track.

The instructor called out Trent's name, and he donned a helmet and strapped himself into the driver's seat. He took a deep breath and decided he'd push his limits today. He was going to catch the bastard in the getaway car, no matter what.

The horn sounded and the suspect peeled away. Trent floored his car and sped after it. He had to maneuver through a course of traffic cones in some sections of the track, while others were clear for passing or other pursuit maneuvers. They'd be scored on how they handled each obstruction and lose points for hitting cones. Trent found himself gaining on the suspect once he was out of the cone zone. The guy swerved sharply around a curve and Trent took a chance trying to pass from the outside.

He needed a lot more speed to make it, and he really had never tested the limits of this vehicle. He saw the quarter-mile marker—they were nearly at the end of the course—and he made a risky move on the next curve, this time skidding to the inside of the suspect's car. The car came close enough to smash its side mirror against Trent's passenger door. His heart stopped as he straightened out of the turn and floored it, letting instinct take over, not consciously thinking about when to brake or when to gun it. His tires screeched before he felt them lose their grip on the track, but he steered into the skid and positioned his car in a way that forced the suspect to stop or ram right into the side of his vehicle.

He'd caught the bastard! Trent's chest hurt, and he realized he couldn't remember breathing. He put the car in park, and before he could open the door, his fellow trainees were running to the car and shouting, pulling the door open and slapping him on the back.

"Jesus, Trent, you nearly killed me on that run, and I was just watching." Randi slapped his helmet so hard he thought he saw stars. "Great job, man!"

Trent fought to catch his breath, beaming at the compliments from his peers and the nods of approval from the two instructors. Then the suspect's car door opened and a man stepped out. He walked up to Trent and his buddies before pulling off his helmet.

"I surrender, Trent."

Reed? Trent wasn't sure he was seeing correctly. Maybe he had hit his head. "Reed? Reed!"

Trent threw his arms around Reed and pulled him into a tight hug. Then he realized what he was doing and stepped back. He could feel warmth spreading across his face. "Ah. Sorry."

The other trainees burst out laughing. "Your boyfriend, I guess?" Randi asked.

"Yeah."

"Gonna cuff him?" That comment elicited couple of catcalls, and had the others laughing, including the instructors. "I sure would." That was Rita Chavez.

"Not yet. I'll give the rest of you a chance to chase him. But he goes home with me, even if you catch him."

"I'd say you passed this unit, Trent," Reed said as he stepped away from Trent. "Now, who's next?" He put the helmet back on and got back into the getaway car.

OUT OF the rest of the trainees, only two others caught Reed: Chavez and Bill Ritter, a tall, quiet man from one of the Carolinas. Trent couldn't remember which since he always got them mixed up anyway. Chavez got the top score, but Trent came in a close second—much to everyone's surprise.

Reed joined them all for dinner and a couple of celebratory beers. Trent's buddies peppered him with questions, about Trent, about Reed's missions, and about the Bureau in general. He answered what he could and kept catching Trent's eye. Trent liked showing Reed off to his new friends and he was glad Reed had chosen today to visit—rather than the day he got three other people killed over in Hogan's Alley. He hoped the instructor wouldn't tell Reed and that the other trainees wouldn't refer to it in front of him.

Finally, Trent got Reed alone back in his room in the trainee dorm. He'd never been more thankful for single rooms. But the Bureau respected its trainees and the new agents who usually used these rooms. This particular "short course" was taught between sessions of the eighteen-week-long New Agent Training. Trent had enjoyed the four weeks he'd spent at Quantico, and he'd been so busy he hadn't had time to miss Reed except for the few moments he lay awake in bed before falling into exhausted sleep. But now he realized how long they'd really been apart. As soon as the door was shut and locked, he pounced.

REED LET Trent knock him onto the bed, noticing how he'd gotten leaner and stronger during the month of daily PT and assorted physical challenges. But he looked good. Reed admitted he hadn't expected Trent to be so daring—and skilled—on the TEVOC. He felt some pride bubble up inside, though he didn't have time to dwell on it because Trent rolled on top of him and began to kiss him within an inch of his life.

Pent-up desire blotted out thoughts of everything besides getting naked and reacquainting himself with Trent's body. Reed slid his hands along familiar but firmer muscles as he inhaled the intoxicating scent of Trent he'd never gotten out of his memory. He traced fingertips across the raised scar below Trent's right hip—an unwelcome souvenir of their trip to Italy the fall before. It had been six months, and the scar had lost its raw, red look, but seeing it brought back Reed's fear he'd lost Trent as if it had only happened that morning.

Trent pushed Reed's hand off the scar and distracted him by licking a hot stripe up the underside of Reed's cock. He was almost instantly hard, and he didn't care what Trent did to him as long as it was soon.

"Missed you so much," Trent mumbled against Reed's balls. The vibration sent pleasure shooting through Reed's core, and he knew what he wanted. "Fuck me, Trent."

"Let me just read you your rights first…."

Reed burst into laughter, ruining the moment, but the desire was too strong to stop the momentum now. He was glad he'd put a bottle of lube on the nightstand before Trent attacked.

Trent balanced on his knees, hovering over Reed, and reached for the lube. "Condoms? Why'd you bring those?" Trent wrinkled his brow. "Not sure what I've been up to when I'm away from you?" They'd been tested and didn't use them at home.

"No. Just seemed less messy here in the dorm. Don't know when you'll have time to do laundry, and with people in and out of each other's rooms…."

Trent appeared to process the information for a moment and then shrugged. "Okay. I'll go with that explanation. It's better than any of the alternatives."

"Forget the alternatives. You're the one who caught me today." Reed grabbed a condom packet and unwrapped it.

"So did Rita Chavez." Trent watched Reed roll the condom on him.

"I'm not in bed with Rita Chavez." Reed slathered lube on Trent's firm, gorgeous cock, getting impatient with Trent's need to turn everything into a conversation. Any other time it was part of his charm. But not the first time they were in bed together in a month.

"Not that she didn't try."

"Trent, shut up and—" Trent pushed in with no warning, the generous amount of lube easing his way with just the right degree of friction. Reed let out a sigh and grabbed hold of Trent's hips. He needed Trent in deep, needed Trent to bring his body and soul back to life. He'd been through hell while they'd been apart, and only Trent's energy and vitality could rescue him. He opened himself wider and let Trent work his magic.

At first their movements were awkward and uncoordinated, but after a few tentative thrusts Trent and Reed fell into a familiar, comforting rhythm. Trent seemed to have more energy than ever and Reed came in thick spurts long before Trent had his fill. He maneuvered Reed into several positions before he let himself go and crumpled onto Reed in a sweaty mess.

They lay together on their sides, facing each other. Reed reached out to brush damp strands of hair from Trent's face. Trent ran his fingers over Reed's side, where they encountered a raised red welt. Reed couldn't help flinching at the touch. The spot was still painful even though the stitches had been removed a week earlier.

"You gonna tell me how you got this?"

Reed shook his head. "I can't."

"Can't or won't?"

"Trent. Don't ask."

Trent let out a sigh. Reed hated that sometimes he had to keep secrets from Trent. "National security," they told him. He used it as an excuse because some jobs he didn't want to talk about. Didn't want Trent to know everything about him, about what he'd been forced to do. About things Reed barely admitted to himself once the mission was over. He looked into Trent's eyes and begged silently for understanding.

Trent blinked slowly and licked his bottom lip. He wasn't happy, but Reed knew he'd let it go. The instructors had briefed Reed on Trent's performance on the tactical exercises. He'd never bring it up unless Trent did. But a part of him was glad Trent couldn't pull the trigger on another person—even with a paintball gun on a controlled FBI training mission. He wanted Trent to learn to protect himself, to get away from danger, but shooting someone changed a person forever.

Reed would do anything to keep Trent away from that regret. Anything.

2

THE LAST two days of Trent's training course flew by. Reed watched him graduate—proof he had mastered at least the basics in all areas of instruction—though he didn't earn any official certificate or qualification. That's all Reed had expected, but Trent had surprised him, performing far better than Reed, White, or the instructors had predicted.

They flew back to LA and spent a lazy weekend in bed before Reed had to report for his next assignment. Trent watched him pack the same overnight bag he always used, no matter where he was being sent.

"Reed, do you know where you're going?" Trent lay in bed propped up on pillows as Reed, naked, tossed items in the bag.

"Yes."

"Same place as last time?"

"No."

"Then why are you packing exactly the same things?"

"I'll pick up the credentials—new name, ID, etc., along with the appropriate wardrobe—from a contact with the local field office. You know that."

"I thought maybe now you'd tell me more."

"I don't always know more, until I get there. But I can't tell you about this one."

"I don't see what harm it would do."

Reed let out a loud stream of air. "Colorado. I'm going to Colorado."

"What's happening in Colorado?"

"Trent!"

He could see Reed's usual calm demeanor slipping, and Trent wished he hadn't started asking questions. That wasn't how he wanted this morning to go. He rolled onto his side and slid the top sheet provocatively down his thigh.

"Trent." Reed's tone was a warning, but not as stern as before. "I don't have time."

"Please? I want to give you a proper good-bye." Not that they hadn't had plenty of proper good-byes during the weekend. This would be the real good-bye.

"Oh, Trent," Reed said as he climbed back into bed.

Which is why they'd left late and Reed was glaring at the back of the taxi driver's head. At least he wasn't glaring at Trent. Trent stroked Reed's arm. "We're almost there."

"Trent!"

When the taxi pulled up at LAX, Reed had thirty minutes before take-off. Plenty of time. Trent went inside with him, and they had one last kiss good-bye at the security line. "Love you. Be careful," Trent said and let go.

He watched Reed show his ID at a special entrance, where he was ushered through a gate without having to go through security. Reed turned and blew Trent a kiss.

That broke his brave front, and he felt warm tears sliding down his cheeks. He blinked a couple of times, sniffled, and acted like he wasn't going to burst into sobs as soon as he got back in the cab. This was one of the reasons he went with Reed in a taxi rather than driving him to the airport. It gave them more time together, and Trent didn't have to try and drive home while he was so choked up. So much for the tough guy he hoped he'd become after that training course. Who was he kidding?

For the next two weeks, Trent filled his days with writing and his evenings with dinners, drinks, and films with his friends Beth and Mick, and once with his agent Cassandra. For the first few days, he checked online news from Colorado to see if he could figure out which case Reed was working on. Nothing in Reed's line of work—retrieving stolen or smuggled art—had been reported. Eventually, Trent had to face the fact that Reed probably wasn't even in Colorado and had just made the story up to stop Trent's questions.

Luckily, the FBI training course had given him some good material for the book he was working on, and the writing flowed quickly and smoothly, occupying his brain and his time and making Reed's absence less noticeable.

He pushed himself and finished a decent first draft in record time, prompting Cassandra to host a celebration dinner with plenty of champagne—Trent's favorite—at a new restaurant that described itself as Silk Road cuisine with California influences. They served cocktails with ingredients like basil vodka and beet juice. Reed would absolutely hate the place.

When he got home from dinner, he found a voicemail from Reed explaining that he had been called directly from one case to another with no time for a break. He'd call Trent again as soon as he had some idea when he'd be home.

God, Trent missed Reed. With the book finished, Trent felt restless. The FBI training course had gotten his hopes up that maybe he could be part of Reed's job in some way, go along on an easy recovery, but Reed hadn't even suggested the possibility.

Maybe he didn't trust Trent. He'd gotten all those other agents killed during the course. Trent was too soft; he should have realized the short training course he'd taken wasn't enough to turn him into the kind of man Reed wanted as a partner.

Trent opened the nearest bottle—pineapple vodka, but he didn't care—and drank half of it before he passed out on the couch.

3

THE FOLLOWING morning, Trent woke with a headache, sprawled on the couch—no surprise. When the pounding subsided, he tried to sit up straight, at which point he recalled the message from Reed and his mood took another turn for the worse. He spotted the half-full bottle on the coffee table and contemplated finishing it, but his head and his stomach screamed for him to stop in time.

He pulled himself off the couch and nearly broke his neck when he tripped over Godiva, his Siamese. She flicked her tail and meowed louder than a cat should when her owner had a monster hangover. She kept at it until he fed her, lest he risk his head exploding. Then Trent swallowed some ibuprofen and dragged his sorry ass into the shower. He washed away as much of the night before as hot water and his favorite body wash could manage but felt only marginally better.

He puttered around the kitchen trying to decide how to spend his day. He'd just finished a book and wasn't ready to start a new one yet. But he had some ideas he'd let percolate for a while before settling in to his usual attempt at outlining.

Percolate. That reminded him he hadn't had coffee yet.

He pulled the Italian espresso maker out of the cupboard and decided he wanted a big cup to sip on all morning, rather than a tiny jolt of caffeine. He put the pot back and got the French press out of the cupboard instead and set the kettle to boil while he measured out some coffee—without scattering too much on the counter. He glanced at the espresso maker, recalling the trip to Italy where he'd gotten it. Which only reminded him of Reed again.

He wished he knew more about what Reed was doing. The lack of communication and information made him seem even farther away. Reed's previous assignment had been investigating several pieces brought in from India by an American college student who said he didn't know he couldn't take them out of the country. Reed had to determine whether the story was true, or if the kid was some kind of "art mule" trying to get around export restrictions. Trent liked hearing about Reed's missions after the fact. That was an improvement. Before Italy, Reed had continued working for the Bureau but kept it secret from Trent so as not to worry him. Now Reed didn't keep secrets—unless the Bureau told him to. Trent could handle plenty, but Reed hadn't started trusting him any more than before. Not yet.

He'd learned more than he'd ever need to know about firearms and Bureau procedures, and more than enough agent techniques to take the luster off his former fascination with the television show *Burn Notice*. Trent wasn't exactly on the Bureau track to becoming an agent, but he knew enough to protect himself and disable anyone who wasn't carrying an automatic weapon. Well, almost enough. Just not enough to protect his team.

One thing Trent had learned was just how much he didn't know about doing Reed's job. His respect for Reed and his fellow agents had grown exponentially. He'd also learned how not to get in Reed's way. That was why Trent was bouncing around the apartment in LA while Reed was apprehending bad guys.

The kettle whistled, and Trent poured boiling water into the French press pot and set the timer. He had four minutes. A soft ding-dong caught his attention. He went to the door to discover his landlord standing in the hallway with a small envelope.

"Came registered mail, and you weren't home so I signed for it. Hope you don't mind." The landlord stared at the thick envelope as if hoping Trent would open it up and share the contents with him. He wouldn't.

"Thanks, I appreciate that," Trent lied as he took the packet. The guy stood on the doorstep, peering around Trent, so he started to close the door. He hated being rude, but he suspected the landlord was checking to see if Reed was there. He seemed to have a crush on Reed, and while Trent wasn't worried, it annoyed him. The guy could find his own man. Trent pictured him still standing on the doorstep, staring at the door, and grinned. He liked having a partner who was the object of someone else's crush. With his shoulders straight and back tall, he padded back into the kitchen just as the timer went off.

He pushed down the plunger and poured strong, fresh coffee into his favorite insulated mug, added a large amount of half-and-half and a spoonful—okay, two—of raw sugar, and settled on the couch with the envelope.

The return address said Gallery LMNO. He took a sip, barely avoiding scalding his tongue, and ripped open the packet. It was a monthly financial statement with a direct deposit receipt.

Trent's former partner Marc Nachman had owned an LA art gallery with his sister Leah, and when Marc had died three years earlier, he'd left his share to Trent. Marc's death had left Trent something of a basket case—even he admitted it—and he'd pretty much ignored the gallery in the intervening time. He made good money writing, and the gallery income was a welcome supplement to his finances, meaning he could live very comfortably. Leah ran the gallery on her own. She'd offered to buy out Trent's share, but he'd been unable to make a thoughtful decision at the time, and she'd never pushed him to sell.

Marc had always thought she'd done a great job with the gallery, and Trent had no reason to question any of her decisions. A year ago she'd offered Trent the opportunity to be more than a silent partner if he wanted, but he hadn't taken the suggestion seriously. He also hadn't been emotionally ready to consider it, still too cut up over losing Marc.

Then Trent had met Reed and his life had turned around. He got over Marc and moved forward, emotionally and romantically. Some days Trent almost forgot Marc had ever existed. Marc had decorated the apartment—from the furniture to the granite counters in the kitchen—and all of the artwork had belonged to him, but even so, he was no longer a presence in Trent's life. He had Reed and they were good together. Never better, even after everything they'd put each other through in Italy and the reappearance of Reed's old FBI partner—and lover—Peter Isett.

Trent took a few more mouthfuls of coffee and brought the gallery paperwork into his office. He generally took a cursory look at the statement before filing it away with a folder full of older statements, but this time he noticed Leah had attached a handwritten note.

We need to renew the lease on the gallery space. Please sign these and return them by the 20th.

Love, Leah

It was a nice sunny day—when wasn't it nice and sunny in SoCal?—and he had nothing on the schedule besides feeding Godiva and… well, nothing. He decided to walk to the gallery and hand deliver the documents.

THE GALLERY was less than two miles away, just off Santa Monica Boulevard in Beverly Hills. Despite its proximity to the apartment, he hadn't been there for months—only once since he'd returned from Italy—though he'd spoken to Leah on the phone a few times since then. She and her husband, Jacob, were expecting their first child. He couldn't even remember when he'd last visited, and he felt a stab of guilt. Leah had been wonderful and treated him like family while Trent and Marc had been together, and she'd helped as much as she could after Marc's death, but it had hit her and their family hard. Trent couldn't rely on her to keep him afloat emotionally, but Beth and Cass had been there when he'd needed a shoulder. Now Trent realized he hadn't given back as much to Leah as he wished.

The stroll down Santa Monica took less than half an hour, and the waves and a couple of whistles he got brightened his mood. Not that he'd cheat on Reed, but he liked knowing someone else was interested.

He opened the door, greeted by a wave of air conditioning that nearly froze him to his toes. He felt his nipples peaking and resisted to urge to look and see if they'd punctured holes in his shirt. He moved through the front room, which featured a display of sepia-toned photographs. They were magnificent, some nearly as tall as he was, and he lingered along the first wall, drinking in their beauty.

There were two couples in the gallery, one gay, the two men arm-in-arm, the other a straight couple standing close enough to touch each other. Trent missed Reed. Of course, he'd probably never be caught dead in a place like this. Reed's interaction with art was more Indiana Jones than Beverly Hills. Trent glanced around, refamiliarizing himself with a place where he'd spent a lot of time during another part of his life. He loved the bright clean lines of the place: pale natural wood floors and display panels suspended from the ceiling, instead of solid walls, to retain an airiness. Marc had wanted to redo it with ugly industrial-looking bare concrete floors and distressed metal walls. Thankfully, Leah had talked sense into him. The gallery looked sleek and elegant, yet still rich and welcoming. The concrete and metal would have been cold, but with Leah's design touches, clients felt at home, which made them want to spend more. Overruling Marc's changes had given Trent and Leah a bond almost instantly.

Marc had introduced him to the art world, one he'd had no contact with before, growing up the son of a USDA official in Oklahoma. At first it had been eye-opening and exciting, but as Trent's interest grew, Marc's had waned, driving him to dangerous hobbies like BASE jumping and cliff diving. Trent would have been content to sit in a museum all afternoon, absorbing the colors and style of Impressionist painters, but it had begun to bore Marc.

These photographs reignited that spark in Trent.

"Incredible, aren't they?"

Trent whirled at the voice, startled to see Leah, extremely pregnant, just behind him. "Wow! Is that a whole basketball team in there?"

"Probably not." Leah's laugh fluttered around the room. She was on the short side, as Marc had been.

Trent bit his lip. He might have just insulted her. "Oh. Shit."

"There are two of them, though. So maybe we've got a beach volleyball team in here." She rubbed her belly, covered in an elegant pale-green silk dress.

"Damn, it's good to see you, Leah." Trent leaned down and hugged her, unable to get very close due to the size of her body. "Oh, sorry. Did I hurt you?"

"No. Just about everything seems to get in my way these days."

"I can't believe it's been this long. I didn't mean—"

"Don't worry about it, Trent. I'm just glad to see you. You look so good. Come in back and tell me all about things. Do you have time for lunch? I can order in, or we can go out. I know you used to…."

Trent almost tuned out her words. She'd always been like that, talking and moving on before he could answer her first question. He'd missed her.

"Lunch sounds great. Let's order in." He made that decision to avoid having to consider eating at any of the places he'd been with Marc. He'd gotten over Marc's death, but maybe Leah would feel something if they visited a place they'd both been with Marc.

"Okay."

Twenty minutes later, they sat at a table in her spacious office, chowing down on bento boxes from a place around the corner.

"Hey. You're good with those chopsticks."

Trent shrugged and avoided her gaze. "I guess." He'd gotten good while in Asia with Reed but wouldn't mention that to Leah.

“Tell me about Reed.”

Trent nearly coughed up a piece of tempura shrimp. “Reed?”

“Yes. I want to hear about your trip to Italy.”

“No, you don’t.”

“Why not?”

So many reasons. And none of them had to do with the smugglers. He didn’t reply and concentrated on chewing carefully to avoid any potential embarrassment with the food in his mouth.

“Trent, you don’t have to pretend you’re single. You know that, right?” She sipped tea from a pretty blue porcelain cup the restaurant delivered with their lunch. Later they’d come to pick up the boxes and teapot and cups. It was a civilized, elegant way to do business, compared with the usual Styrofoam and plastic.

Trent turned his gaze on her but looked away again. She had Marc’s eyes. “Leah, I—”

She waved his comment away with her chopsticks and fixed her gaze on his. “We’ve never really had this discussion, but it’s time. It’s past time.”

Trent’s gut clenched. He tapped his chopsticks on the edge of the bento box until she leaned forward and stilled his hand.

“Trent, it’s okay for you to be happy now. You should be happy now. It’s not your fault Marc died. I don’t blame you. No one blames you.” She squeezed his wrist. “You have no reason to be feeling any guilt.”

He let out a breath and cautiously looked at her. “How did you know?”

“One thing you definitely learned from Marc was Jewish guilt.” She grinned.

“What’s that?”

“Catholics feel guilt for things they do, right? Jews feel guilt for something they haven’t done. Like calling your mother or—”

Trent couldn’t remember the last time he’d called his mother either. He burst out laughing, relieved to let go of the guilt that had been eating away at him for much of the past three years.

“Feel better?”

“A little.”

“Good. Me, too. Now eat your lunch. All of it.”

“Practicing?”

"Oh yeah. I'm having twins. It's going to take a lot of work to be a Jewish mother."

They finished lunch over small talk that eventually touched on his life with Reed and Leah's husband's work as an entertainment lawyer. "I can't say *who*, but someone is suing their spouse, claiming the idea for a blockbuster film was theirs, stemming from a conversation they had in *bed*." Despite Trent's begging, she refused to give even a hint.

They gradually wound their way around to safe conversation topics about Marc, though Trent knew a day would come when they'd be able to talk about him more openly. But this had been a start.

"So, you should take a look around the other exhibition right now, if you've got time."

"Sure, I have time. Reed's away for work, and I haven't started my next book yet. I have too much time."

"And money? You okay for that?"

"Yeah, sure. You want me to buy something? The gallery seems to be doing well, but if you need something…."

"We're doing great. Don't you check the statements I send you every month? And you don't have to buy anything. If you like something, let me know. You can borrow a piece."

Trent nodded. Marc had constantly been borrowing pieces from exhibitions. He'd owned quite a bit of valuable artwork as well, but Leah had to help Trent figure out which pieces rightfully belonged to the gallery. Trent hadn't been sorry for her to take some of them back after Marc's death.

"I don't really look at the statements, just notice the direct deposits." He smiled. Thanks to the gallery he never really had to worry about money. Then the smile faded away. He really had left everything to Leah. Suddenly it seemed insensitive for him to take half the profit when he did none of the work.

Now he wandered around the other exhibition. It was a fantastic complement to the dreamy quality of the sepia photographs in the front room. Those were clearly American, but these illustrated a more ancient dreamworld, that of Japan. He definitely had missed this place. Maybe it wouldn't be such a bad idea to bring Reed here after all. Reed loved art, or at least knew a lot about it. He'd had some spectacular pieces in his place in Bangkok when he was supposed to be a shady dealer trying to interest a Triad leader in the Ruby Buddha. Did Reed genuinely enjoy art or was it just a job to him? Trent didn't actually know.

"What do you think of these?"

"They're incredible. I've always loved the woodcuts. Maybe I would like to take one home."

"Sure. Just tell me which."

"How'd you get these? Are there many outside of Japan?"

"More than there used to be."

"Oh, why's that?"

"The economy. You know a lot of Japanese companies and businessmen paid outrageous prices for art back in the '80s and '90s before the economies of both countries collapsed."

Trent nodded. They had stopped in front of an image of a bathhouse. The figures showed a man fondling a woman who was just coming out of the bath, but when he took a closer look, he realized it was a male figure, touching another man. He looked more closely. The penises were drawn with amazing detail. He could feel his cheeks heating up.

"Is this the one you want?"

"Is this real? From 1890? I didn't know it was okay to be gay then, even in Japan."

"Well, I don't know much about it, but that theme is present in several other images in this collection. It's a big selling point for a large portion of our clientele, actually."

Trent realized this print had a red dot next to it, indicating it had been purchased. He noticed the selling price: $1,000. Wow. A quick glance told him the other gay images had also already been purchased.

"Same guy bought all of them. My client will be happy."

"Your client?"

"A Japanese collector who needs cash fast. We priced everything a little below market, given that even American art collectors are feeling the economic pinch."

"Interesting. I've really lost touch with the whole art market. At least the kind that works through a gallery." He smiled. He'd mentioned the two art cases he'd helped Reed with but had only touched the surface. But Leah had been fascinated about the illegal side of the art world.

"You should come back more often. Bring Reed."

"You sure?"

"I want to meet him. You're still part of my family. At least I want you to be. I hope you feel the same way."

"Oh, God, Leah, of course." He leaned down and pulled her into as tight an embrace as he dared, given her condition. She held him tightly and they stayed there, the warmth comforting and familiar, even though both their worlds had changed in so many ways.

A polite cough broke their hug. "I have a question." It was the straight man who had been looking at photographs. His female companion stood next to him.

"I don't want to keep you."

"See you soon, Trent." Leah gave him a quick smile and headed toward the couple.

Trent spent another fifteen minutes looking at a slice of gay Japanese history he never knew about. Did Reed know? There was still one print that hadn't been purchased. He'd give Leah a call and ask to borrow it. Hell, if Reed liked it, Trent would even buy it. He'd get a hefty gallery discount.

THREE DAYS later Trent went back to the gallery to pick up the print. Leah met him in the front room. Most of the photographs now had sold dots next to them.

"You gonna pull that exhibition down early, since it's all sold? Waste of wall space."

"Spoken like a true gallery owner." She had a cryptic look on her face. A Cheshire-cat grin that seemed out of place. "Which leads me into something I wanted to talk to you about."

Trent felt his cheeks warm slightly. He might own part of the gallery, but he still felt guilty about taking money when he didn't do anything around here. "Yeah, about that. Maybe it's time to sell." He glanced around, wondering why finally saying it hurt a little. It wasn't about Marc, though. It was about not walking in here again and knowing he'd see something thrilling and special.

"Oh. I didn't expect that." The smile on Leah's face faded away.

"Is this a bad time? I guess with the babies coming you don't have the cash to buy me out."

"No. It's not that at all. Well, we don't have that much cash lying around, but I was going to ask you something completely different."

"What's that?"

"Come on back." She turned and headed for her office, and Trent followed, curiosity piqued.

Leah settled down at the table at one end of the room.

"Wouldn't you be more comfortable on the couch?" Trent waved a hand in the direction of a sleek, but comfortable, couch near the desk.

"If I sit down, I won't be able to get up without a forklift."

Trent grinned. "Sure." He seated himself across from her at the table where they'd eaten lunch a few days earlier. "What's up? Is something wrong?"

"Not at all. Well, not exactly." She smiled and put Trent at ease. "I mentioned the Japanese collectors trying to unload their artwork. Well, I have a few prospects with fairly extensive collections that need to be examined in person. Usually, I go or send one of our usual appraisers."

"And?"

"Obviously, I'm not prepared to travel, and my Asia expert is tied up with other clients." She paused and gave Trent a deep, appraising stare. "Would you be interested in going to Japan for me?"

"Me?" Trent sat up and blinked. "I don't know anything about Japanese art."

"I know. But you don't have to. There're a few local appraisers in Japan who come highly recommended. But I don't feel comfortable having them handle the whole process until I know I can trust them. And I like giving our prospective clients the personal touch. Would you be interested in going to Japan, meeting the collectors, and overseeing the appraiser's work?"

"I don't know. I wouldn't want to mess things up if I said the wrong thing."

"I don't think either of the clients speak English. You'd have an interpreter, who would make sure you didn't say the wrong thing. Part of their job is smoothing over whatever you say so you don't put your foot in your mouth, or theirs."

Trent laughed. "What else would you want me to do?"

"Take photographs of everything for me, then e-mail them with the appraiser's report. I'll decide which items to take, and you work with the transport company to arrange shipping. It would be two weeks, probably."

"Two weeks in Tokyo?"

"Tokyo and Kyoto. I have one collector in each city and a possible third in Osaka, which is near Kyoto."

"I've always wanted to go to Japan. Especially Kyoto."

"You could take someone with you—Reed?"

Trent loved that idea. Taking a trip to Kyoto, visiting the famous temples and gardens of the ancient capital. "Reed's away now. And I'm not sure we can afford the trip."

"Don't worry about that. The clients are paying, and they'll cover expenses for two people to travel to Japan, as well as the appraisals and interpreter."

"If they pay for the appraisals, how can you be sure they're accurate?"

"Good question. You know more about the business than you think!"

Trent felt his cheeks warming again. Maybe he wouldn't be useless at this after all. Leah's compliments boosted his spirits. "So?"

"I select the appraisers, and the clients only pay the bill. I only use experts who come highly recommended by people I already trust. So far I haven't had any trouble. But your presence should be additional insurance. If they see I've sent a representative, there's less likely to be any monkey business."

"When would you want me to go?"

"Within a week or two. When will Reed be back?"

Trent inhaled. That was always the question. When was Reed coming home? He bit the inside of his lip.

"What's wrong?" Leah's voice dropped to a consoling tone. "Trent?"

"Nothing. I'm not sure about Reed's schedule." He paused. Then he nodded. "But I can't keep making my schedule around Reed's, right?" He waited for Leah's approval before continuing. "I'd love to go, but…." Then a brilliant idea struck him. "Could I bring Beth?"

"Your friend Beth from college? I remember her. Sure." Trent recalled that Beth had been at several events over the years where Marc had invited Leah.

"Her mom's Japanese, and she grew up there till she was in high school. She's been to visit relatives many times since. She minored in Japanese back at the University of Michigan, probably for the easy As…."

"That's perfect. See if she'd want to work as an interpreter. She'd have an all-expenses paid trip and get paid for the work on top."

"She's a struggling screenwriter, so she'd probably be glad for the job, to be honest."

"Sounds great. Why don't you see if she's interested, then let me know your schedules so I can coordinate the trip with the clients and the appraisers in Japan."

"Just like that? Don't you even want to talk to her about it?" Trent thought Leah might have met Beth once or twice during the time Marc had been alive.

"Just like that. I trust you, Trent. You wouldn't have suggested her if you didn't think she'd do a good job, right?"

"Yeah. Right." Trent wasn't so sure of his own judgment, but he liked that Leah had confidence in him. How hard could this be, after all? Looking at some art, taking photos, and smiling and bowing. Piece of cake, right?

TRENT WAS walking on air when he left the gallery with the woodblock print wrapped and tucked under his arm. He'd decided to buy it. He hoped Reed would like it. If not… well, if not, Trent would keep it anyway.

He pulled his phone out of his pocket to call Beth, slowing his pace. A man brushed roughly against his shoulder as he passed.

"Watch where yer walkin'," the man shouted, but Trent ignored him.

Beth answered on the first ring. Bad sign. "Hi, Trent!"

"You busy?" He already knew the answer to that. She'd been struggling with writer's block the past month and hadn't written more than a few pages. She needed this trip as much as Trent needed a change of scenery.

"Nope." Her tone went from peppy to gloomy.

"I've got some good news. Come over to my place."

"Now?"

"Now."

"Okay. See you in fifteen." She disconnected.

At least her mood seemed brighter. Trent picked up his pace and made it home in ten minutes, slightly out of breath. He skipped the elevator and raced up the stairs, enjoying the burn in his quads. He needed more cardio….

He grabbed a glass of iced tea and was looking around the living room for the perfect spot to hang his new print when Beth's distinctive, soft double knock sounded on his door.

"It's open," he shouted.

He unwrapped the print and pulled down a Matisse reproduction. The woodblock would fit perfectly in the space.

"Hey, is this new?" Beth carefully picked up the print.

"Yeah. I got it at Marc's… uh, the gallery." He still called it Marc's gallery; he had to stop thinking of it that way.

"Wow. I've never seen one like this."

"What do you mean?"

"It's two samurai. That's rare. Usually these prints have a man and a younger male partner who wears a woman's kimono or styles his hair like a woman."

"You know a lot about this, huh?" Trent took the print from Beth and stared at the two main figures. The older one wore the traditional samurai topknot with partially shaved head, while the younger had slightly longer hair, pulled up onto his head. One sword stood on a rack at one end of the room, and a second, shorter sword lay on the mat in front of it. The figures lay together on a brilliant blue bed—the hue a trademark of the *ukiyo-e* style of printing, Trent knew that much. Both men had their robes pulled up around their waists, with two very detailed penises in full view, also typical of the style of the erotic version of the traditional Japanese art form.

"It's called *danshoku.*" Beth smiled. "Literally, it means male colors, but *shoku* often has a sexual connotation." She sat on the sofa and watched Trent hang the print. "Up a little on the right…. Too much… a little more."

Trent stepped back to assess the alignment. "Is that what you sound like in bed, too?"

"I don't know. I haven't been in bed with anyone else for a while." Beth frowned. "God, I hope not." Then she let out a chuckle. "Oh, maybe that's why?" She winked. "Seriously, though, that's been a dry spell too."

"Well, sister, I have just the solution."

"Sorry, Trent, I'm not so hard up I'd consider sleeping with Mick."

Trent responded with an exaggerated cringe. "I'd never suggest that to anyone. Don't worry." He shuddered. "What I have in mind is far better."

"Don't keep me waiting!"

"You say that in bed, too?" He sat next to Beth on the couch, and they both looked at the gay samurai. She punched him in the shoulder. Hard.

"Ow. Maybe I'll change my mind on sharing the solution to your problems."

"No! What is it?"

"A trip to Japan. With me."

Beth wrinkled her brow and gave him a sidelong glance. "Huh?"

"I talked to Leah today. She has a couple of prospective clients in Japan. Big collectors who need cash, so they're willing to sell their artwork, and she needs someone to go over to meet them, assess the collections, and oversee sending the work to the gallery. She asked me to go, and I suggested you as my lovely assistant-slash-interpreter."

"Uh-uh. No way I'm going to suck up to some rich guys. That's one thing I hate about Japan. All the formal, polite rigmarole, especially for women."

"All expenses paid, plus a daily rate as interpreter." He told her how much Leah had offered.

"When do we leave?"

"You are *so* easy."

"I am *so* broke. And I'm not writing, so I can't even call myself a starving artist. This *is* just what I need. A nice break—and some money."

"Hey, if you're having trouble, just ask. You know I'd lend you some money." Trent wouldn't consider asking her to repay him but knew her own pride wouldn't let her take any sort of handout.

"It's not that bad. I'm fine for a while, but if I don't sell a piece soon, next year might be tough."

"You're welcome to come by for meals if the price of Cup Noodles goes up."

"Gee, thanks."

"You just need to do the dishes."

She punched him again. He feigned pain as he rubbed his shoulder. "Maybe we can marry you off to some rich Japanese guy."

"I thought you said these guys needed cash. No deal."

"Otherwise you'd be up for that?" He grinned.

"No way." She shook her head so violently her hair slapped Trent in the eye like a whip.

"Okay. I won't make that joke again. Don't worry." He rubbed his eye, this time in some very real pain. "I'll call Leah and tell her you're on board. Then she'll make the arrangements with the clients."

THE NEXT week went by in a blur of preparations. Leah gave Trent and Beth a quick course on the types of artwork the clients owned and what to look out for. Trent would take photos, and along with the appraisals, Leah would decide which pieces she could sell. Trent and Beth would arrange shipment with a reputable international art courier service.

Learning about art and doing research on Japan kept Trent's brain busy all day. In the evenings, he gorged on Japanese films. Even though they provided no useful background for the trip, he most enjoyed samurai movies. He could handle their violence more easily than the brutal yakuza films.

He only had time to miss Reed when he lay alone in their bed. Exhausted, he fell asleep quickly, then each morning felt a wave of guilt that he hadn't missed Reed more. Solitary breakfasts and showers drove the point home, but the excitement of heading to the gallery or meeting with Beth to discuss Japanese customs and etiquette filled his days. He couldn't wait to leave, glad to have something to keep his mind occupied.

4

REED TOOK a cab from the airport. It was late afternoon, and Trent wasn't expecting him back for another week, but he'd wrapped up the case in Ohio and decided to surprise him by coming home early for a change. Usually, Trent met him up at the airport, and Reed admitted he loved seeing Trent waiting for him at the baggage claim, all bright smiles and warm, strong arms wrapped around his aching shoulders. No one had been there to greet Reed for the last decade of coming back from deployments or missions or jobs, and he had quickly grown to love it and look forward to the greeting. He knew Trent enjoyed it, too. Even more than that welcoming hug, Reed was looking forward to giving Trent a very private greeting back home, in the bedroom—if they made it that far.

Damn, he'd missed Trent more than usual. They'd spoken a week earlier, and Trent had mentioned some sort of surprise for Reed. He'd sounded so excited and animated—a notch above Trent's usual level of enthusiasm—but he wouldn't tell Reed why. He'd find out soon enough, but whatever it was could wait. First he wanted to wrap Trent in his arms and kiss him till he didn't know what day it was. Then fall into bed and forget about the job and everything but Trent until they ran out of lube. Maybe they'd take a break for food.

The afternoon traffic was worse than usual, could be a ball game or just for no reason at all. Reed thought he could run home faster than the cab moved on the impacted freeway. The guy had the AC up so high Reed thought he might freeze to death, but rolling the windows down wasn't an option unless he wanted to inhale fumes so dense you could see them. He'd never hated the traffic this much in Bangkok or Hong Kong. In Asia it was part of the charm of the place, but something about LA made the inconvenience more unbearable.

The cab finally exited the 170 freeway at Highland. Half a mile from home, he had the guy double park as he ran inside to a little florist off Sunset and picked up the brightest bouquet they had. This one was a riot of colors, a daring mix of oranges and pinks with spiky purple things instead of that inane fluffy white stuff on most bouquets. Reed didn't have a clue what any of it was called, and he didn't care. All that mattered was that Trent would like it. Next door was a small wine shop, and he bought a bottle of French Champagne and slid back into the waiting taxi for the final leg of his journey home.

Noticing the elevator was on the fourth floor, Reed ignored it. Old Mrs. Jameson lived there, and she pulled the stop button when she was unloading her groceries. It was faster to walk than to wait for her to release the elevator. Reed slung his pack over one shoulder and raced up the stairs two at a time, adrenaline propelling him upwards, and he was barely out of breath at the sixth floor. He dug for his key ring and unlocked the door as quietly as possible.

The apartment was dark. Reed flicked the hall lamp on to see two golden eyes glaring at him. Godiva the cat—certainly not as sweet as her chocolate namesake—meowed loudly and strode away from the door, tail floating regally behind her.

Where was Trent?

He must have left hours ago because otherwise he would have left a light on.

Warning bells went off for a moment, and then Reed relaxed. This was LA. Even Trent couldn't get into too much trouble on his home turf. He'd probably just gone to the library or maybe out for a drink with Beth or Cassandra. So much for the big surprise.

Reed dropped his bag in the hallway and took the Champagne and flowers into the kitchen. He stuck the bottle in the fridge—surprisingly empty considering Trent's love of cooking—and opened cupboards in search of an appropriate vase for the flowers. He checked in every cabinet, some of them twice, and was rooting around in the hall closet before he finally found one large enough. He spent ten minutes fucking around with the flowers to make them look nice and stuck the whole thing on the low table in the living room.

Still no Trent.

Reed unpacked his bag, tossed the laundry in the bathroom hamper, and put his shoes away carefully in the closet. One military habit he'd never been able to break: keeping his gear clean, well-organized, and in good shape. Trent, on the other hand, was a bit of a mess. Not a slob by any means, but he left things around the place in little piles or clusters and wasn't very good about hanging clothes back up. Reed tidied up the bedroom, hoping Trent would come bouncing in at any moment.

No such luck. He straightened up the whole apartment before he started to worry. Still hoping to keep his early arrival a secret, Reed flipped open his cell phone and called Beth. If she wasn't with Trent, she probably knew where he was.

"Hey, Beth."

"Reed? What's wrong? Is Trent okay?"

"That's why I'm calling you. Looking for Trent."

"He's not with me."

"Oh."

"Where are you, Reed?"

"I wanted to surprise him. I'm home early but he's not here."

"No. He wouldn't be."

"Oh? Where would he be, then?"

"I can't tell you."

"Why not?"

"I can't. I promised Trent."

Promised Trent what? What was he doing that they had to hide from Reed? "Beth, you're on the way to pissing me off. Where. Is. Trent?"

"He has a surprise too, so I can't ruin it. But he should be home by now."

"Where is he?"

"Look, let me call him—"

"No. I don't want you telling him I'm back and ruining my surprise."

"Well, then, you'll have to wait till he gets home. You can't have it both ways."

"Fair enough. Is he in LA?"

"Yeah. Of course. He'll be home later, I'm sure. Don't worry about him."

"Too late."

"He's fine."

“Don’t ruin my surprise, Beth… or I’ll kill you.”

“I’m sure you would.” She forced out a little laugh that didn’t sound particularly amused, then disconnected.

Reed started at the phone and shoved it violently in his pocket.

Where the fuck was Trent?

Reed found some beer in the fridge—the last two bottles of his favorite brand—hiding behind some healthy-looking but foul-tasting yogurt drink Trent liked. He popped the top and took a long swig right out of the bottle, then wiped his mouth with the back of his hand. Damn, it tasted good. Nice and cold, and before he knew it, he’d drained the bottle. He tossed it in the recycling bin, grabbed the second bottle, and headed for the couch. He’d wait there till Trent showed up.

So much for a romantic surprise. Reed popped the cap on the beer and settled on the couch. He sipped at this one, wanting to make it last. Usually, Trent stocked up on beer while he was gone, but Reed hadn’t noticed another six-pack in any of the cabinets. Maybe Trent’s surprise was that he’d finished another book. He must have been so busy he hadn’t had time for shopping—or housekeeping. That was fine. It wasn’t Trent’s job. Writing was.

Reed put his feet up on the coffee table and relaxed as much as he could, considering he didn’t know where Trent was. He half hoped Beth would call him and urge him to come home soon. The thought of Trent’s return warmed Reed a little. A little too much, and he shifted position. His cock sure wanted Trent to come home soon. It made its presence known, and Reed’s jeans felt uncomfortable. He popped open the button at the waistband and tried to rearrange himself to take the pressure off. He’d been busy on the case, and though he could have used the release, he hadn’t even jacked off once on the trip. He’d wanted to save all of that energy for Trent.

Damn. Just imagining everything he’d do when Trent got home set Reed off again. He unzipped his pants and shifted his cock to a more comfortable position. He was tempted to take the edge off but restrained himself. Before he had a chance to get his hand out of his shorts the door swung open and Trent came into the living room. His narrowed eyes and clenched jaw sobered Reed up instantly.

“Surprise?” Reed said as he sat up and tried to zip his pants. Fuck. This was not the way he pictured their reunion.

“Yes, it certainly is. I guess you started celebrating without me, huh?”

“No. I was just… anticipating your return.” Reed grinned and stood up. He knew his breath smelled like beer. What had he been thinking? “Look, I brought you flowers…." Reed pointed to the vase. At least the flowers still looked fresh, even if he didn't.

Trent broke into a smile. "Flowers? Aww, they're beautiful." He dropped the messenger bag from his shoulder with a heavy thud and threw his arms around Reed, squeezing him too tight to breathe. Just what Reed wanted. He wrapped his arms around Trent and their mouths met in a long, hungry kiss.

"I didn't expect you home yet."

"I'm just here for a weekend. Nothing's happening for a couple of days, so I could get away." Later, he'd surprise Trent with the news that this break wasn't just for the weekend. After they crammed as much reunion into the weekend as they could.

"A weekend off. Too bad this doesn't happen more often."

Reed completely agreed. "Now let me show you how glad I am to see you."

"Ah, this is the weekend equivalent of a booty call?" Trent slipped out of Reed's arms.

Reed shrugged. "If you want to put it that way."

"How would you put it?"

Reed snuggled up against Trent again. "*Where* would you put it?" He slid his palm up Trent's thigh, smoothing it across Trent's cock through his pants. This time Trent didn't even try to get away.

REED DIDN'T have a chance to wonder where Trent had been until the next morning. He woke at daylight, barely able to breathe with Trent lying across his chest. It was good to be home. He listened to Trent's even breathing and fought the urge to carefully roll Trent over and suck him till he woke up, then let Trent fuck him into the mattress again. And again. Reed shifted his weight and felt the slight burn, the welcome soreness. The whole trip home he'd thought about how good it would feel to slip inside of Trent's tight heat, then when they'd pulled each other's clothes off all Reed wanted was to feel Trent deep inside. Trent had lasted far longer than Reed had, and Reed's ass was feeling it now. He grinned and laughed, the motion jarring Trent, who shifted position onto his side.

Reed pulled the sheet back and looked at Trent's slumbering body. Smooth skin, a little golden stubble at his jaw and a dark-blond nest at the base of his cock. Trent usually kept that hair trimmed close, but he let it grow when Reed was gone. It was one of their rituals for Reed to trim it when he got home. The anticipation of that joy brought a smile to his face as he reached out to stroke Trent's half erection. A little pressure along the underside and he watched it bloom into a full hard-on, which he'd gladly cherish until he drove Trent wild.

"Mmmm," Trent moaned and pushed against Reed's hand.

Reed wrapped his fingers around Trent's cock and leaned toward his mouth, intending to plant a kiss on his lips.

"About time." Trent opened one eye and stretched, showing off every inch of himself to Reed.

Reed straightened up, the kiss forgotten. "You're awake? Just pretending to be asleep and suffocating me?" He tightened his lips into a straight line, but he didn't let go of Trent's erection.

Trent shrugged, beaming. "I was waiting for the right incentive. That's it. That's just perfect." He bucked up into Reed's hand.

"Not so fast." Reed let go and rolled away from Trent.

"Hey, come back here." Trent slid across the bed and pressed up against Reed's back, cock digging pleasantly into the flesh of Reed's upper thigh. He shifted his leg so Trent's erection slid between his thighs. Trent's moan rumbled through Reed's body, and he felt his own arousal growing. Trent wrapped one arm over Reed's hip, letting his hand fall temptingly inches away from Reed's cock. "I missed you, Reed." Trent planted kisses along Reed's neck and down one shoulder. Then he reached his fingers down to brush at the tip of Reed's cock.

That glancing touch sent shockwaves through Reed's entire body. He'd missed Trent more than he'd say. He'd missed Trent's body, the things he could do with his hands and mouth and… just thinking about it made Reed's nipples ache and forced a groan from his lips.

Trent played with Reed's cock, letting his long fingers brush ever so slightly, making it bounce and tremble. Again and again. Teasing. Taunting. Bringing Reed's desire to the breaking point.

"Trent…." Reed put both a warning and a plea into the word.

"What?" Trent asked softly. "What do you want?" He moved away from Reed's back, taking his warmth and hard body away. Then he rolled Reed onto his back and leaned down to take Reed's cock into his mouth, enveloping it in wet heat.

Reed melted against the sheets and let Trent lick and suck at him, intent on not allowing his body to take control. He wanted this to last.

Trent propped himself up on one elbow and leaned down, alternately using his mouth and hands. Reed's breath caught in the back of his throat. Trent knew just how to play him, like an instrument, drawing out the pleasure long past the point Reed thought he'd erupt.

But it wasn't enough. Not just now. Reed wanted more. He shifted so he could reach Trent's cock, thick and dark with drops of precome welling in the slit. Reed swallowed, imagining how the smooth head would feel against the back of his throat. He moved closer, taking in as much of Trent's hard length as he could until his nose pressed against the dark-golden curls.

He echoed Trent's surprised groan with his own moans and hungrily sucked, wanting, needing as much of Trent as possible and then more. He lost control of his body, hips thrusting, fucking into Trent's mouth as he sought to take in every inch of this man who filled his thoughts, his body, and his life with pleasure.

Reed felt Trent's cock start to spasm, and hot salty jets pumped against the back of his throat. He swallowed as his own orgasm raced up on him and pressed deeper into Trent.

When the storm was over, Reed lay panting against Trent's powerful thigh, the oceanic tang of him still vivid on his tongue.

"READY FOR breakfast?" Trent called from the kitchen.

"Yeah." Reed rubbed a towel over his wet hair and hung it up in the bathroom. He didn't bother to put on any clothes for breakfast. It was part of their routine when he came home. First twenty-four hours were clothing free, unless they were going out.

He walked into the kitchen and was greeted by the sight of Trent's bare ass as he stood in front of the stove. The ties of an apron around his waist curled down over the pale globes of flesh.

"Mmmm," he half growled as he came up and pressed himself to Trent's back.

"Apparently you didn't take a cold shower. But I like that." Trent turned his head and met Reed for a wet kiss. "Sit down, it's almost ready."

"I'm hungry." Reed didn't want to let go of Trent, but he sat at the table.

Trent flipped pancakes from the skillet onto plates and set them down.

"Smells great. But you know the rules." He pointed to the apron. It was pretty small, just enough to protect him from the dangers of cooking while nude. He liked the way Trent's cock pushed it out and away from his body. Trent hadn't had a cold shower either.

Trent presented his back to Reed and bent over just enough to tease. Reed slipped his hand between Trent's legs and cupped his balls with one hand and untied the apron with the other. "Now you can eat."

"Thank you." Trent sat and put a dab of butter and a drizzle of syrup on his pancakes.

Reed looked down at his plate and noticed the pancake had a little smiley face. A sort of smiley face. The mouth was crooked. "I think this guy needs to go to the dentist."

"Oh, you do? How does it taste?"

"Delicious." Reed chewed and smiled.

Trent ate his pancakes in silence.

"Can you make some more? Reed asked.

"More? You want more?" Trent stood up.

"Yes, please?" Reed pulled him in with an arm around his waist. He kissed Trent's navel and intended to move lower when Trent disengaged himself. He went back to the stove, sans apron. Reed enjoyed the scenery.

"Here you go." Trent brought the skillet over and flipped the pancake out onto Reed's plate.

He stared. It was shaped like a dick, with two smaller round pancakes at one end. "That's cute."

"That's for you, you dick. Complaining about my smiley pancake. Dick!" Trent dropped the skillet in the sink and it sizzled as it hit water. "That's the only dick you'll get in your mouth this weekend. Enjoy it!" He strode out of the room.

"Trent, I'm sorry. It was cute. I liked it. Thank you." Reed got up and followed Trent. He was in the bedroom putting on underwear. "That's against the rules."

"Those rules don't count when you're being a dick." Trent turned his back to Reed.

"I don't remember that, Trent. Dickery doesn't cancel out the no-clothes rule." He heard a muffled sound. Trent was trying not to laugh. He put a hand over his mouth, and Reed spun him around. Trent's eyes betrayed his mirth. "You're going to have to take them off, Trent."

"Make me."

"Don't worry. I will." Reed grabbed for the waistband and Trent moved out of his reach but fell onto the bed. He put up a token amount of resistance, but Reed got the shorts off. The struggle had Trent panting slightly and he was half-hard. Reed leaned down and took Trent into his mouth, completing the process. "Delicious."

"Please, sir, may I have some more?"

"Do you deserve it?"

"Yes."

And he did, so Reed obliged.

"SO BETH said something about a surprise? That's the reason you were out so late last night?" Reed had made cheese omelets for a late lunch. That was pretty much everything in the fridge. They'd have to shop or order groceries from a shop down the street.

Trent stopped chewing and stared at Reed. "You talked to Beth? When?"

"Last night. I got home before dinner, and when you didn't show up, I called her to see where you were."

"Why didn't you call me?"

"That would have ruined the surprise that I got home early."

"Right. I didn't know when to expect you, so I didn't realize you were home early." Trent hadn't intended to let any resentment seep into the comment, but he could tell from Reed's expression it had.

"Oh. Yeah. That's true." Pain was evident in Reed's gaze before he looked away.

"Sorry."

"Me too. And I have a surprise too, but I want to hear yours first. Don't worry, Beth didn't even give me a hint."

Trent put the fork down and glanced up at Reed, letting his thigh brush against Reed's. "I'm going to Japan." Trent wanted to ease into the news, but his excitement bubbled over and it spilled right out.

Reed had been sipping orange juice and choked a little at the announcement. "Japan? Why?"

"For Leah. She needs someone to meet with prospective clients, and she can't go right now. She's having twins."

Reed put his fork down on the plate and glanced at Trent. "That's a lot of news at once. I didn't know you were doing anything with the gallery."

Trent tried to gauge Reed's mood, but he couldn't discern whether he was happy with Trent's plans or his explanation so far. "I haven't been. But while you were away, I had to sign some papers—lease renewal and insurance. She mentioned she had this job and asked if I was interested. And I was."

"That's great."

Trent stared at Reed, not sure whether to believe the words. "Really?"

"Yes. Really. I'm glad you're trying something different. But what about the writing?"

Trent shrugged. "I finished the book while you were gone."

"Fantastic." Reed raised his glass and clinked it against Trent's. "Oh, that reminds me, there's some Champagne in the fridge. We should celebrate with that."

"Real Champagne?"

"No, Korbel." Reed grinned at what must have been a look of confusion on Trent's face. He liked bubbly, but not enough to drink Korbel. "Yes, real Champagne from France. The kind you like, Bollinger. The one James Bond drinks, right?"

Trent's cheeks heated. He was torn between embarrassment for selecting his Champagne based on a fictional character and love of Reed for remembering—and not making fun of Trent for it. He chose the latter. He leaned over and pulled Reed into a kiss. "God, I love you."

"Then have some Champagne so I can get you tipsy and take advantage of you. Again."

"You don't have to get me drunk for that."

"I know. But you're so much more compliant when you are. And you don't argue as much."

"I don't argue."

Reed chose not to comment on the irony of Trent's response. "Let me get the Champagne." He stood up and walked to the refrigerator.

Trent stared at his bare ass and grinned. It was good to have Reed home. Even better when it was naked day. He watched Reed grab the bottle and a dishtowel and expertly open it, with just the softest whisper of a pop. He grasped two flutes from the counter, put them on the table, and poured golden liquid into each glass before sitting back down.

They made a wordless toast and drank. The bubbles danced on Trent's tongue, the sweetness perfectly balanced with the toastiness of the wine. He couldn't think of anything better than these reunions. They made the days without Reed bearable.

"So, when is your trip?"

"Monday."

"That's only four days from now."

"You sound surprised, Reed. Don't you have to go back and finish this job up?"

Reed put his glass down and leaned on the table. "Well, that's my surprise." He gave a crooked grin. "This job is over, and I asked for a two-week break until the next one."

That knocked Trent for a loop. Reed taking a break from work? "Oh." Trent's mood plummeted.

"How long will you be gone?"

"A couple of weeks. When I planned it, I thought you were going to be gone the whole time."

Reed's jaw tightened for a split second, but Trent spotted it. He felt Reed's hand squeezing his knee. "I could go with you and enjoy the rest of the time you're there. You won't be with the clients 24/7, will you?"

Trent shook his head. The hand on his knee and the Champagne made it difficult to think clearly. "No. But I'm going with Beth. We've planned things already. It wouldn't be fair if you come along. She'll feel like a third wheel, even if we ask her to join us for meals or sightseeing." Trent's heart raced. He desperately wanted Reed to come with him, but he'd already made a commitment to both Leah and Beth.

"Well, we better make the best of these four days." Reed slid his fingers up Trent's thigh and Trent felt himself trembling, but unable to stop himself from being unbearably aroused by Reed's proximity, his scent, and the Bollinger. Reed tickled Trent's thigh and stroked his balls as he leaned in for a deep, wet kiss. Trent melted against Reed, powerless to resist. He had no intention of resisting.

TRENT LAY on his stomach, Reed half sprawled on top of him, their bodies glued together by sweat and semen. Reed had fallen asleep, relaxed and sated.

Why hadn't Reed been more persistent when Trent said he was going to Japan with Beth? He gave in without any discussion, and Trent felt a little insulted.

Reed woke, probably disturbed by Trent's tumultuous thoughts. He leaned over and kissed Trent. "I'm hungry again, how 'bout you?"

"A little." Trent paused and felt his stomach shift. "Yeah, I'm hungry. I burned a lot of calories already today."

"We need groceries. Want to do an online order?"

Trent sighed. He wanted to think about the trip, and he felt too constrained with Reed around. "No, I'll go to the store. I want a little fresh air." He rolled Reed off of him and headed for the bathroom for a quick shower. He'd barely squeezed body wash on the soap puff when Reed joined him.

"Let me do that for you." Reed took the puff and soaped Trent up and down. They were both sated, and the shower was comforting and intimate rather than arousing. Trent enjoyed the attention but wished for even a few minutes alone to think. Usually, it was the other way around. It felt odd to not want to spend every precious second with Reed.

After the shower, Trent stood in front of the closet trying to decide what to wear, a towel wrapped precariously around his hips.

"Going somewhere special?" Reed asked.

"No. Why?"

"Then what does it matter what you wear?" Reed grabbed the first thing he touched and put it on. "I'll go with you to the store. Help you carry everything."

Trent glared at him, but not because Reed wanted to join him. They were closing in on two years together, and Reed didn't know him at all. He looked at Reed's outfit: it looked fine. Trent stuck his hand in the closet and pulled out a shirt and then went back for some pants. He held them up in front of a mirror. No way. That shirt didn't work with those pants!

Reed came up behind him and yanked the towel off. "Don't even bother getting dressed. You stay here and I'll shop. Conserve your energy. I'm already dressed."

Before Trent could reply, the phone rang. Reed picked it up and headed into the living room. Trent wondered if it was the Bureau calling him away yet again, even though he said he was on leave.

A few minutes later Reed shouted, "It's Beth."

"Why didn't you say so?"

"We were chatting. She welcomed me home." Reed handed the phone over.

Trent tucked the towel back around his waist before speaking. "Hey, Beth."

"Hey, glad to see you and Reed had your reunion."

"It was memorable."

"Don't give me any details. I like to keep the mystery."

Trent shrugged. "Your loss. What's up?"

"Now that Reed's back I wondered if you didn't want him to go with you to Japan instead of me."

Trent tried to gauge her emotions, but over the phone, that was next to impossible. Her tone was neutral, but he knew her well enough to suspect she'd be extremely disappointed if he changed their plans. He paused for a moment before replying.

Beth filled the silence. "Because it's perfectly understandable if you do. I mean, I don't want to keep you two from having some quality time together, since I know that doesn't happen very often." The words tumbled out quickly.

"Hang on, Beth. I wouldn't do that to you."

"It's okay...."

"No, it's not okay. You and I made a plan and a commitment to Leah. I'm not backing down on that."

"Really?" The relief in her voice was palpable.

"Really." Trent glanced into the living room. Reed was on the couch flipping through the LA Times. The scent of coffee brewing floated toward the bedroom. Trent smiled and continued, "He asked if he could come along, and I said I didn't think it was a good idea."

"You did?"

"Yes. It's not a good idea. It wouldn't be the same if he came too."

"And what did he say?"

Trent took a deep breath wondering when he and Beth had turned into high school girls. Maybe they'd never stopped being high school girls. "He said he understood and hoped our trip was successful."

"Just like that? Didn't put up an argument or act disappointed?"

Trent considered Beth's questions. His stomach tightened. Why hadn't Reed sounded more disappointed? "No…." Trent walked into the living room and stood behind Reed, gaze boring a hole through the back of Reed's skull. Reed kept reading, ignoring Trent's laser-beam stare.

"But you're sure about this, Trent? Just you and I going?"

"Yes. Look, I gotta go." He disconnected and put the phone down on the table near the bedroom door. Trent had been sure, but the more Beth asked, the more he considered changing his mind. No. He wouldn't. This wasn't about Reed anyway. Not really. This was about Trent finding his own thing to do, making his own life and not living his life around Reed's. There would be plenty of other times to go away with Reed. He folded his arms and stared at Reed, who still sat reading the paper, back to Trent.

He must have finally felt the weight of Trent's gaze. Reed turned, noticed Trent watching him. "What? Something wrong?"

Trent shook his head. "No. Just watching you. Glad you're home." He stepped to the back of the couch and put his arms around Reed's neck from behind. Reed turned and smiled. Trent planted a kiss behind his left ear when he turned back to the newspaper.

"You want to spend the day watching me read the paper?" Reed's tone turned playful.

"I thought you were going shopping?"

"Come here and tell me what you want me to buy." Reed tugged at one of Trent's arms and used his weight to unbalance him so he toppled over the couch and landed partially in Reed's lap where his towel conveniently unwrapped itself. He grinned and let Reed kiss him, first on the lips, then down his abs—and lower.

"They didn't teach that move at Quantico," Trent said, sucking in his breath as Reed brushed his lips along the length of Trent's cock.

"Good. I wouldn't want you practicing this with anyone else."

"Promise."

5

THE NEXT few days went by far too quickly. Trent had one final meeting with Leah and Beth at the gallery before their trip, and he still had to tackle the most difficult task of all: packing. It was spring and the weather reports indicated the chance of showers, but even in April, Japan could get awfully cold, according to Beth. The silver lining was that they would most likely be there for cherry blossom season, a fleeting week or so where the ethereal beauty of the delicate flowers was celebrated by picnics and parties under the trees.

In the end, Reed packed for Trent. He insisted it would be a measure of his trust in Reed to allow this, but in reality Reed couldn't stand Trent's constant monologue as he debated whether to pack each item. Reed couched his offer to pack by suggesting better ways to spend their last day together. Trent could pack or he could play. Thankfully, Trent had his priorities right.

On Monday morning, they piled into a taxi with the single suitcase, as Trent marveled how he couldn't believe Reed had managed to pack a week's worth of clothing in one case and still have room for body wash and other necessities. As the driver wove through the morning gridlock on the freeway, Reed slid an arm around Trent's shoulders and pulled him close.

"How many times have we been here?" He enjoyed the soft brush of Trent's hair as he whispered into Trent's ear. He inhaled, memorizing.

"A lot. How does it feel to be the one who's staying?" Trent glanced at Reed.

"I'm not sure yet. I won't really know till you're gone."

"Don't you know whether you'll miss me?"

"Of course I'll miss you. And I'll worry. Just a little." Reed tightened his arm around Trent. He had a knot the size of a Hummer in his gut at the idea of Trent leaving. Deep down, he admitted his doubts about whether Trent was up to the challenge hurt as much as the thought of not getting to spend his two-week break together. He wanted so much to trust Trent's abilities, but he didn't want to risk letting him out of his sight in another country.

"There's nothing to worry about, Reed. Isn't Japan one of the safest countries in the whole world?"

"I'm not sure about that…." Reed had checked. Crime in Japan had skyrocketed in the past decade. It was no longer a place where even women felt comfortable walking alone at night. It was still safer than the States, but it wasn't the idyllic paradise Trent believed it was.

The cab stopped outside of the departures counters and Reed paid the driver. Beth would meet Trent inside—she'd kindly chosen to make her own way to the airport so Trent and Reed could have some additional private time. Reed appreciated her gesture and took the opportunity for a nice long kiss before he got Trent moving toward the skycaps, who checked in his luggage.

Beth waited just inside the entrance. She wore a pair of dark-blue slacks and a staid white blouse, and carried a tweedy-looking jacket. Her shiny black hair was pulled back in a thick ponytail at the back of her neck. Reed almost didn't recognize her. She usually wore jeans or skinny black pants and had a fondness for brightly colored tank tops, lots of rings on her fingers, and the occasional gravity-defying hairstyle.

"What happened to you?" Trent asked when they reached her. "Did you get mugged by a Mormon missionary or something?"

"No." She frowned and smoothed her hand down one thigh. "Hi, Reed."

"Hey, Beth." Reed had the same thought as Trent, but he didn't know Beth well enough to comment on her appearance.

"There's a different sense of fashion in Japan. For the clientele we're meeting, I need to present what they consider a professional image. Even to the driver who picks us up."

"Did Leah tell you to dress like that?" Trent asked.

"No, but I think it's necessary. Didn't you pack any professional-looking clothes?"

Trent covered his face with his hands for a second. "Oh no! Are you saying I shouldn't have brought that feather boa? And all the sparkly pants? Uh-oh."

"Trent, you jerk!" Beth finally broke into a grin and punched Trent. "But still…."

"Beth, Japan is one of the most fashion-forward places around. I don't even understand their sense of style, but it's not 1950s vintage Midwestern housewife."

"I—"

Before she got another word out, Trent went on, "And we represent an art gallery. We work with artists, so we have some leeway in being artistic and creative. They probably wouldn't trust us if we didn't look at least a little hip."

Beth twisted her lips and shrugged. Reed didn't think Beth was completely off base in toning down her usual flashy style, but Trent's argument made sense, too. There had to be an appropriate middle ground. Maybe the trip would go smoothly after all with Beth to temper Trent's more excitable side.

"The line's getting longer. We better try to get through security now." Beth waved at the increasingly long line waiting for TSA approval to enter the terminal.

"Yeah, you're right." Trent turned to Reed. "I'll call when we get there."

"Good." They shared a G-rated kiss, and Reed squeezed Trent's hand before he and Beth got on the end of the line.

"Don't worry about anything. We're just going to look at some artwork. What could happen?"

Trent waved, and Reed watched as they snaked their way toward the X-ray machines. He could have used his ID to get into the terminal without a ticket and wait with them at the gate, but he didn't want to prolong the departure. Trent needed to focus on the trip and not on what he was leaving behind. Reed had plenty of experience with that. He walked down to the baggage claim area and the taxi stand, threading his way through groups with carts piled high with bags, already snapping photos of their exciting LA vacation.

He hated that he had doubts about the trip, and Trent's last words—"What could happen?"—put him on alert rather than easing his mind.

Knowing Trent, *anything* could happen.

6

TRENT STRETCHED as the captain announced their imminent arrival at Tokyo's Narita Airport. He recalled the uncomfortable flight to Thailand nearly two years earlier, but this time he and Beth had gone first class—literally. The clients had provided them with business class tickets on Japan Airlines. Complimentary Dom Perignon, amazing seats that turned into beds, and Shiseido toiletries. They ate and drank like kings.

With the time change—they flew across the International Date Line—they arrived the following afternoon, even though the flight was only eleven hours. Trent wouldn't have minded a longer flight, since the bed and the robe and slippers were so comfy.

"I can't wait to tell Reed about this!"

Beth sighed. "I know."

"Sorry." Trent realized he'd said that about ten times so far. He wasn't a ten-year-old on his first trip out of Oklahoma, and he didn't need to tell Reed about everything that happened.

Trent pressed his face to the window. They were low enough to see individual structures, and as far as he could see were buildings, and more buildings. He knew the airport was miles outside of the city, and he'd expected some countryside, not this uninterrupted landscape of squat gray boxes. The only natural landmark was a thick river snaking its way toward a more concentrated bundle of buildings—including some high-rises. He saw a few patches of green, but mostly just more concrete and glass. Tokyo was disappointingly unexciting at first glance. He hoped Kyoto would be as beautiful as all the photographs he'd seen.

Narita Airport was bright and clean and bustling when they left the gate, and Trent stared around him, taking in everything. There were many more English signs than he'd seen in Bangkok. Beth moved them quickly through baggage claim, immigration, and customs, speaking Japanese to the airport staff. The woman stamping their American passports clearly didn't expect Beth to speak Japanese to her.

Once they'd officially entered Japan, Beth located their driver—arranged by Leah. They'd ride in style to their hotel.

"Welcome to Japan. I am Takeda. I can take your bags." The guide, a middle-aged man wearing a formal but slightly shabby black suit and a less-than-crisp white shirt, bowed and hoisted their suitcases onto a cart and led them toward a sleek black limousine. Takeda handed Beth a package containing two cell phones they'd use during their trip. As soon as Beth changed Trent's phone to display English instead of Japanese, he called Reed, before the limo had even made its way out of the enormous airport.

"We're here!"

"Sounds like the flight went well."

Had Trent expected Reed to miss him already? That was silly. But he wished Reed didn't sound so businesslike. They never spoke while Reed was away, and Trent realized they'd hardly talked to each other on the phone at all. "Yes. The flight was fine. We're just leaving the airport."

Reed chuckled. "You could have waited to call from the hotel."

"I know."

"But I'm glad you didn't. The bed's too big without you. I've never been here on my own before. It's strange."

"Don't snoop in my drawers." Trent felt warm and tingly when Reed mentioned the bed.

"No fun snooping in your drawers if you're not wearing them."

"Hold that thought." Trent glanced at Beth, who was staring out the window, clearly pretending not to be listening. "I'll call you later." He made some kissing noises only because he knew it would embarrass Beth. Reed had already hung up.

Then he settled into the back seat and peppered Takeda with questions about the journey.

"I am Takeda. I will take you to the hotel." Takeda smiled and started the car.

Trent squinted at Takeda and then at Beth. "Why didn't he answer?"

"He only knows a few phrases."

"I don't believe that. His English is very good."

Takeda turned to them when he stopped in traffic. "Our journey will take approximately two hours."

"See?" Beth turned one corner of her mouth up in a smirk.

"He does sound a little like one of those recorded voices."

Beth nodded, then asked Takeda a question. In the rearview mirror Trent could see his eyes widen, and then he replied in rapid-fire Japanese. He let out an audible sigh and carried on a cheerful conversation with Beth.

"What was that all about?"

"I asked him if we'll be in time for *sakura*—cherry blossoms. He said they have already started blooming near the palace, and the blossoms will hit their peak when we're in Kyoto. He even told me his favorite place to see them."

"Do we have time for cherry blossoms?"

"Sure. We're meeting Maeda tomorrow morning, but we have the whole afternoon and evening free today, if you're not too tired."

"Nope." He was a little nervous about meeting the appraiser the following day, but since the flight had gone so smoothly, he sat back and tried to relax. The seats were upholstered with plush black fabric, but there wasn't enough legroom. He rotated so he could stretch a little better and stared out the window, asking Beth—and she in turn Takeda—questions about the landmarks they passed, though he recognized the tops of the rides as they passed Tokyo Disneyland.

Once in the heart of Tokyo, the roads narrowed and the traffic slowed. He stared at people walking along the street.

"They all look so normal. Suits, ties, skirts, light coats and jackets."

"What did you expect? All the women in kimonos and the men with swords and *chonmage*?"

"Huh? Cho-what?"

"Chonmage are those topknots the samurai wore."

"Oh. Well, I don't know. Maybe." Trent stared out the window, avoiding Beth's gaze. He had expected people to look different here and now he realized how idiotic that was.

Takeda drove carefully, avoiding other cars, buses, and random bikes. The streets were a maze, and neon and lights seemed to cover every building's upper stories, already lit in the late afternoon darkness of early spring. People crowded and bustled on the sidewalks, and he felt a sense of excitement he hadn't yet experienced since they landed. He couldn't read any of the Japanese characters but recognized a few familiar symbols for electronics companies.

The taxi stopped in front of the Park Hyatt Hotel. Trent went for the car's door handle, but before he could open it Beth grabbed his arm. "Don't open the door."

"Why not?"

"The driver does it. They're automatic. Supposed to be more polite that way. He'll let us out."

Trent waited and sure enough, the back door opened and he and Beth slid out of the car. He'd been expecting them to get out of the right side, then recalled they were on the left side of the road.

The hotel occupied the top floors of a high-rise. They rode to the forty-first floor just to check in. The lobby of the hotel was elegant, immaculate, and bright, befitting the outrageous prices they charged. Leah said their suite was two thousand a night, but the collectors were paying, so they should enjoy themselves.

After they checked in, the elevator whisked them to the fiftieth floor in efficient silence. The spacious suite featured a mixture of western and Japanese style. Trent kicked his shoes off and enjoyed the thick carpet under his feet. He strode toward the floor-to-ceiling window to get his first real look at Tokyo—from the top of the high-rise hotel.

Beth also kicked her shoes off and headed into her bedroom. He heard her plop herself onto her bed. "Oh, it's nice to travel in style!"

Trent left the living room window and joined her, letting himself fall backward onto the bed next to Beth. As college buddies they'd spent plenty of time lying on one bed or the other and commiserating. Though they'd stayed friends long after graduation, Trent had missed that intimacy. "Comfortable!" he agreed, staring up at the ceiling.

"I could get used to this. Probably not a good idea." Beth rolled over so she faced Trent.

"Used to being in bed with me?" he teased.

"No, silly. To living a life of luxury." She let out another sigh and flopped onto her back again.

This time Trent rolled over and propped himself up on an elbow. The suite was luxurious, but not the best place he'd stayed in. He hadn't realized just how lucky he was to earn a good living from writing and his share of the gallery. Marc had brought him along on gallery buying trips around the world, always staying in Michelin-rated hotels. And on the trip to Italy with Reed, they'd stayed in first-class accommodations, thanks to the reward money Trent had received from the Thai government. Was his life that much more comfortable than Beth's? Maybe he should take her away for a weekend somewhere special after they got home or treat her to a spa weekend where she could pamper herself.

"I'm gonna unpack some things for tomorrow and have a shower. Then if you want, we can wander the streets of Shinjuku for a while. Or we can go to the palace grounds to see the sakura. We call it *ohanami*, which means flower viewing."

"What's the best time to see the cherry blossoms? Don't we want to go while it's still light?"

"They look gorgeous after dark too, illuminated with special lights. *Yuzakura*, or nighttime sakura. But I think you'd enjoy seeing the transition between day and night, before the lights go on. So we better hurry up. I guess that shower can wait."

Trent squished up his nose.

"Oh, that bad?" Beth sniffed an armpit. "Smells fine to me." She leaned toward Trent and sniffed. "You, on the other hand…."

He gently pulled a lock of her hair. "I smell fresh as a daisy."

"Then let's go."

THEY TOOK a taxi to the Imperial Palace and walked through the gardens outside the high gray stone walls. Lush masses of pale-pink cherry blossoms clustered on nearly every tree lining the path. The actual palace was surrounded by wide moats, guardhouses with traditional Japanese pointed roofs at each corner.

"It looks just like something from a samurai movie!"

Beth frowned. "Seriously?"

"Well, it looks ancient. But beautiful."

They joined crowds of Japanese enjoying the scenery and atmosphere. As the sky darkened, the air chilled, and Trent pulled his coat around his body.

"You hungry yet?" Beth asked.

"More cold than hungry."

"I can fix that." She led him to a row of makeshift concession stands at one edge of the park. All the signs were in Japanese.

"I want some of that." Trent pointed to a stall with a line snaking away. He had no idea what they served, but it was the busiest stall, so it must be something good.

"That's sake. They heat it up."

"Sake? At a picnic?"

"Yeah, ohanami is a big time to drink."

The line moved quickly, and she got them a large bottle of heated sake and two small ceramic cups. She purchased food from another stall, though Trent didn't have a clue what it was. Then Beth suggested they sit under one of the trees and enjoy their traditional ohanami feast.

All the trees already had clusters of people underneath, and Beth asked if they might join a group sitting under a tree of a particularly spectacular dark pink—less common than the pale pink Trent was familiar with.

They sat and had a toast of sake. "*Kampai*!" they said and drank the contents of the small cups.

"Oh, that's good," Trent said, trying not to choke as the potent heated liquid went down his throat. He coughed, and the Japanese sitting near them laughed.

A man shouted something, and Trent looked to Beth for a translation. "He wants to share a toast with you. To celebrate your trip during the sakura season."

"Really?"

The man moved to sit by Trent and poured clear liquid into his cup. He sipped. "Woo-wee. What's this?" He thought it might make him choke worse than the hot sake.

"*Shochu.* It's a kind of Japanese vodka. Made with potatoes usually." Beth laughed and accepted a cupful from the friendly Japanese man.

Soon warmth spread through Trent's body and after a few bites of the tasty snacks—Beth still didn't explain what he was eating—he was in a fine mood. The Japanese group had spread to include them and everyone was sharing drinks, shouting "Kampai" and trading food. Beth did her best to keep up the translations, but after a while it didn't even matter. Body language and alcohol smoothed over any issues of language.

By the time all the drinks were consumed, it was dark. As dark as it gets in a city of twelve million people and about a billion light bulbs. The raucous laughter quieted as the whole group stared up. The cherry blossoms were even more beautiful at night with each petal illuminated, shimmering an eerie pink. In the distance the orange glow of Tokyo Tower reminded Trent they were in ultramodern Tokyo.

Trent and Beth got a taxi back to the hotel and rode up the elevator, Trent humming a song the Japanese had taught him, though he couldn't remember any of the words.

They were both exhausted, and Trent barely remembered to wash and get undressed before falling into bed. Out of habit he rolled toward the middle and remembered he was in Japan, thousands of miles away from Reed. He put his hand out and smoothed it across the space Reed would occupy. He felt a little twinge of guilt that he hadn't thought of Reed at all while they were enjoying the sakura-viewing party. But he fell asleep with the memory of Reed's arms around him.

7

THE NEXT morning, they woke to headaches and room-service breakfast before packing up again in preparation for their trip down to Kyoto that afternoon. They would leave the suitcases in their room during their morning visit to meet Naoko Maeda, the appraiser Leah had hired.

They got in a taxi, and Beth handed the driver a card with the address of their destination. There was a short discussion before the driver put the car in gear and started driving. Trent was busy watching the cityscape and the bustling sidewalk activity, but when Beth continued to talk with the driver, he got curious.

"What are you talking about?"

Beth fluttered a printout on her lap. "I'm giving him directions." Beth paused to guide the driver again, referring to her map as they seemed to get into a disagreement. "He turned the wrong way back there, and I'm trying to get him headed in the right direction."

"He doesn't know how to get to the museum? Why didn't we get in a different cab?"

"They're almost all the same. Many of the drivers don't know how to get anywhere without your help."

"You have to be joking." In the States drivers used GPS, and in London the cabbies were famous for knowing every single street and alleyway. They even have to pass a test to get their license.

"No."

"I thought the Japanese were meticulous and did everything perfectly."

"Maybe some things, but this isn't one of them. It's like the drivers are in the Dark Ages. Even when they have GPS, they don't always use it."

"How hard is it to find an address?" Trent couldn't quite understand the problem, though he had noticed the streets didn't seem to be laid out in a grid as in most cities. Everything went off at an angle and many of the streets were narrow, exacerbating the traffic.

"I'll explain later."

The driver pulled over to the side of the street and stopped.

"We're here?" Trent asked and reached for the door until he remembered not to touch it.

"No."

The taxi driver raised his voice, arguing with Beth. Trent was stunned. Everyone had been so polite. The driver kept saying "Chica, Chica."

"Why's he talking in Spanish?" Trent asked.

Beth laughed. "It's not Spanish. He's telling me to get out and take the subway. '*Chikatetsu*' means subway."

"Will it be faster?"

"Probably."

"Fine by me."

Beth said something to the driver and Trent readied himself to leave. Then the driver started shouting again. "Now what?"

"He won't let us out until we pay."

"So give him the money." Trent looked at the meter. It said 9940. He saw Beth hand over a 5,000-yen note and say something to the driver. He still wouldn't open the door.

"He wants the whole fare!" Beth said, shaking her head. "He drove us around in circles. I don't want to pay for that, plus the hassle of the subway!"

Trent wondered if there was something else going on. He hadn't seen her this upset since they'd arrived. "The meter's almost 10,000, Beth. That's not right."

"Yesssss…." Beth bit her lower lip. "Oh fine," she shouted in English and peeled another note from the pile she had in her wallet. The door opened, and Trent and Beth scurried onto the sidewalk. The driver shut the door before Trent was out of the way and it clipped his knee. He let out a howl and noticed pedestrians staring at him. He looked down and rubbed the aching joint.

Beth started moving almost immediately and Trent stopped her with a hand on her shoulder.

"Beth, why are you so upset over the taxi? The expenses are covered. It's not your money."

"Not important." She pulled away from him.

"Hang on. What is it?"

She stared up at him, her mouth a tight white line. "He said something rude when you got in, under his breath, before he realized I speak Japanese."

"What did he say?"

"Just leave it, okay?"

He nodded, and reached for her hand. She pulled her hand out again, then took hold of it and started moving down the street.

The subway entrance was on the next block. Beth put money in the machine and got them tickets; then they walked through what seemed like endless corridors until they took an escalator to the platform. The train arrived and people streamed out like ants heading for water, then the new passengers got on and the train moved out of the station. The train was crowded and they were pushed along inside, then had to stand.

Trent towered over everyone, and his head nearly brushed the ceiling. People stared at him. A man sitting in front of Trent put his foot out, right up against Trent's foot, comparing the sizes. Trent's foot was huge compared to the man's. The Japanese man looked up at Trent and laughed, then he said something to his traveling companion—another gray-suited man with slick combed hair. The two stared at Trent and chuckled.

Trent stared back and didn't know how to react. He'd gotten separated from Beth, and she was a few feet away from him. He raised his eyebrows and she shrugged. When they reached their destination, he told her what had happened and she chuckled.

"You are quite fascinating to some Japanese. I'm sure it will happen again. They'll probably ask all sorts of personal questions about you. Just be prepared."

"Oh, great. Why didn't you warn me?"

She shrugged again. "I guess I didn't really think of it till now. Don't worry, I'm the interpreter. I'll figure out what to say."

They exited the station and walked into what appeared to be a huge city park.

"This is Ueno Park, one of the largest parks in Tokyo. Maeda-san works at the Tokyo Metropolitan Art Museum, and it's located inside the park." They strolled through the park, which had more concrete than trees. But when Trent glimpsed the rows of cherry blossom trees in full bloom flanking the main path, he realized it was much more beautiful than he'd thought.

At the museum entrance Beth spoke to the guard at the door, and they were escorted inside and taken to an office in the back. Along the way, Trent glanced at the exhibition on the ground floor. It wasn't Japanese art at all. It was all about Leonardo da Vinci. He slowed down to look at one of the drawings on the wall—a mechanical study of some incredible machine.

"Trent, we can look around the museum later. Let's not be late for this appointment."

Trent nodded and pulled himself away from the exhibit.

When they entered Miss Maeda's office, Beth was the one to get the surprise. Miss Maeda sprang up from behind her desk, and Beth's jaw nearly hit the floor. Instead of the severe, conservative outfit Beth was wearing, Miss Maeda wore a short skirt fashioned from ruffles of plaid fabric edged with white lace. She had on white stockings dotted with little black Scottie dogs and a top made from black velvet and more white lacy frills.

"Glad to see you fit right in, Beth." Trent tried not to laugh out loud. He could tell from Beth's pinched expression the irony of the situation wasn't lost on her.

Beth offered her a business card, holding the corners, using both hands, and bowing as she did so. Trent followed suit with his own card. He loved how his name looked in Japanese on the cards Leah had made for them. He bowed and used one of the greetings Beth had taught him, but he knew he'd made a hash of it when Miss Maeda grinned.

"So pleased to meet you both. Please have a seat." Miss Maeda's English was precise, though accented—British, not the Japanese accent he was already becoming familiar with. She waved them to chairs, and they sat. "Please feel free to call me Naoko, at least when we are not with the clients."

"Okay, Naoko-san," Beth said with a smile. "I adore that skirt. May I ask where you got it?"

"A boutique in Harajuku."

"Maybe we'll have time to stop by there before we leave for Kyoto," Trent said, and he could see the color coming back into Beth's face. She nodded. The two women chatted for a few moments about fashion and Trent glanced around the office. Glass cases of delicate antique pottery bowls flanked one wall, while an impressive collection of swords adorned another. They seemed so disparate: the violence represented by the swords juxtaposed with the beautiful craftsmanship of the blades and the exquisitely decorated handles and scabbards.

Based on what Leah had told them of Maeda's experience and qualifications, she must be in her mid-thirties, and she spoke confidently and knowledgeably about art, which soon dispelled Trent's initial doubts at her high-school-girl appearance. They spent an hour discussing the two clients whose collections Naoko would help them value. She was familiar with both collectors.

"Motofuji-san is a well-known and well-respected collector within Japan. He has had many of his pieces for a very long time. I examined the list of pieces Leah sent me, and I've done some preliminary research in terms of authentication protocols and current market trends. There are a few items I won't be able to estimate until I've seen them, but it will be a good basis for valuing the work once we've seen it."

"What about the other collector? Waseda?" Trent asked.

Naoko's face took on a sudden ashen cast that disappeared as quickly as it had come. Trent thought he'd imagined it. "He's what you might call 'new money' in comparison to Motofuji-san. He came almost out of nowhere in the art market and acquired an impressive collection, both Japanese and European, many at inflated prices. I can see why he might need to sell, for economic reasons, but I doubt he would get what he paid for most of his pieces, which will be something we'll need to finesse once we start talking numbers. I also did some background research on him as well as his collection."

"Thank you, Naoko-san." Trent glanced at Beth to see if she had anything to add. To his surprise she spoke in Japanese. Trent frowned, and Beth gave him a mild glare from the corner of her eye. She and Naoko spoke for several minutes in Japanese before Beth translated anything, but he caught the name of the collectors, Waseda and Motofuji.

"Naoko-san indicated there may be some question about the authenticity of some of Mr. Waseda's collection. But she'll reserve judgment until she sees which items he intends to place with Leah."

"I see. We can deal with that in the event he wants to sell anything shady."

"Yes. I think that's best," Naoko said. "Now, did you have any other questions for me? If not, I will meet you at Tokyo Station this afternoon for our journey to Kyoto. It should leave you plenty of time to get to the shop in Harajuku." She gave Beth a conspiratorial smile and walked them to the door.

Beth bowed and Trent followed her lead. Naoko also bowed and said something in Japanese.

Once they were back in the main hall of the museum Trent stopped and put a hand on Beth's arm. "What did she say?"

"She just gave a standard good-bye, a formal phrase one uses with business acquaintances, even though we had an informal talk."

"No, that's not what I meant. When she was talking about Waseda." Trent thought they'd discussed far more than that simple piece of information about his shady art collection.

"I told you."

Trent sighed and chose to leave it there. He didn't want to openly accuse Beth of hiding something, but he wondered why she hadn't told him the truth. Could he trust her interpreting, or was there another reason she hadn't explained everything? He only knew a few words in Japanese, and he thought he'd recognized one of them, because both women had used it.

Yakuza.

8

BY MUTUAL agreement, Trent spent a few hours in the museum while Beth went shopping. He wouldn't have minded going with her—he loved shopping, even if he wasn't buying anything for himself. But he wanted to think about what Beth hadn't said and felt some space from her was the best way to decide how to bring up the topic again.

She called him when she was done shopping. It had been a great idea to get the local cell phones. Thankfully, Beth had programmed his in English and showed him how to find the time in California. She'd also written down instructions in Japanese for him to show someone if he got lost, so he could get back to the subway at Ueno Station and ride down the Yamanote Line to meet her back at Shinjuku to retrieve their luggage and get to Tokyo Station.

Trent was proud of himself, riding the subway on his own. Most of the signs in the station were also written in English. Apparently both Ueno Park and Shinjuku were popular stops for tourists, so there were plenty of well-marked signs. And lots of ads in English, though Trent discovered some of them used English in a way he couldn't quite understand. He'd ask Beth about that too.

Back in the hotel, Beth showed off her new clothes. "These aren't from the place Naoko mentioned. An outfit there would cost a year's earnings for me. I found a few cheaper places with really cute clothes. Art experts must rake in the bucks. I studied the wrong thing."

"Naoko isn't going to have her name on an Academy Award winner."

"At this rate, neither will I." Beth frowned. "Oh, I got something for you too!" She dug in her shopping bags and pulled out a bright-green bag and handed it to Trent.

"Thanks." He opened it up and found a white T-shirt showing a skyline of Tokyo with Godzilla looming menacingly behind it. He collected all kinds of film-related things. "I love this! Really love it." He hugged her for thinking of him.

Beth discovered she couldn't fit all her new clothes into her suitcase without discarding some of what she'd brought. It took her about a minute to decide what to pitch, so she left a pile of blouses and skirts for the housekeeping staff.

"I don't think they'll take them," Trent said as he examined one of the blouses.

"Why not?"

"The maid's uniforms in this hotel are cuter than any of this stuff."

Beth frowned. "Yeah, I know. Should I just burn them?"

"No. Last thing we need is to get arrested."

"Funny you should mention that." Beth laughed as she sat on her suitcase to close it—she'd bought plenty in her short shopping excursion.

"Mention getting arrested?"

"Yeah. That awful cab driver. He threatened to drive us to the police station if I didn't pay the full fare."

"That's crazy. Can they do that?"

"Well, why do you think the drivers use those door controls? Extortion. But I don't think the police would actually arrest us. My Japanese is too good for a shady cab driver to put anything over on us."

"Good to know." Trent put an arm around her shoulders and gave a squeeze. A knock sounded at the door and the bellboy entered with a cart for the luggage.

They were on their way to Kyoto.

9

TOKYO STATION was unlike anyplace Trent had ever seen or imagined. So many people. Mostly, he saw a mix of gray and blue suits dotted with the more brightly clothed younger Japanese, many with blond or wildly colored hair. Beth had to drag him through the masses of commuters to get to the gates where the *shinkansen*—bullet trains—departed.

They joined Naoko Maeda at a prearranged gate and together made their way to the platform. They piled themselves and their luggage into the train and settled into the comfortable seats. Comfortable at least to the Japanese, Trent thought, as he debated where to put his legs so they wouldn't be in anyone's way. As the train filled, he kept them toward the window, but once they departed, he was able to stretch out into the aisle, carefully moving them when anyone tried to pass.

"How fast are we going?"

"Three hundred kilometers per hour. We'll arrive in Kyoto in under three hours," Naoko said.

"Wow. We don't have many trains in the States. Subways in big cities—even in LA for the past ten or so years. But no one takes trains between cities anymore."

"Didn't government programs favoring highways make trains almost obsolete? A favor to the oil industry. Back before oil prices got so high," she replied. "Now they don't need favors but still are so profitable."

"Uh, I'm not sure, but that sounds about right." Trent glanced at Beth, who was looking out the window. He wondered how on earth Naoko knew so much about American politics and business. "Did you ever live in the US?"

"No. I studied there for a semester during college. But many Japanese have read and studied a lot about the United States. We want to know what your country is like, and whether we can learn anything to do—or avoid—from the successes and failures of your policies."

"I didn't realize that. I thought there was more interest in films and television."

"Sure, there is a huge love of American pop culture here. And in trade we've sent you anime, which I hear is very popular even with adults in the US."

"Manga, too, but I admit I haven't read any. Or watched anime. Am I missing out on something?" Trent waited, wondering if he'd insulted this well-respected art and antiquities expert by asking about anime. Maybe he should keep his mouth shut as Beth had suggested. And as she was doing.

"To be honest, I have a few favorite anime." Naoko launched into a discussion of plots and characters that had Trent's head spinning.

"Oh, I love *Psycho Pass* too," Beth chimed in, a huge smile on her face. "It's one of my favorites."

The two women chatted about more incredible plots, and Trent wondered if it would be rude to call Reed while they were bonding. A few minutes later, Beth had switched to Japanese, and Trent had his answer. He grabbed the cell phone and got up. He could use the opportunity to stretch his legs and call Reed from the end of the car. He wanted to wander around the magical train. He'd heard about these super-fast trains for years, and finally he was on one. He felt like a kid again. Beth and Naoko seemed blasé about the train, and with their minds on demons and unrequited high-school romances, they barely noticed the scenery zooming past.

He strode through two more cars, both identical to the one he was riding in. The passengers were mostly silent, heads bent, intent on phones, laptops, or other electronic devices. Younger passengers wore ubiquitous iPod headphones. Trent remembered how when he was a kid everyone had a Sony Walkman. Now Apple had conquered the world on the electronic front.

Trent pulled the phone out of his pocket when he got to the end of the next car. He accessed the world clock app Beth set up so he would know what time it was back home. She remembered his middle-of-the-night calls from Thailand and wanted to spare Reed the same.

"One o'clock," Trent said out loud for no reason. Or perhaps just to hear another American voice besides Beth's. Somehow, even when she spoke English here, she seemed like a different person. She might have changed her outfit back to something more normal for her, but she'd retained that odd politeness, that deference he'd noticed.

"Good evening," a middle-aged man with dark strands of hair plastered over a smooth, balding pate said.

"Oh, hi. Good evening."

"Are you American?"

"Yes." Trent wondered what prompted the man to speak to him.

"How tall are you?"

He stopped wondering. "Six foot three."

"In centimeters?"

"I don't know."

"May I take a photo with you?" The man smiled eagerly. He looked like a forty-year-old kid.

Trent couldn't think of a good excuse, so he nodded. The man whipped a phone out of his jacket pocket, sidled up to Trent, and snapped a few shots of both of them, the flash blinding Trent. He was still blinking away the white spots on the inside of his eyelids when another man approached him. Trent quickly turned and rushed back to the car with Beth and Naoko. The man got caught by the sliding door between carriages and gave up. Trent ducked to the side of the door and speed dialed Reed.

"Acton." He sounded like he was underwater.

"Reed? You okay?"

"Trent, it's after one in the morning. Are you okay?"

"One a.m.? Oops." Trent considered snapping the phone shut, but since he'd already woken Reed, they might as well talk, right?

"Trent? I thought Beth got you the clock app. Have her show you how to use it."

Trent gave the phone a nasty look. If they had video calls, Reed would know what Trent thought of that suggestion. "She did, but she must have set it up wrong. It says 1:00 p.m." He wondered if Reed would buy that excuse.

"Yeah. Right. You just read it wrong." He paused. "Hey, I miss you. Maybe I was dreaming about you."

"Really?" Trent's indignation melted away with Reed's admission. He got a nice warm feeling in his chest because Reed had said it first. "I miss you too. Every time I see something wonderful, I want to call and tell you."

"So, what's wonderful enough to call now?"

"The train. We're on the bullet train. It's only going to take like an hour to go three hundred miles. How cool is that?" Trent probably had the numbers wrong, but it sounded impressive. Reed had so many more experiences; Trent felt like the country cousin.

"That fast?" Reed laughed. "But that's cool." His voice was gravelly. It sent a shiver down Trent's spine. He looked around to notice a couple of passengers were looking at him. He ducked into the bathroom at the end of the car and slid the door shut.

"Reed, are you naked?" Trent leaned against the mirror. He closed his eyes and waited for Reed's response.

"No. Not exactly." Was it Trent's imagination or did Reed's voice get a little lower, a little more whispery? He could feel himself hardening already at Reed's mysterious response.

"Not exactly?"

"I'm wearing one of your T-shirts. The fabulous unicorn one."

Trent tried not to laugh. It wasn't particularly sexy. In fact it was silly, a unicorn braiding its tail. But Reed could make anything look sexy. "Anything else?"

"No. Just the T-shirt." Trent had worn that shirt when he went for a run the day before he'd left LA. He smiled at the thought of Reed choosing that shirt. Then the image of Reed in Trent's T-shirt, lying on the bed, the T-shirt riding up to expose Reed's cock, took center stage. He pictured Reed nice and hard and imagined taking Reed into his hand, feeling him harden as he squeezed and stroked the hot flesh. Damn, now Trent was hard as a rock. "Oh, God, Reed, I wish you hadn't said that." Trent's voice was low now, too. He was sure Reed knew just what effect he'd had.

"Where are you, Trent?"

"In the bathroom on the train." Trent unzipped his pants and freed his dick from his boxers. "I wish you were here." He hadn't meant to say that so soon. Not just for sex, but because he did want Reed to share in his new experiences.

"What would you do?" Reed's breath came in audible pants. Trent knew he was stroking himself by the little moans Reed let out.

Trent's nipples tingled and his shirt felt rough against them. He squeezed around the base of his cock, knowing if Reed said one more word he'd come all over the wall in the tiny bathroom. He grabbed a wad of toilet paper and closed his eyes again. "Reed, I wish I could suck you right now. Run my tongue along the head of your cock then take you deep." He imagined how Reed tasted and smelled and how he'd squirm as Trent slid his hands up under the T-shirt and pinched Reed's nipples. Trent could make Reed come in less than a minute if he did that, though usually he made the ride last much, much longer.

"Deeper, Trent." There was a catch in Reed's voice. He was close.

Trent stroked himself, up then down, wishing he had Reed's cock in his hand and not his own. He groaned the way Reed liked him to do during oral sex, so the vibration went through Reed's body.

"Yeah, Trent—" The rest of the sentence got cut off as he heard Reed coming, grunting softly through his orgasm. The combined image and sound had Trent coming a second later. He minimized the mess with the wad of tissue.

"Reed. I'll call you when we get to the hotel in Kyoto, okay?"

"Yeah, you can tell me more about the train."

"The train." Trent chuckled. He'd never think of trains the same way. A knock on the door brought him back to reality. "I have to go."

"Bye." Reed clicked off. Just the sound made Trent feel a little lonely again.

Trent cleaned himself up and checked his appearance in the warped mirror on the wall. Then he slid the door open to see an elderly woman, tiny and stooped, holding the hand of a girl about ten years old. Trent's entire face and neck felt as if they had caught fire. He avoided eye contact and moved into the aisle with one last glance at the bathroom, hoping he'd cleaned up carefully.

He walked slowly back toward his own car, giving himself time to calm down before he rejoined Beth and Naoko. As he slid into his seat, they barely looked up, still chatting amiably in Japanese. When Beth finished her sentence she glanced over.

"Hey, Trent. How's Reed?" She grinned and looked toward Naoko. "*Bōifurendo*," she added. Naoko nodded.

"How did you know I called him?" Trent asked.

"You're smiling. The way you do when you're together." She gave a wistful smile.

Trent hoped he wasn't smiling *too* much. "He's fine, except I woke him up."

"Got the time backwards, didn't you?" She laughed.

Trent didn't think that deserved an answer.

"Would anyone care for dinner?" Naoko asked, clearly sensing Trent's dissipating good mood at Beth's ribbing. "The *shinkansen* no longer have dining cars and now only serve sandwiches from a trolley cart or a vending machine."

Trent's stomach rumbled at the mention of food. "We didn't eat before we got on board."

"I suspected you might not have time. So I stopped for *ekiben* before I met you."

Beth gave an excited little clap.

"What's ekiben?" Trent asked.

"A Japanese tradition," Naoko explained. "Each station has a specialty food and the ekiben—station lunch—is a meal that includes the local specialty."

"You know bento boxes, right?" Beth asked and Trent nodded. They were the take-out meals from Japanese restaurants. "Same 'ben' as in 'ekiben.'"

"Oh, got it." Trent nodded.

Naoko smiled and dug into one of the large bags she'd brought on board. She handed each of them a small flat box wrapped in a colorful scarf.

"Wow, it's like a Christmas present!" Trent didn't want to mess up the pretty wrapping. He waited until Beth and Naoko opened theirs before he unwrapped his. All three meals were different and Trent didn't recognize anything except the rice.

"One is *tonkatsu*—pork cutlet." Naoko pointed at Beth's. "That's *unajū*, a kind of marinated eel. And the last one is *kamameshi*—vegetables and meat cooked with seasoned rice."

They all looked and smelled delicious.

"Which would you like, Trent?" Beth asked. "I think you'd like *unajū*, but if you don't, you can trade with me." She slid the box over to Trent.

"It's eel?" He looked at it and sniffed. It smelled fantastic, not slimy or eely, though he really didn't know what an eel would smell like.

"It's a very popular dish here. A special treat."

"So are Rocky Mountain Oysters, but you wouldn't get me to eat one," Trent said. "But when in Rome…." He picked up his chopsticks and separated them, waiting for the women to sort out which meal each wanted. Beth got tonkatsu and Naoko took the casserole meal.

"Oh, we can't forget this." Naoko opened another bag and pulled out three cans of beer. They all popped their cans open and made a toast. "Kampai!"

Trent took a tentative bite of the grilled eel. It was coated with a sweet and salty sauce and the tender meat almost melted in his mouth. It was delicious. "Oh, wow. This is incredible. I love it!" He collected another bite of fish and rice on his chopsticks and popped it into his mouth, smiling.

"Trent, you are very skilled with chopsticks. You didn't drop anything. Not even one grain of rice!" Naoko complimented him.

"I eat a lot of Asian food, so I've had some practice." He appreciated the compliment. "Why haven't I ever had this before? Do they serve it in the US?"

"Yes. At all sushi places. But when we go for sushi you're always too squeamish to try the eel."

"Really?" Trent munched away at his meal. In addition to the grilled eel, it contained some marinated vegetables cut into flower shapes and small segments of rice sprinkled with different seeds and flavorings, each just one bite for an average-sized person. For Trent, he could easily fit a couple into his mouth at once.

"Naoko, thank you so much for bringing the meals. It was very thoughtful." Beth finished her beer and relaxed back in her seat. "*Gochisōsama*," she said with a smile at Naoko. "Those were such a treat!"

Trent tried to repeat the phrase, one Beth had told him was very polite. Naoko smiled and collected the empty meal boxes.

"I'll take care of that, unless you wanted to keep one of the special boxes?" Beth asked, and Naoko shook her head. "I want to stretch my legs anyway. Should I get some more beer while I'm up?"

"We have about another hour until we arrive in Kyoto, so we have time," Naoko replied.

"Trent, do you want to help me?" Beth asked as she stood.

"Sure." He grabbed the boxes and followed her toward the rear of the train. At the end of the next car was an open section filled with brightly lit vending machines. He dumped the boxes in a trash can and joined Beth in front of one of the machines. It was filled with rows of beer cans. Silver, gold, or covered with images of flowers or samurai.

"What is this?" He asked, feeling like a kid in a candy store.

"Beer vending machine. Which one do you want?"

"Why are there flowers on some of the cans?"

"Those are special for ohanami."

"How does it taste?" Trent angled his head to look more carefully at the array of cans.

"Like beer. Only the can is different, and what's inside is pretty much the same as all the other cans. Each beer company makes different cans for each season. Just pick the one that looks nice."

He debated for several minutes until Beth glared at him and he chose the Kirin with an illustration of cherry blossoms. Beth selected one with a dragon and another with a samurai on it.

The rest of the journey went quickly as they sipped their beers.

"So, Naoko, what can you tell us about Motofuji-san?" Beth asked. "Have you met him?"

"Yes. He's loaned some of his pieces to the museum before and I've been asked to appraise portions of his collection as well. He asked me to authenticate a few pieces last year when he wished to purchase something, but in the end…." Her voice trailed off and she left the thought unfinished.

"What kind of name is Motofuji anyway?" Beth asked. "I've never heard it before."

"It's quite an interesting story, but I should allow him to tell you himself. He's quite proud of the tale."

"Really?" Beth gave a thoughtful nod. She turned to Trent. "Usually it's not polite to ask people about their family or background, the way we do at home. Here someone may choose to tell you something, or you ask a mutual friend."

"Oh." Trent was glad Beth was here. He was certain he'd embarrass himself without her. He could trust her to translate only the polite version of whatever he said. Or so he hoped. He recalled how she hadn't told him everything earlier in the day when he thought she'd been talking to Naoko about yakuza. But then again, maybe he'd just misunderstood. So many Japanese words sounded the same to him.

The memory gave him a niggling little ache in the pit of his stomach, and he wished he hadn't drunk the second beer.

10

THE TRAIN arrived right on time, neither a minute early nor a minute late. They collected their luggage, and as soon as they exited the platform, Naoko spotted a uniformed limo driver waving a placard identifying their group. He whisked them away to a charming Japanese-style inn.

They had to take their shoes off right inside the front door and put on the indoor slippers. Trent had to try a couple of pair before he found ones that would fit his larger-than-Japanese feet.

Naoko had her own room, but Trent and Beth shared a small suite. Once Beth explained how traditional the place was, Trent didn't want separate rooms. He wasn't sure he'd figure out the shower, bath, or even the toilet. And once they got into the room, Beth admitted the clerk hadn't wanted to leave him on his own in a room, worried he'd mix up the floor slippers with the bathroom slippers or damage the tatami.

Trent pretended to be interested in the artwork on the walls as he willed his embarrassment to fade. This suite was almost completely opposite the one they'd had in Tokyo. The whole city—or what Trent had seen of it—seemed very different from Tokyo. Less traffic, less bustling, more trees. It felt much more relaxed and much more traditional.

If only *he* could relax. He considered calling Reed for advice and decided this was something he had to handle himself. He'd known Beth since they were eighteen—more than ten years. Reed wouldn't have any advice, and Trent had to stop relying on him to handle the unpleasant things. This wasn't a spider in the bathroom. Trent had to sort it out.

He waited until Beth had freshened up from the journey and unpacked some of her new clothes before he said anything. Thankfully, he didn't even have to start the conversation.

"Trent, honey, you're so quiet." She sat down on a floor cushion next to him. The room had tatami mat floors and no furniture, just cushions. They didn't really fit Trent's size and he wasn't particularly comfortable folding up his legs underneath his body the way Beth did. "Just sit cross-legged, whatever works for you," Beth whispered as he shifted around.

He took a deep breath. He could smell the fresh, almost grassy aroma of the flooring. He gave a weak smile.

"Okay, something's wrong. Usually you can't shut up asking questions, looking into everything. You got jetlag or just missing Reed?"

"Neither. I feel like something is wrong. Between us."

"Nothing's wrong. What do you mean?" Worry crept into her voice and she put a hand out toward his arm.

"What's with Naoko? When we—"

"Naoko? You're mad because we were talking in Japanese? I didn't think you wanted to join in the discussion, but I'm sorry if you felt we excluded you."

"I did feel a little left out on the train, but I'm talking about this morning, in her office. We asked her about the collectors, and I know you didn't translate everything she said. What aren't you telling me, Beth?"

Beth pulled her hand off Trent's arm and looked down at her knees, which were peeking out from under her short skirt as she sat on the floor cushion. "I didn't know what to think about what she said, and I was waiting until we were alone before I brought it up."

"We were alone right after that, until you ran off to go shopping."

"Hey, don't act like that with me, Trent."

Trent paused before he said what was on his mind. Mentally, he rephrased it before speaking. "I'm not criticizing your shopping trip or your priorities. But we're here to do a job for Leah. I made a promise to her, and I need your help. If I can't rely on you, let me know now, and I'll hire another interpreter. But I have to trust you'll tell me what's going on or figure some tactful way to discuss it in private."

Beth nodded, but Trent could see the conversation had drained the joy out of her face. His stomach ached again at having to broach this topic. Now he understood Reed's situation more clearly, all those times when Trent got in the way of something bigger and more important than their plans for the day. He didn't want to regret bringing Beth on this trip.

"She told me something that worried me, and I wanted to find out more before I shared it with you. I also wanted to see if we could trust her before we believe everything she says."

That seemed reasonable. "I just need to be in on it. What don't you trust about her? And what did she say?"

"She said there were rumors that Motofuji was the leader of a yakuza gang. He's quite old, and his gang is very old fashioned, traditional. He's not the flashy young style of gang member who shows off money and doesn't care what the police think of him, which is a common stereotype in popular culture."

So Trent had heard correctly. What did this mean for their job here? "Is it dangerous to meet him?"

"No. I don't think so. She's not afraid of him. The issue is whether his collection is genuine. I don't know that we'll ever know how he obtained the pieces. I suppose some of them might be stolen." Beth looked around as if someone might be watching or listening to them. Trent tried not to think of paintings with the eyes following them around the room. He couldn't help glancing at all the pictures: all flowers or calligraphy. No portraits. He let out a little sigh and relaxed.

"Well, that's part of what we need to research. What Naoko has to research. Can we trust her?"

"I think so. I wanted to engage her in chitchat, girl talk. I don't think she could relax and talk about trivialities if she were trying to lie or cheat us. She seemed genuine."

"Okay. I need to talk to Leah about this. Do they have Wi-Fi in this place? It's like we walked into a scene from *Shogun*."

"Yeah, let me get the instructions." Beth padded over to the desk, which was situated near the door on a portion of the floor that was carpeted and not covered with tatami. Apparently, you couldn't put a desk and chair on a tatami mat, or so Trent surmised. Beth unpacked her laptop and tapped away at the keyboard, occasionally referring to a small card on the desk. Two minutes later she let out a little cheer.

"Yup, Wi-Fi is connected. Get your computer and I'll set you up."

Trent did and settled back on the floor with it. "Okay, what should I say to Leah?"

Together they crafted an e-mail summarizing the situation for Leah and asking whether they should meet Motofuji as arranged. "We should have an answer by our morning. If we need to cancel, I'm sure he won't kill us. Will he?"

"Trent, don't be so melodramatic." She paused and glanced at her own computer for a moment before turning back to him. "You didn't watch a bunch of yakuza movies before the trip, did you?"

Trent shrugged and Beth threw a slipper at him. "Trent, you scare the crap out of yourself for no good reason."

"We're supposed to see a yakuza boss tomorrow. That sounds like a good reason to me!"

"Keep your voice down. We don't know who's listening."

"Thanks, Beth, you had to remind me."

"Sorry. Do you want to get something else to eat? If not, I'll have the maid set up the bedding."

Neither of them had any appetite despite their small, early dinner on the train. Trent sent Reed a quick e-mail instead of calling. He wasn't in the mood for more phone sex. If he heard Reed's voice again, he'd feel more worried and not less. And he certainly didn't want to sound needy or "melodramatic." Best not to say anything about the yakuza stuff.

Beth called the front desk, and a woman wearing a pale-pink and gold kimono came in and unfolded thin mattresses onto the floor for them, each covered with a thick quilt. "Futon," she said to Trent and gave a shy smile. Then she bowed and left them.

"That's a futon?" The flat mattresses didn't look anything like any futon he'd seen.

"Yes. This is what a futon really looks like. What we call futon back home is nothing like the real thing. They are much more comfortable than they look. You'll see."

Trent quirked one corner of his mouth, wondering how he would ever sleep on the floor on the thin padding. But compared to worrying about yakuza and fake artwork, the futon was the least of his concerns.

You can figure everything out, he told himself as he lay on the futon trying to sleep. The bedding was simply a longer, slightly thicker version of the floor cushion and Trent could feel the tatami through it. Once he found the right position, he was surprised how comfortable it was. The tatami gave under his weight, just enough to cushion and support his body. The fresh scent and the slight squeaky-crunching sound relaxed him and he let the worries of the day flow out of his brain.

THE NEXT morning they took quick showers in their own Western-style bathroom, rather than the traditional bath down the hall. Trent had been looking forward to that. He knew how to shower first before getting into the tub. But there wasn't time for the whole Japanese bathing ritual, which Beth explained most people did at night. Naoko joined them for breakfast, served by the hotel staff in Trent and Beth's room.

The woman who served them wore a traditional kimono and brought in what seemed like a dozen small dishes. Eggs, nori strips, assorted vegetables, a flattened grilled fish over a tiny flame for each of them, and plenty of rice. She poured tea for everyone then backed out of the room on her knees.

"What is all of this?" He didn't recognize most of the food and none of it looked at all like breakfast.

Naoko and Beth explained a traditional Japanese breakfast. "This hotel serves a very special meal, so you have a chance to try many local dishes. For dinner they serve about three times as much food. It's spectacular." Naoko smiled and went to work, taking pieces from each of the dishes and placing them on her bowl of rice before picking up a mouthful with the chopsticks. Trent tried to repeat her movements, but he wasn't quite that skilled.

His mood had improved over the night before. Leah had responded, and Trent and Beth had a chance to discuss her e-mail before Naoko joined them. Leah didn't know whether the accusations of Motofuji's yakuza connections were true, but he had an impeccable reputation as a collector. She'd sold pieces for him before, and he'd worked with other galleries. He'd even paid for their travel in advance, rather than out of proceeds, so she felt he could be trusted as a businessman, but if they really felt uncomfortable, she understood if they didn't want to go to his home. Naoko could go on her own, then appraise his collection and inform them if anything wasn't authentic or had questionable provenance. There was another local appraiser whom they could consult if Naoko wasn't forthcoming with either the authentications or appraisals. Leah knew enough about some of the pieces that Naoko couldn't fool her. Trent's stomach stopped complaining and he enjoyed this traditional but unusual breakfast.

THEY WERE scheduled to meet Motofuji at his home that morning at ten, and a hired car—arranged by Motofuji—took them. Naoko had a special camera and a case full of notebooks. The driver stowed everything in the trunk and took them on a scenic route through the city on their way. Beth and Naoko pointed out famous landmarks—temples, the ancient palace, and several important shrines—as they wove their way up into the hills. The journey reminded Trent of the winding route to Elvio Milaccio's secluded home on the exclusive island in Italy, where he and Reed had discovered much more than drug dealers during their erstwhile vacation. He didn't mention the similarities to Beth.

The house was nestled in a forest. Trent had never seen so many shades of green at one time. As the car pulled into the drive, he noticed the house looked like a small version of a palace, with peaked roofs and a sand garden to one side of the door. There was also a cluster of cherry blossom trees—near their peak. It was so beautiful and peaceful. Trent tried to ignore how the man who lived here earned his fortune.

A middle-aged woman wearing a simple, dark kimono opened the door and bowed profusely to everyone in the group. After they removed their shoes and put on slippers, she backed away, leaving them in the entrance hall, presumably to alert their host. Trent glanced at the several displays of ikebana arranged around the entrance hall. He found the styles too spare for his taste, though each blossom was perfect. A variety of gorgeous pottery vases held the flower arrangements, and from the way Naoko peered at them, they were possibly more valuable than they looked. If this was how the man decorated his entrance hall, what treasures awaited them in the rest of the house?

They didn't have long to wait. A man in his sixties, nearly bald and very slender, soon entered the hallway. He wore a well-tailored Western-style suit.

"Welcome to my home. I am Motofuji." He bowed and said something in Japanese.

Trent bowed, trying to go lower as he'd been schooled. "I'm Trent Copeland." He resisted the urge to shake hands.

Motofuji bowed again. "Welcome, Cōpurando-san."

Then Beth introduced herself and finally Naoko, in a mixture of English and Japanese.

Beth quickly translated the brief formalized introductions they had made in Japanese. Trent recognized the phrases, though he didn't necessarily understand the introduction ritual. He didn't need a translation but assumed Beth was showing him she would interpret everything.

They were invited for tea in a large front room overlooking the city below. It was another ritual before they would approach the business that brought them here. Trent fought off his impatience to get to the collection. Something told him to get out of here as quickly as possible. That ache in his gut. It couldn't just be the little fish he had for breakfast, could it?

As they had tea, Motofuji asked Trent in slow, careful English about his visit to Japan so far. When he struggled with a word he said it in Japanese and Beth translated.

"May I ask after Lei-a-san's health? Did she have her baby yet?"

"In two weeks," Trent replied. "Twins."

After some more discussion of Kyoto and Los Angeles, Naoko spoke up. "Motofuji-san, perhaps you could share the story of your name for Cōpurando-san. He was very intrigued by it."

Trent felt self-conscious about his nosy question until he saw Motofuji's face break into a broad smile. A few teeth were crooked or missing, giving him the look of a lopsided jack-o-lantern, far less scary than the yakuza butcher Trent pictured every time he glanced at the man, despite his politeness and genteel exterior.

"Oh, that's quite a story." Motofuji nodded and poured more tea for everyone. Then he settled back onto his heels and sipped his cup. "Back in samurai days—three hundred years ago—no one had a last name. Not a real last name. Everyone had a first name, and generally they were called by their profession or skill. 'Ichiro the butcher.' Only samurai could have family names. The rest of the people were prohibited. Until 1875. The new government was modern and tried to end the feudal practices under the shogun." He took a break for another sip and Trent wondered how long the history lesson would go on. "Everyone had to have a name by a particular date. People in my ancestors' village lined up to choose a name."

"Choose?" Trent put a hand over his mouth at his interruption.

"Yes. Choose or the mayor would choose for you." Motofuji chuckled. Trent glanced at Beth, who seemed to be as curious as Trent now. "Those at the front of the line chose regal or important sounding names. As you know, Fuji-san—Mount Fuji—is very special to all Japanese. So the name 'Fujimoto,' meaning originating on Fuji-san, was in high demand. My ancestor was in the middle of the line. His family was from a town in Fuji-san's shadow, so he wanted the name very much. But when it was his turn, the mayor said there were too many 'Fujimotos' already. He gave my ancestor the name 'Motofuji' instead, if he was so intent on having 'Fuji' in his name. The men behind him laughed, but he took it anyway. Proudly. It's a very uncommon name, unlike Fujimoto. There are a million Fujimotos, but not many Motofujis." Motofuji laughed so hard he began to cough. When the coughing subsided, he laughed again.

"Thank you for sharing such a unique story with me," Trent said sincerely. He smiled and glanced toward Naoko who nodded and scrunched up her nose. Even Beth nodded her approval of his response.

"Cōpurando-san, what is the origin of your family name?"

"I don't know. But now I am curious to find out."

"Perhaps you can share the story next time we meet." Motofuji gave Trent a big grin.

With tea finished, Naoko steered the discussion to Motofuji's collection. They moved around his house as he spoke a little about each piece, including where he had obtained it. He had documents for many of the pieces and handed them over to Naoko. She took photographs of each piece and asked additional questions. Beth whispered the translations of the discussion into Trent's ear, and he made notes for Leah.

They had only made it halfway around the collection when Motofuji suggested a break for lunch. His maid served grilled fish with pickled vegetables. Motofuji complimented Trent on his skill with chopsticks—he was getting used to that. The discussion centered around the *netsuke* carvings and some exquisite ancient ceramics they had seen that morning.

In the afternoon Motofuji showed off the real gems of his collection: several dozen woodblock prints by the most well-known artists and another dozen by almost unknowns. Naoko explained that these artists died before they created enough works to become as well-known as Hokusai, Utamaro, or Hiroshige. Trent thought some of these were even more exquisite, including one with a danshoku theme: a military officer kissing a young man. Trent's cheeks warmed up when Motofuji noticed his interest.

"It's very rare. Very rare. At the time the owner probably hid it. But you can see this window overlooks a temple—" He pointed to the print. "—and if you look closely you may recognize it as the Ryōan-ji." Motofuji grinned and looked toward Naoko. "Maeda-san, do you recognize that view?"

"I think there are many buildings which face that side of the temple. Now. Though most have an obstructed view." She licked her bottom lip. "But at the time it was made, perhaps very few." A grin spread across her face. "Was this a window of Kyoto Imperial Palace, the emperor's former palace?"

Motofuji nodded. "I believe so." He grinned his Halloween grin.

“So was the officer in this print supposed to be the emperor?” Trent asked, not sure he understood.

“Who knows? Maybe. Or someone of high rank in his court. So many secrets buried with the dead.”

They took notes on the rest of the prints in the room, but Trent’s gaze returned to the one that might depict an emperor kissing another man. As they gathered up Naoko’s equipment to move into the next room, Motofuji approached Trent.

“Cōpurando-san, I would like to give the print to you, as thanks for doing business with me. I know it will go to someone who will value it as more than an investment on a wall.”

Trent’s heart pounded. He didn’t know what to say. He couldn’t possibly accept it, but he wasn’t sure whether he was supposed to take it or to refuse it. He glanced at Beth and her gaze gave him no clue. “I can’t take such a valuable gift. But thank you for the offer. It is lovely and perhaps I might be able to afford it, once we have appraised it.” Trent looked to Naoko for help.

“Cōpurando-san, the value of this print is in your heart, not in Maeda-san’s knowledge.” Motofuji made a polite bow to Naoko and apologized to her in Japanese. “I haven’t yet decided which pieces to part with yet. Once Maeda-san completes her valuations, I will decide with Leah which pieces to sell. But my mind is made up on this print. It is a gift to you.”

Beth nodded and whispered into Trent’s ear. “Say thank you. We can sort it out later.”

“Thank you very much, Motofuji-san. I will cherish the gift as a memory of our meeting.” Beth nodded approval and Trent relaxed.

“Motofuji-san, I have never seen so many pieces from outside Japan in a private collection,” Naoko said when Motofuji brought them into a room filled with Chinese and Korean pottery spanning millennia. “You have an excellent eye for beauty, whatever the source.”

“I am pleased you like the collection” was all he said, somewhat ill at ease until he began to discuss the objects again. He gave them a primer in Asian art history as he pointed out his favorite pieces. Occasionally Naoko remarked over a piece of particular beauty or significance. Trent’s brain had hit art overload a thousand years earlier and was on autopilot as he helped Naoko and took notes. It wasn’t until the next room that anything caught his attention again.

The jade room. Trent had never imagined jade could take on so many different shades and hues and shapes. From tiny intricately carved pendants and charms to large Buddhas, dragons, and even pitchers, and *was that a phallus?* But the place of honor in this room was held by something Trent had never imagined. He strode toward the display case in the center of the room. Most of Motofuji's art was on shelves or cases set into the wall. This was one of the few pieces set in a display case with specialty lighting. He walked around it twice to take in the beauty of the thing.

A dagger carved from pure jade.

"Impressive, isn't it?" Motofuji stepped up behind Trent. Beth and Naoko came around the other side of the case and stared down at the dagger.

Trent nodded, feeling as if he were under its spell. The dagger was perhaps ten inches long, with a curved blade that came to a sharp point. It was thin enough for the light to shine through, making the thing seem to glow a brilliant emerald. The handle was intricately carved with lions or perhaps dragons. Even the blade had been engraved with another fantastical beast.

"I never saw a blade made from stone like that. Is it sharp?"

"During the stone age, techniques for sharpening stone without breaking it were perfected," Naoko said. "I imagine this one is carved as thinly as possibly without fracturing the jade. It's quite an accomplishment for both its artistry and its functionality as a weapon."

Motofuji nodded and turned to Naoko, speaking in Japanese. Beth came over toward Trent to translate, but the discussion soon turned technical about carving, and Trent gave up trying to follow it. Beth listened and occasionally translated portions she thought might interest Trent.

But Trent remained transfixed in front of the case, still drawn to the glowing jade inside. Was it a trick of the light, or was there something truly magical about this dagger? He wondered how valuable it was. Perhaps it was one of the pieces Motofuji intended to keep.

As if reading Trent's mind, their host went back to English. "I won't be selling this one. It has some sentimental value for me. But I would like Naoko-san to prepare an appraisal for my insurance company." Motofuji paused. "Just in case."

"Of course," Naoko responded with a small bow.

As she moved around the room photographing and cataloging the other jade pieces, Trent couldn't help glancing back at the dagger. Had he never seen the piece, nearly any other item in the room would have impressed him.

But the dagger put everything else to shame. No wonder Motofuji wanted to keep it.

When they finished cataloging all of Motofuji's pieces it was nearly six o'clock, and the sky was beginning to darken. The driver and the maid helped stow Naoko's equipment in the car, and they stood in the entrance hall, making their good-byes, along with a great deal of bowing.

"I would like to treat you all to dinner tonight, if you do not have other plans," Motofuji said as they were about to leave. "There is a small restaurant which is famous for its *Kyoto-ryori*—our local delicacies. Kinmata has been serving for over two hundred years. It may be Cōpurando-san's only chance to try it. Will you all join me?"

Naoko took in a sharp breath. "It's quite an honor to be invited there. I have heard of it, but have never been."

"I'm honored again by your thoughtful invitation." Trent paused for a moment. The words had come out without his taking time to think. A few hours ago, he'd thought this man some kind of monster, and now he was flattered by Motofuji's dinner invitation and wouldn't dream of turning him down. This on top of his giving Trent the gift of the woodblock print—though Trent hadn't asked about it and Motofuji hadn't given it to him yet. Maybe he intended to present it at the meal. "Yes, we would all be delighted to be your guests tonight."

"Very well. I will have the car return you to the hotel and then bring you to dinner at eight o'clock if it suits you."

With the plans agreed to, Trent, Beth, and Naoko got in the car and returned to the hotel. Trent was about to speak as they drove down the hill, but Beth shook her head and squeezed his wrist—one of the warning signs they had agreed upon in private before joining Naoko that morning. Trent nodded and smiled. It was something he'd learned at Quantico, and he was thrilled to get a chance to use it.

Eat your heart out, Michael Westen!

11

MOTOFUJI'S DINNER was sumptuous and elegant, though Trent had no idea what half of it was. Beth explained the best she could, and Trent tasted it all. He suspected she outright lied to him a few times about the ingredients to make sure he would try everything in order to be polite.

During the meal Motofuji suggested his favorite sights for Trent to visit on his first trip to Kyoto. "I'm certain I'll see you again, Cōpurando-san. You'll be down to supervise the shipping, and perhaps there will be additional pieces in the future."

Trent hadn't thought that far in advance. He and Beth still needed time to digest their day with Motofuji and to consider Beth's impressions of whether or not Leah could trust Naoko's appraisals. They would have time once she left the next day. Beth and Trent intended to stay in Kyoto for another two days to tour the city and then meet with Naoko later in the week. They also had another collector to visit in Tokyo. Motofuji was the older, and thus more distinguished, client, so they had gone to see him first.

After dinner Motofuji again surprised Trent. "Cōpurando-san, I promised the woodblock print to you, yet I have not brought it tonight."

"It's okay. As you said, we'll be back next week to arrange shipping."

"I was hoping perhaps you would accompany me back to my home tonight and allow me to present it to you there. I have something else I would like to share with you."

Trent glanced at Beth who blinked twice. Another sign. *Say yes, but if you want I can get you out of it.*

"We can stay for a short time, but…." Beth said.

Motofuji glanced at Beth then back to Trent. “Just you. I do not intend to say anything so complicated you would require an interpreter.”

At that moment, Trent wished he’d presented Beth as a friend rather than an employee. They had thought she would seem more neutral as such, and Motofuji would not pay her much attention. That plan had worked a bit too well. He didn’t know how to back out without appearing rude, so he agreed. Then he felt ungrateful for his reluctance to collect a valuable gift.

The hired car left with Beth and Naoko while Trent and Motofuji waited for the hostess to arrange a taxi for the drive to his house. When they arrived it was dark, with lights showing in only a few windows. The taxi’s tires crunched on the gravel as it turned into the driveway.

“Will the taxi be back?” Trent asked.

“No, I’ve arranged for the hired car, which is now taking the women to the hotel, to come back to retrieve you.”

Trent nodded, feeling the night’s chill more fiercely.

They stood outside, looking down on the bright lights of the ancient city, the temples spotlighted. Cherry blossom petals floated in the air like late spring snow, and Trent felt them land soft as a kiss on his hair.

Kiss. The word reminded him of Reed. Would Reed come alone to the Godfather’s house? What had he been thinking? He tried to recall the training course: slow down and listen. Watch and listen. Danger moves in fast, and you can see it coming if you remain still and alert. The advice sounded like Reed’s Zen training. Maybe there was a connection.

Trent nearly jumped out of his skin at the sound of a twig cracking. He turned toward the noise—Motofuji shifting his weight as he took in the scene below, silently. After a few moments where Trent thought he heard footsteps, Motofuji spoke. “Cōpurando-san, you impress me. You have an eye and appreciation of beauty rare in the Americans I have met. You understand the importance of silence. Words are not always necessary.”

Trent didn’t know how to respond, so he just smiled. It was dark, and he didn’t know whether Motofuji could see him. He didn’t care. Motofuji took a step toward the front door, and reluctantly, Trent followed. His host unlocked the door himself.

“I’ve given my maid and driver a few days off—which is why we used a taxi tonight.” He took a breath and glanced around the room, his gaze lingering on an item here and there. “I want to sit here alone with my collection and my memories while I decide which items to sell. Perhaps you think me a crazy old man." Motofuji chuckled and motioned for Trent to follow him.

As Trent did he wondered again how smart it was to come up here. But what would Motofuji gain from harming him? Nothing. The realization put Trent at ease. Motofuji led Trent into the jade room. With most of the lights in the house off, the jade dagger seemed to glow even more intently in its display case.

"You admire this piece. Would you care to examine it more closely?"

Trent leaned down so his face was near the glass. Motofuji chuckled.

"Allow me to remove it from the case for you." Motofuji switched off the light in the display case. Despite the loss of its spotlight, the dagger still shone as if lit from within. Motofuji unfastened some latches and pulled the glass box off and set it down. He gestured to the dagger.

Trent glanced at him for approval, and only then did he reach out to touch it. Slowly.

A sound from the back of the house startled him and he stood up straight. Breaking glass? Footsteps?

"My cat. Nothing to fear."

Trent shrugged and reached for the dagger again. He was afraid to touch it. He let his hands hover for a moment before finally touching the cool surface. He caressed the carved handle before taking hold of the dagger and bringing it close enough to examine.

"Come into my office. There's a good desk lamp."

Trent followed Motofuji and settled himself in a chair in front of the desk. The jade felt odd in his hands. At first it was cool to the touch, lifeless stone. Beautiful, but still no more than that. Then the jade seemed to warm to his touch. Under the light he felt it almost pulse with life in his hands. With each beat it glowed more intensely. Like a heartbeat.

He turned it over in his hands, feeling and seeing the skill of the artist. He touched a finger to the blade's edge. It wasn't sharp enough to cut his skin, but he knew with the right amount of force it would rip flesh. At Quantico they told him it took only a pound of pressure to break skin with the point of a sharp knife. This one might take two or three times that. He jabbed the knife into the air, feeling what it might have been like for its original owner to use it for protection—or had it been for something more nefarious?

Motofuji finally broke the silence. "The dagger has a bloody history." The words came out in a raspy whisper that echoed in the eerie stillness of the room. "It is believed to have been originally carved in about 200 B.C. Its owner received it as a wedding gift and thought it so beautiful he immediately had it displayed on a wall in the bridal chamber. The next morning, both the bride and the groom were found dead, and the dagger was returned to its display in their bridal room. No one knows who used it."

Trent shivered upon hearing the story, and he nearly dropped the thing. The heartbeat was back. Was it a memory of the victims and the blood pumping out of their bodies?

Okay, he had to stop thinking like this. Reed wouldn't let him watch horror films, yet these images flashed into his brain anyway. He needed to write a children's book. Something about bunnies. *Fatal Attraction. Oh, shit, I'm going crazy.* He put the dagger onto the desktop.

"I see my story has shaken you, Cōpurando-san. I'm sorry. I am afraid for all its beauty, this dagger has drawn much blood since it was carved."

Trent settled into the chair and tried to relax his shoulders, which were up around his ears. "It answers my question of how sharp it is."

"Yes. We Japanese love the interplay between beauty and pain. It's like a dance—how far can one go before being drawn to the other? Our most famous stories all have tragic endings. The most beautiful things are the result of someone's suffering." Motofuji looked off into the distance as if speaking to himself and not expecting an answer from Trent.

As he recalled the beautiful things in this man's collection, Trent also remembered the violence that must have been part of how he'd accumulated the wealth to afford these masterpieces.

"Yes, Cōpurando-san. I, too, have earned beauty with pain and death. Sometimes I was responsible for the pain, and other times I had to endure it. That dagger had a twin—almost a twin—made of black jade. A rival used it to kill my wife."

Trent looked up in horror and caught Motofuji's gaze. "Oh, how terrible."

"I destroyed that dagger. But I kept this one to remember her beauty."

Trent glanced at the dagger on the desk again and shuddered. "It must be time for me to go. I think I heard the car pull up in front of the house."

"Yes. I believe you are right. Would you mind putting the dagger back into its case for me? I prefer not to touch it."

Trent was even more reluctant to touch it again. Why wouldn't Motofuji touch it? Was this actually the one used to kill his wife, rather than its black jade twin? Had *he* killed her? Trent felt like he was in some twisted

Japanese version of *Rebecca*, and he was the new wife… happy until he discovered how the old wife had died.

Reminding himself it was just a piece of jade, Trent picked up the dagger and moved quickly into the jade room and put it back in the display case. He didn't know how to fasten the case again, so he left it and headed for the front door.

Motofuji was waiting for him with something in his hand.

Another knife? Trent instinctively put his hands up and was ready to defend himself.

"This is the print I promised you." Motofuji bowed and held out a tube of the sort used for holding paintings and prints. Trent took the tube with both hands the way Beth had taught him. Then Motofuji handed him a second, slimmer tube. "And this one contains the frame. You can easily put it together when you get home. There is also an official letter indicating it is a gift. In the event you have any problem with customs."

Trent tried to slow his racing heart and took the tubes. He felt like such a heel, nearly accusing this man of trying to harm him when all he wanted to do was to offer a gift. Along with some creepy conversation. But Trent figured the man didn't have many friends, and he would take companionship where he could find it.

Motofuji opened the door, and Trent bowed low and said goodnight in the most polite Japanese he could recall. The limo was waiting in front of the house with the rear door already popped open. He slid inside and waited for the door to close, but it didn't. He tried to look through the partition, but it was dark. Even the ceiling light in the passenger section was out. Trent thought he heard footsteps. Maybe the driver was admiring the cherry blossoms in the moonlight.

Trent was exhausted. A long day, then a late dinner and that strange discussion with Motofuji. He closed his eyes. They'd be back at the hotel soon. He was glad to be sharing the suite with Beth, because he was certain Motofuji's story would give him nightmares.

HE WOKE up to the sound of someone speaking loudly in Japanese, then felt a hand gripping his shoulder.

"Misutā Cōpurando. Purīzu weiku appu! Jis izu za hoteru."

Trent blinked and got his bearings. The limo had brought him back to the hotel in Kyoto. He thanked the driver and headed inside, remembering to take his shoes off and don the slippers. The lights were low in the lobby except for a tiny light near the front desk. The woman who had checked them in was waiting at the desk and gave him the "*Irasshaimase*" greeting he was coming to anticipate. He hadn't expected her to wait up so late, so he gave her a bow and meekly took the key she shoved at him like a knife. God, he was seeing daggers everywhere now!

When he opened the door to the room, Beth was waiting for him, cell phone in her hand.

"What happened? Are you okay?" She reached out and ran her hands along his chest and arms, as if checking for injuries.

"Yeah, I'm fine. I guess. Why are you so worried? Have I been gone that long?" He brushed her hands off as gently as possible.

"You have blood on your face and your hand… and on your shirt." Her voice rose. "What *happened*?"

Trent looked down. He hadn't noticed any blood. "I guess I had a nosebleed. I get them sometimes. I have a headache… maybe there's a connection."

"What happened? What do you mean, you guess?" Worry—near panic—was evident in her tone and wide-eyed expression. "Do you have any idea how worried I was about you?"

"He just wanted to show me something and give me the print." He held up the tubes.

"That's it?" Her downturned mouth indicated she was unconvinced.

"Yes. That's it." Trent put the tubes down on the desk and plopped down onto one of the floor cushions.

"It's nearly 3:00 a.m., Trent! What did he have to say that was so important?"

Trent rubbed his eyes. "I lost track of time. I didn't think I was there that long. But there's nothing to worry about—you and Naoko kept telling me that. He's a harmless old man. And look, I'm fine. No scratches." He held his arms up so she could examine him. "See, Ma?"

"What was so important?"

"Nothing was important. He just wanted to talk to me. I'm not really sure why. He told me some gruesome story about his wife getting killed with the twin to that jade dagger I thought was so beautiful."

"Shit." Beth blinked and stepped backwards until she came to the other cushion and sat down, eyes still unfocused. She gave a shiver. "Creepy."

"He said it while I was holding the damn thing, too."

"Oh, Jesus."

"Yeah, I'm pretty spooked, and I don't want to talk about it. Maybe tomorrow. I'm beat. I think I could sleep for a week. If I don't have any nightmares, that is."

THE NEXT morning Naoko joined them for an early breakfast. She didn't look like she'd slept very well either, but neither Trent nor Beth mentioned the dark pockets below her eyes. They discussed her schedule for completing the appraisal of Motofuji's collection. She left for Tokyo after breakfast, leaving Beth and Trent to spend the day making the rounds of the Imperial Palace and the most important temples, interspersed with food from the best restaurants in the region.

They went for dinner in the Gion district, the former red-light zone, where they had less elegant fare than the previous night but enjoyed themselves just as much. They had time the next day for more sightseeing before their return journey to Tokyo. They arrived just before dinnertime on Saturday and returned to the Park Hyatt Hotel, where they would stay until their return visit to ship Motofuji's collection to Los Angeles.

12

ON SUNDAY morning they met up with Naoko in order to visit the other collector who wanted to sell a portion of his collection through Gallery LMNO. He lived in a trendy part of Tokyo, known for cafés and exclusive clothing boutiques and hair salons. They arrived by subway. Since Tokyo traffic was so much worse than Kyoto, it was actually quicker and more convenient than a taxi. Trent still remembered the awful taxi driver who had threatened Beth until she paid him, even though he hadn't driven them to their destination.

Naoko was waiting for them at an outdoor café. The day was sunny but cool, and heat lamps kept the clientele warm.

"Before we visit, I wanted to discuss Waseda-san with you both." She ordered tea for them when a waitress appeared and then returned her attention to Trent and Beth. "He's quite different from Motofuji-san. Waseda is younger, mid-fifties, and very… I don't know how to say it." She said something in Japanese.

"Aggressive," Beth responded.

"Aggressive. Yes, that works. He is newer money and from a generation that likes to show off how they got it. But despite those differences of style, he is in many ways very much like Motofuji-san."

"What do you mean?" Trent asked. The waitress returned with their order and he sipped at his tea.

Naoko glanced from Trent to Beth and back to Trent. "He is also yakuza." She barely even whispered the last word.

"Oh." Beth looked worried. "You never mentioned this regarding Waseda before. You only mentioned the issue of provenance." She glanced at Trent, then back at Naoko. "You had us so worried about Motofuji's connections, but he turned out to be harmless."

Trent was surprised at Beth's response, but he wouldn't say anything in front of Naoko. "Yes, Motofuji-san was very nice. I don't know what I was afraid of." Trent grinned. He realized he actually liked the old guy. Despite that strange late-night conversation, he had the sense the man had wanted to share something important with him. He'd complimented Trent and given him a beautiful gift, but that wasn't what had changed Trent's mind about him.

"I didn't want to frighten you or give the impression all art collectors here are criminals. Waseda is of no danger to you, but I felt you should know. And reiterate the strong rumors in the art world that some of his collection was obtained by unorthodox methods." Naoko kept her voice low so Trent and Beth had to lean in to hear her. "Leah is aware of the rumors, but she may not have shared all of her knowledge with you."

"Does she know he's yakuza?" Trent asked.

"Not from me," Naoko replied. "But in their own way, the yakuza are honorable. They don't harm average citizens. Their violence is directed at other yakuza—a gang member who commits an infraction, or a rival gang. They don't go looking for trouble, but they protect their territory if it's threatened. Outside of gang activity, they are simply businessmen—or art collectors. You are completely safe."

"Thank you for your honesty," Beth said. Trent saw that her hand shook a little as she put her teacup down on the table. He rubbed her arm and she smiled at him, but her mood stayed cloudy even in the lovely spring sunshine.

They finished their tea and walked through the neighborhood as trendy shops made way for quiet residential streets, until they reached Waseda's home. A high brick wall defined the perimeter around the home. Through a wrought-iron gate, they could see the house and surrounding garden. It was rather modern, though still clearly Japanese. No shoji screens or pointed roofs here, but like Motofuji's home, everything seemed to be of high quality. As Trent neared the gate, two enormous Dobermans lunged from out of nowhere and barked and growled menacingly as they leapt at the bars. Trent stepped back quickly and Beth hid behind him.

A young man with slicked-back hair and a stylish gray suit walked up to them and mumbled in Japanese. Naoko handed him her business card and one of Trent's. The man looked them up and down before opening a cell phone and smashing a few keys aggressively.

He nodded profusely and bowed a couple of times while speaking on the phone, then his demeanor toward the guests changed to complete hospitality. He grunted a few times to another young man—possibly a twin to the first one—who came to the gate and leashed the dogs so thug No. 1 could let Trent and his companions into the yard.

These two guys looked like they'd stepped right out of a yakuza movie. Were the films so accurate, or was there an advantage to looking the part? The one inside handling the dogs even had the obligatory missing pinky. Trent shuddered. He wouldn't think about how much that would hurt.

They were shown to a door where they were greeted by Haruo Waseda. He also looked like he'd walked out of central casting. Trent found this so funny he had to stop himself from laughing. Their style was so stereotypical it was difficult to be afraid of these guys. It was their hidden power—like Motofuji's—that was much more frightening. You wouldn't know when it might strike, like a coiled cobra.

Waseda welcomed them into his living room. It was furnished with sleek modern chairs and tables. The only comfortable-looking piece was a plush sectional couch, and he invited them to sit. Trent was grateful he didn't have to perch on one of the wood-and-chrome chairs. In stark contrast to the furniture, the walls displayed an impressive collection of swords, from the traditional samurai blades to short daggers, all of which appeared to be in near-mint condition.

After the obligatory introductions, during which Waseda demonstrated his near total lack of fluency in English despite his enthusiasm for using it, they were offered coffee or cocktails. No traditional tea in this house. They made more small talk, and then Waseda took them through his collection.

He had a series of rooms set out along one side of the house, reminding Trent of an art museum. They moved through each room, cataloging and photographing, with the exception of one room halfway down the hall. The door was closed, and Waseda didn't bother to even mention it as they passed it and entered a room on the other side.

He pointed out his favorite pieces, including two Monets even Trent suspected might be forgeries. He had a large collection of French Impressionists and some modern sculpture, which Trent didn't find particularly attractive. Someone must like it. Waseda explained—via Beth—which items he wanted to sell and how much he wanted to get for them. He also explained his desire to get out of the art market before prices dropped on his investments. Trent and Naoko took more notes and photographs.

They had one last room to visit, but a loud commotion outside the house prompted Waseda to excuse himself while he went to the front of the house. Trent heard sirens and more intense barking from Waseda's vicious-looking dogs. Were the cops coming here? His pulse raced and he glanced to Naoko; she didn't look concerned.

When the doorbell sounded, Waseda himself opened the door.

Beth and Naoko strained to hear what was being said, and Trent quietly made his way back to the room Waseda had bypassed. He couldn't help his curiosity. What was so special as to be held behind closed doors, and why hadn't Waseda shown them these pieces? Were they nudes on black velvet? Dogs playing cards? He tried the door and, to his surprise, it was unlocked. He opened it and peered inside. He didn't enter the room or flip on the lights, but he could see the paintings were of classical European style, though Trent couldn't name any off the top of his head. He glimpsed a heavy-framed painting of a boat on a dark background and a sketch of a bearded man, but it was too dark to get a good glimpse of anything. He saw movement at the end of the hall and shut the door before one of Waseda's guards noticed him snooping.

By this time the commotion at the front door had increased, and from the volume of noise, the police had entered the home. Waseda strode toward them with a herd of uniformed police on his tail. He looked amazingly unconcerned for a man who had cops in his house. Maybe Naoko was right and the yakuza weren't that dangerous after all. Trent knew those films were just exaggerations, totally unrealistic.

"Oh, crap," Trent whispered to Beth. He couldn't tell what Waseda was saying, but he seemed to become more animated. No surprise since he had half the Tokyo police force in his house.

Waseda stopped and nodded his chin toward Trent. "Kare ga Cōpurando da."

Trent's heart stopped.

The police surged forward and one officer started speaking to him in Japanese. Another had Trent's hands pinned behind his back before he could ask Beth what was happening.

Cold metal handcuffs tightened around his wrists and someone held his head so he couldn't turn around. Trent's heart pounded and his stomach felt like it was blocking his throat. Footsteps sounded and then a voice in his ear,

“Trento Cōpurando you are under arrest for murder.” The man spoke with a slight accent, but a clear grasp of English.

“Murder?” he sputtered. His throat was tight and dry, and the word was a croaky rasp.

“For the murder of—Motofuji Daikichi.”

Before he had a chance to reply, someone pulled him away from the wall and marched him toward the front door. He thought his knees would buckle. His first instinct was to stop, but the police kept moving.

As he was taken out of the house, he passed Beth, hands over her mouth and eyes wide with fear. She ran toward the car as they shoved him in the back, but no one would let her speak to him.

The English-speaking cop was in the passenger seat. “You’re in big trouble now.”

“Oh, yes!” Trent said, then shut his mouth. He hadn’t been talking to the cop.

He just remembered why those paintings seemed familiar. He’d seen at least one of them in a documentary he’d watched recently while trying to learn more about the world of fine art. He just wasn’t sure which doc, and why one painting in particular stuck in his brain.

At the moment, however, he had much more pressing issues to worry about.

13

TRENT DIDN'T have a chance to even think about Waseda's secret paintings. How could someone think he'd killed Motofuji? Was Motofuji dead? Apparently. He couldn't see cops arresting someone without a body. But when, and how? And why Trent? He hadn't seen Motofuji for two or three days. They had visited him on Thursday night. Today was Sunday, right? He wasn't sure anymore. He couldn't recall if they added or lost a day when they arrived. He tried to glance at his watch—but with his arms cuffed behind his back, he couldn't.

And every time the car went around a turn, he thought he'd end up smashed against the window like a bug. They didn't have seatbelts for suspects, apparently. All the while the cop in the front seat was speaking to him in some mix of English and Japanese. Trent felt sick to his stomach. For a millisecond, he considered escaping but quickly gave in to the realization that nothing he'd learned at Quantico would help him get out of police custody. Even if he did, he couldn't exactly blend in with the populace and avoid detection. He was screwed.

After what seemed like ages, even with the siren blaring and the car swerving around Tokyo traffic, they slowed. Trent looked out of the window as they approached what looked like a high-rise office building. Rows of police cars were lined up across the street, along with several TV news vans. Cameramen rushed up to the car as the driver slowed to enter the ramp that led them down to an underground parking garage. At least the reporters couldn't follow him inside. That would be embarrassing. Then Trent remembered no one here knew him.

The only people who cared about him were back in the US. Except for Beth. Hopefully, he'd get to talk to her at the police station. He just wanted to find out what was going on so he could explain that he was somewhere else whenever what happened had happened.

The car stopped and Trent was yanked out of the back seat and taken up in an elevator along with the English-speaking cop and six or seven uniformed men. No one looked at him as the elevator sped upward. They were discharged into a room that looked like any police department in any television show—and Trent had seen a lot of cop shows. Rows of desks, the sound of phones chirping, both uniformed and plainclothes officers bustling around. He was taken to a tiny room where a uniformed cop frisked him and pulled everything out of his pockets and removed his watch. His cuffs were removed so he could be shackled to a table. For a smaller person than Trent the room would feel claustrophobic, but for him, it was like being locked in a lunchbox. Then he was left alone.

There was no clock on the wall. Without his watch, he had no idea how long he sat there. Reed had given him that watch. He hoped he'd get it back.

Reed. God he missed Reed right now. If he'd come to Japan with Reed, this never would have happened. Not that this was Beth's fault, but Reed would know what to do. Or he would have made sure Trent never got arrested in the first place.

Had he been arrested? He wasn't sure. Do they have to read you your rights in other countries? Well, he hadn't said anything, but they also hadn't actually asked him anything either. He'd remain silent and ask for a lawyer. Or someone from the embassy. If he could call them, he could get real help. He knew the code that would get someone from CIA or FBI. If he got his one call… or should he call Reed?

But Reed wasn't here, and the embassy would know how to help. Beth would contact Reed. Trent nodded, secure in the fact that he'd made one useful decision. That was a start.

He thought back to the Quantico training. They'd had only one lecture on what to do if taken prisoner. Reed had joked that given Trent's proclivity for getting locked up, he should stay for a longer course. Now Trent searched his brain for what he had learned, but it eluded him. Hopefully, he'd remember later once he had a chance to collect his thoughts. He might be released before that, once they figured out they had the wrong guy.

Best case scenario.

Trent attempted one of Reed's Zen relaxation exercises to calm himself. It was simple: just count. He was up to 2,149 when the detective came back. He flung the door open so forcefully it slammed against the wall, shattering Trent's paper-thin veneer of calm. Probably the intention.

The cop flipped his chair around, sat on it backward, and stared at Trent for a few minutes. Trent waited, wondering how many American cop films this guy had seen. He was at somewhat of a disadvantage and snappy banter wasn't going to help. He stared back with more confidence than he felt. Up close in the bright lights of the cell, he noticed the guy had three moles on his left cheek, forming a perfect triangle.

Then another man came in and sat in the other chair. He was stockier than the first one, with glasses and a rounder face that made him appear kind.

The two cops spoke to each other in Japanese, further disorienting Trent.

Finally, the first cop turned to Trent and spoke. "I'm Officer N—."

His accent was thick and Trent didn't understand him or catch his name, but he nodded anyway.

"I'm Takahashi. Do you know why you are here?" The second cop spoke slightly better English.

Trent shook his head.

"You are under arrest for the murder of Motofuji Daikichi," Takahashi said.

"Can I talk to a lawyer?"

"No," Triangle Cop said.

"Can I call or speak to my interpreter?"

"I speak English. You don't need an interpreter." This time it was Takahashi. Trent had to look from one to the other, like at a tennis match.

"Can I call anyone?"

"No." This seemed to be the limit of the first cop's vocabulary.

Thankfully, Takahashi added, "Here in Japan you have no right to a lawyer or a phone call. We can call the embassy for you, and they can arrange a lawyer."

"Please call them." Trent kept his voice calm but inside his nerves were screaming. He just had to keep it together until the embassy could get in touch with Reed or get him a lawyer.

The two men left for another extended period of time. Triangle did the same door-slamming thing when they returned.

"It's Sunday. Everyone at the embassy is at a *hanami* party or something. I left a message." Takahashi spoke.

The other cop started laughing.

Trent didn't think it was particularly funny. Well, maybe it was. All the Americans out doing some traditional Japanese activity while he was stuck in a Japanese police station. "Now what?"

"We'll process you, and you can wait in a cell until someone shows up."

"Are you going to question me?" Trent addressed his question to Takahashi.

"Do you want to answer questions?"

"No."

"So, we won't waste our time," Takahashi replied. "This case is easy. How do you say it? Open and shut. Witnesses, forensic evidence. Kyoto might want you. We're waiting on their decision."

"Open and shut," Triangle repeated with a grin, then looked Trent up and down.

Trent didn't respond. What forensic evidence? What the hell happened to Motofuji and when? He'd been with Beth every minute since he'd stepped foot in the damn country.

"They have better food in the jail down there, though. Well, it's up to the prosecutor. I still have to type up the report, but we've got an appointment for tomorrow afternoon. Then how do you say it? 'We'll lock you up and throw away the key!'" Takahashi said, shattering Trent's hope he might be as kind and gentle as he looked.

Triangle opened the door and shouted into the hallway, and two uniforms came in and took Trent to get fingerprinted and photographed.

He was still in his own clothes, minus his belt and shoelaces, and he shuffled along with the guard. He had to take his shoes off and put them in the ubiquitous shoe cabinet before he entered the large open cell already containing four other men—all Japanese. Surprisingly, the floor was made of tatami. There were four futons and a screened-off area near the back of the cell. Each of the others sat on a futon. Trent sat on the floor and waited. He looked around. It wasn't as dirty as he imagined a jail cell would be. Not that it couldn't use Martha Stewart's touch, but if he had to sleep on the floor, he didn't think he'd be overwhelmed by insects. He shuddered at the thought.

A guard walked by the cell and glared at the prisoners every so often. On his third pass, one of Trent's cellmates shouted something to the guard. All Trent could make out of the reply was "Motofuji." The other prisoners chatted for a moment in hushed tones, then one of them stood up and patted his futon, motioning for Trent to take it. He waved away the offer, but the man tried again. When Trent finally stood and moved toward the cot, the man—much shorter than Trent—cowered in genuine fear and scuttled away to a spot in the far corner.

Great, Trent thought, *I'm the big scary bully in this jail, the killer of a Yakuza leader*. It would be funny it if wasn't such a mess.

An hour or so later—by Trent's estimate—a guard brought in trays of food. Rice, some vegetables, and fish, plus water for everyone. Trent wasn't sure if it was lunch or dinner. He didn't know how long he'd been here. It was only midday when the cops came to Waseda's house, wasn't it? Everything blurred together. Trent wasn't sure about the fish, but once his stomach growled, he decided to eat it. He didn't know when they'd get food again. If he was still really hungry and felt mean, he could scare one of the other guys into giving up his next meal. Trent had never felt that mean before in his entire life, but he'd seen every episode of *Prison Break*, and he needed to be ready for anything.

The meal turned out to be dinner because the guards put the lights out sometime later. In the morning, two of the men were removed from the cell and one new occupant arrived.

Breakfast and lunch were the same rice and vegetables as the previous night's dinner.

Where the hell was the embassy person? Now Trent started to really worry. They should have had him out of here by now, since he hadn't done anything. He almost wanted to talk to the detectives again just to find out what kind of evidence they had on him.

A guard came to the cell and shouted for Cōpurando, so Trent stood up. He was cuffed and escorted to a small room. A Caucasian woman in a blue suit was waiting for him.

"I'm Nora Paul from the American Embassy. Are you Trent Copeland?"

"Yes. What's going on?"

"What have they told you?"

"They think I killed a guy."

"Yes. Daikichi Motofuji. He's the head of an organized crime syndicate."

"I know."

"You know him?"

"Yes."

"Ah."

That didn't sound good. Trent wished he hadn't said anything. "Are you a lawyer?"

"No, but I can arrange one if you can give me a contact in Japan or the States who can guarantee payment."

"That won't be a problem." He wrote down Reed's cell number and Leah's number at the gallery. He'd nearly forgotten about her and the appraisals, but he knew she'd take the money out of his share or he'd pay her back. He knew she'd feel responsible at some level, but he could deal with her guilt later—once he was free and back on US soil.

"I also have a message from Beth Conti."

"Oh yes, she's traveling with me. She also speaks Japanese and—"

Nora pulled a pad out of her purse. "She tried to reach Reed, left voice mail, and e-mailed, but he didn't get back to her yet. She'll keep trying." Nora looked at the names and numbers Trent had written. "So we don't need to call this first name, I take it?"

Trent's heart sank. "Yes, please keep trying him. He works for the FBI. They should be able to find him."

Nora gave him a look that swept away any hope Trent had left.

A knock sounded at the door and someone opened it and shouted. Nora stood. "They're taking you to the indictment hearing now. The police will present their case to a prosecutor, and he will determine whether there is enough to bring in front of a judge or let you go."

"But I don't have a lawyer."

"You don't get one at this stage. You only need a lawyer if they decide to prosecute. I'll explain as we go."

MORE HANDCUFFS and elevators. Trent felt like a bum with his pants loose around his waist and his shoes flopping on his feet. He entered what looked like a courtroom. He and Nora sat at a table with uniformed police while the kind-faced plainclothes detectives who had processed him stood at a podium with a thick folder and addressed the man sitting there. “The prosecutor,” Nora explained. “Like the DA.”

Trent nodded and waited. In five minutes this might all be over. He hadn’t done anything. Then the detective opened the folder and started reading from the first piece of paper. In Japanese.

This might take a while, Trent realized. Based on the number of documents in the folder, Trent wouldn’t be heading back to the Park Hyatt for a steam shower and fluffy robe anytime soon.

14

REED PUSHED the hotel room door and untucked his shirt before he heard it slam shut. Damn, he'd forgotten how hot Texas could get, even in mid-April. It was a waste of vacation days while Trent was in Japan, so he had volunteered to do some back-up on another agent's case with South American art being smuggled up through Mexico. It would take a week, tops, and he expected to be home before Trent.

The A/C didn't work in this room, but the place was full and he didn't feel like finding another dive. He debated taking his weapon out of the small of his back, where it probably was coated with sweat. He didn't know what was what in this town yet, so he'd better not. Instead, he flipped on the television—CNN—and went into the bathroom.

He filled the sink with cold water and splashed some on his face, then poured handfuls over his head until his hair was wet. It would dry soon enough in this heat. He dipped a threadbare washcloth into the cold water, put it against the back of his neck, and went back to the bedroom. He flopped onto the rickety bed, hoping it wouldn't crumble under his weight.

Then he turned his attention to the television. The sound was muted but when he spotted the dateline of Tokyo he cranked the volume. An American had been arrested for assassinating a top yakuza leader. Nothing to worry about, Reed decided, and was about to mute it again when a familiar face appeared on the screen.

Not just any American had been charged: it was Trent.

Reed leapt up and sat at the foot of the bed and concentrated on the reporter's words. Trent had been arrested, charged, and indicted within twenty-four hours. He'd only been in the country for a few days. How had he gotten into this much hot water so quickly?

That was Trent. It would be funny if it wasn't so fucking serious. Reed reached for his prepaid burner phone, and before he had it in his hand, it rang.

"Acton?" It was Tom White, Reed's boss.

"Tom, I—"

"I know. Don't worry about the Flores case. I've got someone else who can take it." Not many bosses were this proactive. Had he been watching CNN, too? "I just got word from the State Department. I wish they'd notified us before the indictment—we might have been able to clear him immediately. Now he's in their legal system and it's more complicated. Just take whatever time off you need and call me once you know what you need."

"Thanks, boss." Reed disconnected, grabbed his bag, and headed back to the airport.

IN TOKYO, Trent's head was spinning. He could barely follow the hearing, even with Nora's assistance. The Triangle Cop sat down next to the first one, though he didn't stand up to speak. Apparently they had wrapped the whole case up, and the prosecutor sent Trent back to jail until trial. He didn't even get to plead "not guilty."

Nora didn't say a word or protest anything. None of the evidence was true, but the cop twisted it around until even Trent thought he'd done it by the time the uniforms dragged him back outside the hearing room, where a line of reporters shoved microphones in his face and photographers snapped so many photos he couldn't see.

At one point he thought he heard Beth's voice, but the white spots marring his vision prevented him from seeing her face. Nora could talk to her, but Trent didn't know when Nora would arrange another meeting with him. Or when he'd get that lawyer he wanted.

This time he was taken back to the detention center and put into his own cell. Unlike the previous night, this one was a closed room with a door and a barred window his only connection to the outside. The floor was covered with four tatami mats, the futon was identical to the one in the holding cell, and there was small pillow and clean-looking sheets. A sink and a toilet were at the far end of the room, with a little privacy screen. This was much nicer than the cells on *Prison Break*, not that Trent wanted to stick around longer than necessary. A small shelf was set into one wall, though Trent had no idea why. He didn't have anything to put in it.

No one came by until a guard shoved a tray through a slit in the middle of the door. The same meal he'd already eaten several times, but this time they gave him two bowls of rice and vegetables. Small mercies.

When the guard came to collect the tray, he shoved a plastic bag through the opening. Trent got up from the futon and stared down at the thing, wondering what was inside. Should he pick it up? It couldn't be a bomb, so he was probably safe in checking it out. Then again, he hadn't expected to get arrested for killing a guy, so he didn't exactly trust his own judgment anymore.

After staring at the bag for what seemed like an hour, he bent to pick it up. Seated on the cot, he snapped it open to find several pairs of his underwear, a couple of shirts, and some socks. Beth must have retrieved them from the hotel, and thankfully, either Nora or the police had allowed them through. He wouldn't mind a second pair of pants, but the clean underwear was welcome. He carefully folded everything up and put it on his little shelf.

He smiled. Not that this place would ever feel homey, but a pile of clean underwear could still put a smile on a guy's face. It sure beat thinking about what the sentence was for assassination in Japan.

THE NEXT morning Trent washed up and put on a clean shirt, underwear, and socks before the breakfast tray came around. After he ate, the guard indicated through an elaborate pantomime that he was wanted in another part of the detention center. Trent let himself be cuffed and led down a corridor of other closed cells. He could see a few faces at windows—some Japanese, some other nationalities—but even the Westerners stayed quiet. No one shouted out to him, nodded, or even cracked a smile.

That wasn't a good sign.

He was taken to a small room where Nora and another woman sat.

"Trent, this is Tane Tanaka, your lawyer."

"Hi." Trent reached out to shake her hand and then stopped. The woman looked Japanese and she probably wasn't a hand shaker.

"Mr. Copeland," Tane began in perfect English, with a noticeable British accent, similar to Naoko's. "I'll act as your lawyer at least for the initial proceedings. Once you get your bearings, you may choose to change your representation."

"Are you Japanese? I mean, a Japanese citizen?" He wanted to make sure she knew her way around the Japanese legal system, even if he didn't feel comfortable trusting her yet.

"Yes, though I grew up in the UK. My father worked at the Japanese Embassy in London and I was educated there, until I returned here for law school. My main practice is with *gaijin*—foreigners—in Japan who can't make head nor tail of the legal system, even if they speak Japanese."

"What do I need to do?" Trent asked.

"I should leave now," Nora said. "Tane will explain how you can contact either her or me in the event you need anything. Good luck, Trent." She stood and shook hands with him before knocking on the door. She gave Trent a small smile as a guard let her out. A pitying little smile that drove home how deep a pile of trouble he had landed in.

"Mr. Copeland—" Tane began.

"Trent."

"Trent. I'll need you to sign a paper authorizing me to be your attorney. It's in Japanese, but I have an English translation for you. Go ahead and sign both. I'll make sure copies of all nonconfidential documents go to Nora at the embassy."

"Okay." He read the contract and signed it. "Can you tell me what's going on here? I don't know how any of this happened or why I've been accused."

"Yes. I understand. The Japanese system isn't very transparent, nor is it as protective of suspects' rights as in the US. I don't have much information for you. Once I file this contract, I'll have access to the specifics of the evidence against you. Then I can give you better advice about what sort of trial strategy we should use."

"Trial? I kind of hoped you'd get all these charges dropped. Get them to let me out."

"Even without seeing the evidence, I don't think there's much chance of that. We should work on minimizing the charges. That's the only realistic defense."

"Minimizing the charges?"

"Manslaughter… the penalty is much less. Maybe as low as five years, especially if you tell them who hired you to kill Motofuji."

Trent's head was spinning again. He thought his heart would fly out of his chest it was beating so violently. "No one hired me. I didn't kill anyone. I don't want to go to jail at all for this."

"Manslaughter would be a good result. Because with this sort of crime, they usually ask for capital punishment. Hanging."

Trent reached for his throat. "Hanging? But I didn't kill anyone!" Trent felt like he'd throw up. This wasn't happening. He couldn't breathe. Maybe he'd just die of heart failure now and not get—executed. "No, this can't be happening. I'm just dreaming this." His stomach roiled.

"Trent, you must be realistic. The police have released the information that they have your fingerprints on the murder weapon. There's really not a lot you can do to explain that away. And your alibi...."

"What murder weapon?"

"A jade dagger."

Trent heard a loud whooshing and everything went dark.

15

BY THE time Reed got to DFW, he had already booked a flight for Tokyo. It would take him nearly twenty-four hours to get there—no direct flights—but flying to LA first wouldn't save him much time with the schedules. He considered calling ahead to the FBI liaison in Tokyo and arranging a lawyer in advance, then decided against it. There was always the chance the charges would be dropped before he could get there, and he didn't want to make a big fuss for nothing.

Not that Trent was nothing, but an extra day in a Japanese jail wouldn't be that bad. They had none of the gang violence of American jails or prisons and the food was good. Reed had been in one before—as part of the set up for the job in Thailand. Reed had the unfortunate benefit of knowing about most of the prisons in Asia, either through personal experience or training.

He did call ahead and make sure he'd be seen as soon as he arrived and updated on Trent's case. From the few details his colleague had, it looked pretty bad for Trent. There was a lot of forensic evidence against him, though Reed couldn't understand how. He'd figure it all out when he hit the ground in Japan.

The next call, as he waited for the first leg of his journey to board, was to Beth.

"Reed? Is that you?" she asked, her voice rising, sounding tight in her throat.

"Beth?"

"Oh, Reed." Whatever she said next dissolved into a series of sobs that blended together into a loud wail. "Reed, I've been calling you for two days!"

"Calm down, Beth. I'm on my way. I couldn't get my messages while I was on a job."

"Reed!"

"Beth, tell me what happened. Did you see Trent? Is he okay?"

She let out a few more sobs before calming herself again. "Sorry. It's been awful. Just awful." She sniffed loudly. "I'm not allowed to see Trent. Japanese law. No visitors except embassy staff or attorneys. I tried to say I was his interpreter…."

"So the embassy sent someone?" Reed hadn't asked too many questions when he'd called the Bureau guy.

"Yes. She seems nice enough, but she didn't have much information. She found a lawyer for Trent. That's all I know. The lawyer won't tell me anything. She just let me know Trent was okay, and I made sure he had clean clothes. You know they don't have uniforms. You have to bring your own clothes to jail in Japan."

Reed didn't know if that was supposed to be a good or a bad thing from Beth's perspective. He ignored it. "Don't worry. Nothing will happen to him before I get there. The legal system doesn't work that fast in Japan." Reed considered that a win. Had this been Myanmar or some countries in Africa, he might have already been too late to help Trent.

"So why would anyone think Trent killed this guy? Who was he exactly?"

"He was a big shot yakuza leader. And Trent was up at his house—alone—when it happened."

"Trent went to a yakuza guy's house. Alone?"

"Yeah." She said it like it was an everyday occurrence in Japan. "He's selling a portion of his art collection. We were all there. But he asked Trent back that night…."

What the hell made Trent think that was a good idea? "Well, that's all circumstantial. Was there a witness?"

"I don't know about a witness. But Trent's fingerprints are all over the murder weapon."

Oh fuck. This might be more difficult than Reed thought.

AS SOON as he landed, the Bureau guy from the embassy, Christopher Hammel, met Reed at the gate and expedited him through Customs and Immigration. No one even bothered to stamp his passport. After quick introductions and a discussion about past cases and colleagues in the car on the way into the city, Hammel spelled out what he knew.

"Motofuji was head of a yakuza organization. Had been for maybe thirty years. He was the old-fashioned kind of Japanese criminal. Nothing big or flashy, they just chip away at the edges of respectability and concentrate on the vices: girls and gambling. Nothing underage. Some money laundering. He didn't get into any of the modern stuff with corporate extortion or stock market manipulation. He only took money from people who deserved to lose it, like the gamblers."

"A crook with a conscience?" Reed gave a half smile.

"As crazy as that sounds, yeah. There was a code, and even the gangsters have their own system of ethics. This guy was one of those gentleman criminals. If you were a law-abiding citizen, you'd never even cross his path."

"But he was at odds with some of the younger criminal elements?"

Hammel put his finger on his nose and nodded. "Got it in one."

"There must be plenty of actual suspects?"

"Yes, three or four realistic candidates."

"And somehow Trent stumbled onto the scene and ended up the scapegoat."

"Yeah. He's wrapped up pretty fucking tight, though. I've got a guy in the police, and he told me about the evidence." He shook his head. "Your poor pal's got to be sweatin' bullets if he knows what they have on him."

Reed didn't respond. His mind was already racing ahead to what he'd need to do to help Trent. "What evidence?"

"You name it, they got it."

"You're supposed to be helping me here, not planning Trent's funeral."

Hammel cocked his head and looked Reed in the eye. "So, what's this Copeland guy to you? I couldn't find him in the Bureau database. He someone you worked with before on one of the art recoveries?"

"No. He'd probably be my husband, if it were legal in California." Reed paused. "Which might happen later this year. But in the meantime, you treat him like you would any agent's spouse." Reed didn't even have to think twice before he answered. It would have made him feel great, except for the mess he was here to help Trent out of.

A serious look came across Hammel's face. "Oh, shit, man. Why didn't you say? I'm sorry. I thought you were just doing a favor for someone. Not that he's that important to you."

"He is."

"Enough said."

"Thanks." Reed waited a moment then plunged ahead. "The evidence?"

"Fingerprints. On some jade dagger. Ancient Chinese thing with a carved blade, and really valuable. The maid said Motofuji usually kept it locked in a case. But Trent's prints were all over the thing—the murder weapon—and the display case. And all over the guy's house and office."

"Any other prints?"

"Just the victim's."

"Isn't that suspicious? No other prints?"

"The maid said she cleaned that day. It's not unheard of."

"But Trent wouldn't leave his prints if he'd done something like this." Fuck, what was he saying? Of course Trent hadn't done it. Or if he had there was a really, really good reason. "He's done the short course at Quantico. He knows better."

"Shit, really? Huh." A look of respect crossed over Hammel's face. "But you might not want the prosecutor to know that. He'll twist it around that Trent left the prints so no one would suspect him."

"What about witnesses and alibis?"

"A taxi driver took Trent and Motofuji up there late at night from the Gion district and dropped them off. He said Trent looked strange. Well, he might have said that about any gaijin. We all look the same, and strange. Then a hired limo driver picked him up about a couple of hours later, and he said Trent looked like he'd seen a ghost."

"A ghost?"

"Actually, his words were almost the Japanese equivalent of that phrase, according to my inside guy. There's a local phrase: *obake demo mita yo-na kao o shite ita.*"

Reed narrowed his eyes.

Hammel held up his hand. "Hey, there is a real superstition here about ghosts. Rational or not, it's part of the culture. Even in law enforcement." He paused. "Ghosts aside, there's nearly two hours of time that's not accounted for. The friend—the Asian-American girl—"

"Beth Conti."

"Yeah, she waited for Trent at the hotel, and she also said he was upset and frightened when he came back, but she couldn't vouch for his whereabouts for that period of time."

Reed would have to talk to Beth. Why had she revealed that? Not that he advocated lying to the police, but did she have to admit it? There was a lot he didn't know and would have to find out. He didn't trust the Japanese police.

"Based on what you've told me, we can't rely on a trial to prove Trent's innocence," Reed finally said. "There's evidence that might be explained away with a good forensics team, but from what I hear, the Japanese police won't do much more than what they've already done. And they have no reason to keep looking for another suspect. Waste of resources."

"I agree. We could get the Bureau or the Agency in…."

"I think we'll need to. The only way we can get Trent out of this is to find out who actually did it."

"And make sure they get prosecuted. That's going to be a lot harder."

"Good to know." Reed took a deep breath and leaned back in the leather seat in the embassy car. He didn't feel good, but at least he had information and he had a plan. For the first time since getting in the car he glanced outside to take in the scenery. They drove past the Imperial palace where the trees were full of pale-pink cherry blossoms.

Reed hoped like hell Trent was okay. Just a few days ago, he'd been strolling under those trees without a care in the world. Well, now he was here, Reed would do whatever he had to in order to get Trent freed.

Whatever it took.

THOUGH HE really wanted to get to the embassy and start strategizing with Christopher Hammel, Reed asked to stop at the Park Hyatt first. Hammel hung out in the lobby while Reed went upstairs to speak with Beth in her room. If he didn't see her in person, he knew she'd keep calling.

He sped upward in the elevator and knocked at the door of 5004. The sight that greeted him made him look again at the room number: Beth wore a black mini skirt, white lace top and red-and-white tights that made her legs look like candy canes as the colors spiraled up under the tiny skirt. Last he'd seen of her, she'd been dressed for a weekend at an Amish farm.

"Oh, Reed!" Beth threw herself at him and wrapped arms and legs around his body, squeezing, in a perfect imitation of an octopus. "Have you seen Trent yet?"

"No. I came here from the airport." He dumped his duffel bag on the floor, taking in the large suite. Much nicer than the fleabag dive he'd been in when he'd gotten the news. He scratched his head and wondered when he'd last showered. That could wait. If Hammel weren't waiting downstairs, Reed wouldn't mind a shower here.

"What are you going to do?"

"I'm not sure yet. I'm working with a guy at the embassy. We'll probably have more questions for you at some point, but for now, lie low here. Don't leave the hotel without telling me. We might want you to move to another place, just in case."

"Just in case what?" Her eyes widened and she started biting on a fingernail. "What can the embassy people do? They couldn't even get him out or make a phone call. They're useless."

Reed couldn't tell her Hammel was a Bureau agent. She didn't need to know. And just in case things got dangerous, it was best if she didn't know what Reed was up to. No one's cover would get blown. He shook his head, recalling how insistent Trent had been back in Thailand, and then in Italy, landing himself in the middle of two different cases Reed was working.

"Don't worry what I'm going to do. I will get Trent out. He'll be fine." Reed took the opportunity to convince himself as much as Beth. He knew he could crack the case if they were back home, but he was out of his element with the yakuza. On his earlier missions in Asia, he'd been undercover, dealing with Chinese triads. "And don't call me Reed. I had to travel on a different passport." Beth started to ask a question, and he put up a finger to silence her. "I'm Randall Archer. Can you remember that? Randall or Randy."

"Okay."

"Say it: Randall Archer. Say it ten times."

"Randall Archer." She looked up at him, hesitating until he nodded. "Randy. Randy. Randy. Randy. Randall Archer. Randall. Randy. Is that ten?"

"Another ten."

She followed directions. "Randy, what are you going to do?"

"I don't know yet. But don't worry. I'll call you when I do know. And if I send someone from the embassy, they'll use a phrase so you know I sent them." He thought for a minute. "Take your vitamins."

"What?"

"That's the phrase. If anyone says that, or asks about that, you can trust them. I sent them. Do whatever they say or go wherever they tell you."

"R-Randy, you're scaring me." She backed up a few steps and let herself fall onto the couch.

"I know Trent didn't do this."

"You think he's innocent?" The way she asked the question surprised Reed.

"Don't you?"

"Y-yes, but the fingerprints. And he was gone a long time. I had to tell the cops that he wasn't with me, and supposedly it was when… you know." She put a hand on Reed's arm and he pushed it away roughly.

"You think he could have done it? Why the hell would you even think that's possible?" Reed fought to keep his voice and temper down. Why did Beth suddenly suspect Trent had done something this terrible?

"Maybe he was drugged. We were drinking with dinner. And who knows what he ate or drank up there. He was acting so weird when he got back to the room. I knew something had happened."

"And the something was Trent murdering a guy you'd just met that day? Why?"

"No. I know he wouldn't do something like that. He liked the guy, Motofuji. But everything looks like he did it. I don't know why or how, but he really looks guilty. I'm so scared they'll just stop looking for the real killer."

"That's why you should be scared, Beth. Because the people behind this are so powerful they almost have you thinking your best friend could be a killer."

Beth let out a high-pitched sob and covered her face in her hands. "Oh, God." She wrapped her arms around herself and looked at Reed, fear and embarrassment raw on her face. He stood up quickly and grabbed his duffel. He couldn't wait to get out of this place. If Trent's closest friend thought he looked guilty, how would a jury of total strangers vote if Trent ever got to trial?

He headed back to Hammel and the car. He didn't have a minute to spare. Forces much more dangerous than he'd expected were involved. He hoped Hammel had a good team out here.

HAMMEL TOOK him to a safe room at the embassy. No windows, only one door, and a bug sweeper on constant alert. Reed didn't ask who might be listening in. The Chinese, North Koreans, Russians, or organized crime. Or all of the above. Shortly after Reed sat down at the table, a knock sounded and a Japanese guy in his midthirties entered. He wore an off-the-rack suit and his tie was loose.

"Randy, this is Osamu Kobayashi, from the Tokyo Metropolitan Police Department. Detective Kobayashi."

"Sam," Kobayashi said with a grin and a slight accent. "Call me Sam." He took a seat across the table from Reed. He had a shadow of stubble and a shock of thick, shiny black hair that wouldn't stay smooth no matter how many times he ran his hand over it. And, as Reed noticed, he did that about every three sentences.

"Sam's gotten himself assigned to the case. The police don't know he works with us and keeps us informed on matters we have an interest in."

"Anything with foreigners, even non-Americans, especially from countries hostile to the US. Also anything involving terrorism or potential WMD."

"You pretty busy?" Reed had no clue how much of any of that went on in Japan.

"All the time. With the money around here, wackos are always showing up trying to get funded. Luckily, Japanese organized crime has taken a financial hit lately. They don't have money to spare blowing up things in other countries. It won't make them money here."

"You on the OC taskforce too?" Reed asked. He needed someone with deep knowledge and contacts in organized crime.

"I've worked there. I can get onto a case if needed, or get the files. Just let me know what you need."

"We don't know yet." Reed looked at Hammel. "I'm hoping some brainstorming with you and Christopher will give me some ideas where to start."

"From what I can see, Trent Copeland looks as guilty as they come."

Reed started to stand up, but Kobayashi held up a hand. "Looks." He poured water from a pitcher on the table and took a sip. "He looks too guilty. It has to be a set-up. But it's nice and clean and convenient for the police to let the gaijin take the rap. Finding out who did it and why is going to be messy. Japanese don't like mess."

"Can you do some further investigation, enough to establish an alibi, another witness, some other forensic evidence that points to someone else?" Reed asked.

Sam shook his head. "They don't want to mess with perfection. The legal mandate of the police doesn't involve finding the correct guilty party. They stop when they find an answer unless there's political pressure to keep looking."

"And where do the politics fall in this case?"

Hammel let out a dry laugh. "On the side of blaming the foreigners, so they don't have to look inside and see what really happened. Ignorance is bliss."

Kobayashi nodded. "He's right. I won't be able to turn the investigation in another direction. All I can do is slow it down and maybe lose some evidence for a while. I mean, it might happen that way if I wasn't as diligent as I should be at doing my job." He grinned.

"He's a good cop, but a better American." Hammel grinned.

"American?" Reed asked. He hadn't asked, but now he was curious.

"Dual citizenship. My mother is Japanese-American, and I grew up here but went to college in the States. They let me join the police without giving up American citizenship. I try to act much more Japanese when I'm at work."

"How do you do that?" Reed asked.

"My ingurishi is notto so gooddo in za offisu." Kobayashi grinned. "It's pretty easy to fool most of my colleagues," he added with almost no trace of an accent. "Let me get copies of the files and bring them back tonight. In the meantime, I'll see what connections I can make to rival yakuza and pull those files. We can brainstorm over dinner."

"Sounds good." Hammel stood and shook hands with Kobayashi, and Reed did as well. "Look, Archer," Hammel went on, "you look like you haven't slept in a while and you smell like—well, you get the idea. Take a break, clean up, and have a nap until Sam gets back."

"Isn't there any way I can get to see Trent?" Reed had wanted to ask the moment he landed, but he knew it was vital to get the ball rolling with an alternate investigation first.

"Not tonight. We can pass you off as an embassy official replacing his assigned liaison. But you might not want the police to see you, in case you need to go undercover for any part of this investigation. There's too many cameras—surveillance all over the detention center. You're better off keeping off the official radar."

Reed knew Hammel was right, but he had to know how Trent was doing. "I'm worried about him."

"Japanese jails are pretty safe. But I may be able to get a note to him. Something small or cryptic so if it's found no one will know what it is, even if they can read English."

Would Trent remember the code he'd explained back in Italy? Even so, it used roman characters—English letters. It had to be a symbol that Trent would know came only from Reed.

"Give me a piece of paper."

Hammel slid a pad over to Reed and he drew a simple shape. He showed it to Hammel before folding it up. "That's innocent enough, right?"

"I guess so. Let me have this delivered to the detention center. Depending on the schedules, he'll get this with dinner or tomorrow's breakfast. But you won't be able to get a reply."

"I don't need one. I know what he would say."

Hammel cocked his head and looked at Reed for a long moment. "You two are really that close?"

"Closer. We've been through a lot together… you heard about Italy, so you have some idea." Reed gave a shallow smile. "But he always surprises me. I know he can handle this, but I wish he didn't have to. If he knows I'm here now, it will make all the difference."

WHEN TRENT got his dinner that night, he was famished. He hadn't felt like eating lunch. Hadn't felt like eating at all since the trial or hearing or whatever it was. The lawyer hadn't come back yet, and there was no word from the embassy. He gobbled the rice from the bowl. Only one bowl tonight. Maybe he'd get another later if he was lucky. When he dropped the empty bowl back onto the tray, a piece of folded paper caught his eye.

He glanced down, noticing the Japanese writing on it, just a pencil scribble. Slowly he reached toward it and stopped. What's the worst it could be? He probably wouldn't be able to read whatever was inside. If it was a death threat or an escape route, it would be useless. He didn't want to get his hopes up that it was anything good.

"Definitely a death threat," he said out loud, surprised to hear his own voice echo back at him in the confined space. "But hate mail is better than no mail."

He finally picked up the paper and lay back on his cot. Then he unfolded it.

And smiled.

There was no note. Just a hand-drawn smiley face with a crooked mouth.

Reed.

Reed was here! Reed would know how to get him out. Excitement and relief jumbled in his stomach, and his heart pounded. He felt a little dizzy and put his head on the pillow.

Reed. But what was Reed going to do? Based on what the lawyer and the cop had said, there was a mountain of evidence against him. How was Reed going to prove that wrong? Or was he going to help Trent escape? No, he was just being silly. Most of the day guards were sway-backed old men who shuffled down the hallway, but a few were younger, swaggering up and down the hall, smacking their batons against their hands so the sound echoed along the corridor. That described the guy out there now. The one who only gave him one bowl of vegetables. All the other guards got him two bowls of veggies since he didn't really like the fish.

Asshole. Trent fantasized about Reed kicking the guard's ass and freeing him. They'd run down the hall and down the stairs. Where they'd be caught like fish in a barrel. No stolen guard uniforms or fast moves could hide the fact that they were tall Caucasians. They'd stick out like Madonna in a convent.

The image made him laugh. A few chuckles turned into a long burst of uncontrollable laughter. His stomach ached when he finally calmed himself enough to stop laughing. But it had worked. He felt a tide of peace, of relief, wash over him. He slipped the little note under his pillow and curled onto his side. With Reed's message close, Trent fell into the first peaceful night's sleep he'd had since he'd arrived in Japan.

REED ALSO had his first sleep since he'd left for Texas. Dozing on the plane didn't count. Once he'd sent the message to Trent, that worry was off his mind, so he could concentrate on how to get the charges against Trent dropped.

Kobayashi came back later that evening after his shift was over. They met with Christopher Hammel again in the same hidden room at the embassy.

"I made copies of the files. It was tricky, which is why I had to stay late, after nearly everyone had gone. I have access, but I wanted to bring everything here for you."

"It's all in Japanese? What good is this going to do me?" Reed flipped through the thick file on the table.

"None. Which is why you need me and a translator you can trust."

"Beth…."

Kobayashi shook his head. "There's pretty obscure legal language and forensic stuff in here. She probably can't read it." He paused, then explained. "Japanese language uses both a phonetic alphabet and Chinese characters. The average Japanese knows about two to three thousand characters out of the twenty thousand. Only people who study law or science have ever even seen some of these."

"How do people read, then?" Reed asked, unclear how this supposedly highly educated populace couldn't even read a police document.

"Usually people learn the specific characters for their field. Other times the documents are written with the phonetics as well as the characters. The average person knows the word, just not how to write it."

"It's like not knowing how to spell something in English even if you know what it means and how to use it in a sentence." Hammel laughed. "The opposite of those spelling bee words. Those kids can spell them but wouldn't know what to do with them after that."

"Okay, so Beth's out. Is there someone you trust, Christopher?"

"Yes. I'll arrange some time with her for tomorrow. But Sam can summarize them now."

"Thanks, Sam." Reed nodded.

"Speaking of Beth," Hammel continued. "I had her moved to another hotel. Motofuji had been paying for that room, and I can't spend that kind of cash on her. Sorry. She's in a middle-range Japanese hotel. Perfectly comfortable. You should stay here until we figure out…." Hammel stopped. Reed understood. He didn't want to divulge Reed's location or identity—or that he might change identities—in front of Kobayashi. Good thinking. And it made him trust Hammel even more. No matter how well he knew Kobayashi, Bureau protocol had to be followed. Sloppy procedures lead to disasters. He also hadn't mentioned where Beth had been moved.

"Sounds good. Now Sam, tell us what the evidence is against Trent." Reed grabbed one of the notepads from the center of the table and a pen.

"There's some pretty conclusive evidence. Motofuji was killed with a knife, stabbed repeatedly and his throat slit." He slid photographs across the table to Reed. Hammel glanced through them and slid them back to Kobayashi. "Time of death was Thursday night/Friday morning approximately 2:00 a.m. However the body wasn't discovered until Sunday morning when the maid reported for work. Motofuji had given her the Saturday off. She left at some point on Friday, after Beth, Trent, and Maeda left, but before Motofuji went to dinner."

"Wasn't there a driver?" Reed leaned forward as he spoke, then, aware of his interruption, settled back into his seat. "Sorry, you've got the floor. I'll save my questions."

"Yes, there was a driver. I'll get to him in a minute." Kobayashi didn't appear to let Reed's intrusiveness bother him. "The time of death might be one hour earlier or later. The length of time until the body was discovered made determination difficult. But the weather is still fairly cool."

Reed made notes on the pad and turned his attention back to Kobayashi.

"The driver is a long-time employee of Motofuji. He drove Motofuji to meet the others for dinner on Thursday at a well-known and exclusive restaurant, Kinmata. He was dismissed from duty at that point, and he drove the car to his own residence where he lives with his wife. He didn't go out again from Friday night until Saturday afternoon when he drove her grocery shopping."

"Now to Trent and Motofuji's movements that night. Motofuji is a regular at Kinmata, and there is no dispute about when he left. He treated the others to an elaborate meal, so the staff was very aware of his presence and his departure. He asked the hostess to call him a taxi. The two women left in a hired car, which Motofuji had arranged for the duration of their stay in Kyoto. Trent and Motofuji left together in the taxi. The driver remembers dropping them off at Motofuji's residence. The taxi company has records and sent him out on another call to the Gion district immediately after, so his movements for the time in question are well documented."

"Okay, so Trent went up there in a taxi. How did he get back to the hotel?"

"The hired driver went to get him at midnight. The man said he waited in front of the house until Trent came out, then took him back to the hotel. According to the hotel owner and Beth, Trent didn't get back until after 2:00 a.m."

"The driver waited for two hours up there and didn't knock on the door or anything?"

"That is what is expected of hired limo drivers. They drive and wait until they are told to do something else. They often wait for several hours outside bars and restaurants. It's not a difficult job."

"So Trent has no alibi?"

"No. The theory is he killed Motofuji while the limo driver waited outside. The man is broken up with guilt. He wished he had thought to knock."

Reed made some more notes. "Poor guy. What about forensic evidence?"

Kobayashi flipped a few more pages. Reed could see a ten-card—Trent's fingerprints—and a printout from a fingerprint matching program. Similar to what US law enforcement agencies used.

"Trent's prints are on the murder weapon." Kobayashi slid several photographs of the dagger to Reed along with the print-matching report. Reed didn't need to read Japanese to understand the dots and lines indicating matching points.

"Did he say he touched it?" Reed asked.

"He wouldn't answer questions yet. His attorney wanted to see the files herself before she would allow him to be questioned again."

"Good." If Trent didn't admit to touching it, then they might be able to prove the prints had been planted. It would at least be reasonable doubt. Would that matter in Japan? He had no clue what standard of proof was required for conviction here.

"What else?"

"The method of the murder points to Trent."

"What does that mean?" Reed dialed back his anger, but it settled into his gut and boiled as he listened.

"This sort of stabbing and throat-slitting isn't particularly Japanese." Kobayashi put up a hand before Reed could respond. "We have many knife and sword murders here. But the doers use moves they saw in a samurai movie most of the time. Many of them have training in kendo or other martial arts. This generally results in slashing injuries to the arms and torso. Often they aren't even fatal. This technique doesn't fit usual Japanese crime patterns. And it doesn't fit the way the yakuza kill each other."

"Okay, now we're getting down to it. The yakuza. That has to be an angle here. Why aren't the police pursuing those leads? Because he wasn't killed the right way?"

Kobayashi let out an ironic laugh. "Yes. That's part of it. The police are trained to recognize patterns and connect dots. They don't see a common pattern here, but the dots connect right to Trent."

"And the big red arrow pointing to Trent hasn't set off any alarms?" Reed didn't bother to disguise his bitterness now.

"A closed case is a closed case."

"But why would Trent kill this guy? They just met. There's no motive."

"You know motive is on the optional list. They don't care. But the theory—since they won't go to court without one—is that Trent wanted some artwork and that he stole some documents associated with the missing pieces."

"The guy owns half an LA art gallery. He doesn't have to steal art. Is anything missing?"

Kobayashi dug into the pile of papers again. "A woodblock print—which they found in Trent's hotel room at the Park Hyatt. And they are still in the process of cataloguing the full collection against Motofuji's personal records and insurance inventory. Naoko Maeda, the appraiser, also has a list and photographs. She's been cooperating with the police but hasn't turned over her records yet. But it's just a formality. Even if nothing else is missing, they have a motive—even if it's flimsy."

Had Trent taken the print for some reason, or had it been placed in his hotel to frame him? Reed scribbled down his unanswered questions. He needed to speak with Beth. "And that's enough?"

"At the moment, the prosecutor is happy with just the one print as motive and proof. But the team hasn't wrapped up the investigation. They are looking into the yakuza connection."

"About time. It had to be one of them behind this. It's so obvious even I can figure that out."

"I don't disagree. But that's part of the problem." Kobayashi consulted another document near the bottom of the pile. "The prosecutor wants us to prove Trent was hired by a rival gang to assassinate Motofuji. That he showed up, looking like an innocent American tourist, and he deliberately used a non-Japanese style killing technique."

"That's the most ridiculous thing I've ever heard. Trent writes romance novels for fuck's sake. He's not an international assassin."

"Supposedly he completed a specialty course at your FBI Academy, which included the skills necessary to carry out this crime."

Reed rubbed at his eyes, trying to stop the throbbing in his skull. He wasn't sure he could breathe and knew he couldn't speak even if he knew what to say. Reed had sent Trent on that course to learn self-defense techniques, and now it was being used as proof he was a trained assassin.

Someone somewhere really had it in for Trent. There was only one way to get him out of this mess.

"So we're going to have to find out who actually did it." Reed pulled his notes from the pad and shoved them into his breast pocket. "How hard could that be?"

16

AFTER KOBAYASHI left, Reed and Hammel got down to specifics. Hammel had some new IDs made for Reed with several choices of name, appearance, occupation, and date he had entered Japan.

"This one is actually a real embassy employee. Except for the mustache, you two look pretty similar. You could pose as him for a visit to the detention center tomorrow. Trent's got an appointment with his attorney, and she can bring an embassy rep with her. That's a one- or two-time thing only. The others are if you need to move around in various circles."

The way Hammel emphasized the last word piqued Reed's interest. "Which circles?"

"Art, for one. You can poke around the other collectors who knew Motofuji and Naoko Maeda. Not that I suspect her, but I don't completely trust her either."

"That's certainly an angle. But probably not the one that's going to get the most traction. I don't think it was a rival art collector, do you?"

"Depends on what's missing. But it's more likely a rival gang leader. Or one of Motofuji's own gang. He was old, on his way out, but still in charge. Still calling most of the shots. He'd been bringing the organization into more legit businesses, and they hadn't been earning as much. It's entirely possible a lieutenant decided to off him and take over."

"So why didn't Kobayashi suggest that?"

"He's good, but he's not perfect. He also hasn't had a chance to dig into the yakuza side yet. He's only been on the team for a day. He can't poke his nose up too many asses without someone suspecting something. He's still digesting the facts and, most of all, listening to the other members on the team."

Reed nodded. It was the most difficult skill to teach new agents. They wanted to go out there and knock down doors and take action. But the most powerful way to gather information was to listen to the people who had it—many times they didn't even know they had it or that you wanted it. People will keep talking as long as you keep listening. Once you start asking questions, many sources will clam up. He remembered how many hours of interview technique lectures he'd sat through and the role-playing. It was still his weak spot.

Hammel arranged quarters for Reed to use at the embassy. First thing in the morning, he planned to talk to Beth about that print. He'd invited her to breakfast in the embassy canteen. Then Reed would put on his disguise and go to the detention center to see Trent face-to-face. The thought almost kept him up. He needed to see Trent was doing okay and reassure him that he was doing everything possible to get to the bottom of this frame-up.

Despite his dread at the enormous task ahead of him and the excitement of seeing Trent, Reed slept like a rock until his alarm clock roared him awake the next morning. Sleeping under any conditions had been a necessary skill back in the Army Rangers. You took a few minutes or an hour where you could and had to be rested no matter what was going on around you.

BETH HAD toned down her appearance for the embassy breakfast. Instead of looking like a candy confection, she had dressed in an olive-green skirt with matching tights and a blouse that looked like a chessboard made of jewel-toned silk squares. He'd never seen tights with little pink flowers embroidered on them, but trust Beth to find them. But her stylish ensemble couldn't hide her obvious distress.

They grabbed food from the cafeteria-style line and settled at a table near the edge of the dining room, with Reed's back toward the wall. He wanted to see who might be watching or listening to them.

They received a few curious glances—they were strangers—but no overt attention. Reed had a special visitor badge that gave him access to any room but the ambassador's personal office. The badge garnered respect from embassy employees, who thought he could be a big shot from Washington. No one would risk offending him and getting a black mark in their personnel folder.

"They moved me to a different hotel. Not far from here. And I've got Trent's suitcase and his stuff. The stuff the cops didn't take. Do you want it?"

Reed had started to tune her out, thinking she was complaining about the drop from luxury to the Japanese equivalent of HoJos, but mention of the suitcase caught his attention.

"I'll have the case picked up. I'm going to see Trent later this morning."

"Really? How'd you manage that?" Beth bit into a thick stack of pancakes and a little syrup dripped on her chin. Reed decided not to tell her. He was still annoyed she even considered Trent might have killed the guy. He spread jam on some buttered toast. The thought of pancakes depressed him a little. The last time he'd eaten them had been with Trent.

"I have connections. But I need to ask you about that night. They say Trent stole something from Motofuji. The cops found a print in the hotel room. What do you know about that?"

"Yeah. Well, no. He didn't steal it. Motofuji gave it to him. He saw Trent liked the print—one of the gay prints—so he offered to give it to Trent."

"Gay prints? I don't get it."

"Oh, right. Did you see the print Trent got from Leah? The samurai and another guy?"

"Yeah. He showed it to me. What does that have to do with anything?" Reed let his knife clatter onto the plate and Beth jumped at the sound. He hadn't realized how on edge she was over this ordeal.

"They're very rare. It wasn't exactly illegal back then, but it wasn't openly discussed."

"Beth, get to the point. We can discuss Japanese art history when we're all home and safe."

"Sorry." She sniffed and stared at her pancakes while she collected herself.

Reed felt like a jerk again. He didn't want to bully her, but he didn't have all day. *Listen*, he reminded himself….

"So, Trent spotted this print, and Motofuji could see he really liked it. Said he wanted to give it to him, rather than sell it. Naoko had it down on her list to appraise, but he had no intention of sending it to Leah to sell. That was why Trent went back there that night after dinner. To pick up the print."

"He didn't give it to Trent that day during the appraisal visit?"

"No. I don't know why. And we were supposed to go back there this week after the appraisal was done to ship off the items to LA. He could have waited to give it to Trent then. It was creepy." She blinked. "That's just what Trent said."

"What was creepy?"

"The house that night. The talk with Motofuji. The jade dagger. But the whole thing—"

"Back up to the dagger."

"Oh, yeah. More than creepy. Macabre. *Grisly*. Trent had noticed the jade dagger during the day too. It was in a special case by itself. It was beautiful. I've never seen anything that stunning carved from jade."

"That was the murder weapon?"

"Yes."

"And did Trent touch it?"

"Yeah. That was the creepy part. Motofuji let Trent take it out of the case that night while they were alone, and while Trent was holding it, Motofuji told a story about how his wife was murdered with a twin dagger."

Reed dropped his coffee cup this time and spilled its searing contents all over his lap. He leapt up and the people sitting nearby turned at the commotion. He nodded and laughed and sopped up the mess with napkins, but he was badly shaken by the story—and the proof the prints hadn't been planted.

When he looked up from the mess, he spotted Hammel coming toward him, cell phone plastered to one ear.

"Morning, Randy." He sat down and nodded to Beth. Reed didn't introduce them. Beth looked at him expectantly, but he only said, "Beth, that's it for now. I'll send someone for Trent's stuff later."

"Actually, Randy," Hammel piped up. "You should get it yourself. Now."

"Why?"

"I just got a report that an American couple were killed at the Park Hyatt last night. Room 5004."

This time Beth dropped her cup. A few more people turned to look, then looked away quickly as Hammel glared at them.

"W-what? Killed?" Beth's voice trembled. "In the room we were staying in until last night?"

“It’s connected. It has to be. Someone’s looking for something they think Trent has, and that’s how far they’ll go to get it. Randy and I will collect Trent’s belongings. Beth, you need to stay at the embassy until we get back.”

HAMMEL ASKED his assistant to arrange an embassy room for Beth while he and Reed went to her hotel to get the suitcases. Reed put everything in his own room and had some of Beth’s clothes sent to her room. He wanted to go through everything in those suitcases himself before letting anything else out of his sight.

He stared at the suitcase, remembering how he’d packed it for Trent so they’d have time to make love once more the night before Trent and Beth had left for Japan. He thought about the way Trent had complained Reed hadn’t packed enough socks and too much underwear and why couldn’t he bring one more pair of pants? And about the way Trent had tasted and how soft his lips were when he brushed them against Reed’s nipples. And how he couldn’t wait to wake up again with Trent pressed up tight against Reed’s back as he licked the lobe of Reed’s ear.

If Hammel hadn’t banged on the door, Reed might have noticed how his eyes stung and his nose felt tickly and his chest felt like there was a huge, aching hole in the middle. He had to pull himself together to see Trent or he’d do more harm than good.

“Yeah!” Reed shouted and wiped the back of his hand across his eyes before Hammel could see anything.

“Makeover time!” Hammel had a small suitcase with him, one Reed had seen plenty of times, full of fake noses and little beards and sideburns. A few small changes could alter an agent’s appearance enough to avoid recognition by the average person. New facial recognition software worked on the features you couldn’t alter, like the distance between eyes, width of the mouth, or shape of the ears.

It only took ten minutes for Hammel to add a few little touches and a cheesy porn mustache so Reed would pass for Clark Porter to anyone but his mother, girlfriend, and some advanced software. Reed took an embassy car to the detention center at police headquarters and met Trent’s lawyer, Tane Tanaka, in the lobby. Together they signed into the detention center. The guard frisked him and searched the bag of clothes he’d brought. Reed asked if he could see Trent before he met with the lawyer, so she stayed in the waiting area.

He didn't know what to expect when the guard escorted him to the tiny meeting room. Through the small window, he could see Trent cuffed to the table, eyes downcast, shoulders slumping. Reed got a painful lump in his throat and had to blink a few more times. What was he waiting for?

The guard opened the door and Reed went in with the bag. Trent glanced up quickly and then away again, in obvious disappointment.

"Where's Nora?" Trent asked, though this tone indicated he didn't really care. His voice sounded raspy, like he'd just woken up.

"She's sick. I'm Clark Porter." Reed knew Trent would recognize his voice, but hoped he'd realize not to let on. These rooms were bugged except for meetings with attorneys.

Trent's head shot up, and he narrowed his eyes at Reed's altered appearance. He blinked a couple of times and then gave Reed a sideways look. "Do you like pancakes?" Trent asked.

Reed could kiss him. He sure as hell wanted to, and that question made it even harder not to reach out and touch him. He'd certainly learned something at Quantico.

"Yes, I do." He smiled. "Nice to meet you." He put out his hand for a shake and Trent gripped it tight. The emotion between them turned electrical, communicating so much about what Trent must be thinking, as if he'd spoken directly to Reed. Trent's touch felt almost frantic at first, until he relaxed, hopefully comforted and invigorated by Reed's visit. "I have some more clothes and things for you." Reed pushed the bag across to Trent, using it to shield his hand from the surveillance camera as he pushed a note into Trent's hand. "Open that later."

"Any news from the States?"

"Yes. Your friend Randall Archer has arrived. He's doing some background research on your case. If all goes well, you should be out before the end of the ten-day investigation period."

"Really?"

"Really. He won't be able to visit you—Japanese rules, as you know. But he's got some leads that the police haven't followed yet."

"Okay. Will *you* be visiting again?" Trent's expression screamed hope and expectation, and Reed hated disappointing him.

"Not me. I'm being assigned another project, and I may need to leave Tokyo."

"Oh."

"Tell me about the lawyer."

"She wants to plead down to a lesser charge. Manslaughter." Trent's voice trembled as he said the word.

"Don't listen to her. Don't answer any questions if you can avoid it. And don't sign anything unless Randall or I can read it first."

"How can I let you know what's going on?"

"Someone from the embassy will visit you each day with news. Someone who likes cats. Siamese cats. Got it?"

"Yes." Trent nodded. "I'd rather have pancakes."

"I know a great place. When you get out, I'll take you."

"Thanks. Good luck with that new project."

Reed leaned his chin against his hand, elbow on the table, and ran a finger across his lips. *I love you.* Their secret code. Trent had wanted something only they would understand and Reed never expected it would be necessary for actual communication.

Trent looked like he was tearing up. Time for Reed to go. He stood up and knocked on the door, and the guard let him out.

TRENT HAD dreamed of seeing Reed here since the moment he was arrested. Actually, even before that, when he'd second-guessed his choice of Beth over Reed. But he never expected to actually see him. Not that he looked exactly like Reed. He had thicker eyebrows and a super cheesy mustache. It took all Trent's composure not to laugh his head off at Reed's ridiculous appearance. But it certainly broke the tension. It also served to remind Trent that something far more serious than he realized was going on. Reed using a fake ID and showing up as another person meant he was in full mission mode. Otherwise he would have just used his own name and not worn a disguise.

He just hoped he understood Reed's code correctly. Someone from the embassy who liked cats. If the person didn't mention cats, Trent shouldn't trust him. Was all that necessary? Why?

Trent was better off not knowing for the time being. He trusted Reed to find out how to get him out, whether it meant finding the real killer or figuring out who had framed him. He had only heard smatterings of the evidence against him, but he knew it was serious, and it wasn't accidental. Someone had planned this. But who?

While waiting for the guard to bring his lawyer, Trent snuck a peek into the bag Reed had brought. It was heavy, containing a pair of shoes, pants, two more shirts, and… Trent had to look twice.

A bottle of his favorite body wash. He couldn't help smiling. At first Reed had teased him mercilessly about it, then he'd brought it halfway around the world to make Trent feel safe and comfortable.

Everything was going to be fine now. No matter what happened or how long he had to brave it out in here. Reed would make sure he got out.

17

BACK AT the embassy, Hammel's assistant—another Bureau employee—told Reed Kobayashi had arrived. Since Hammel was out on another assignment, Reed met with him alone.

"I have some news. I just don't know what it means." Kobayashi sipped tea the assistant had brought while Reed waited for the actual news.

"What did you find out?"

"I went back to the evidence room, intending to check out Trent's folder, but once I got it back to the team office, I discovered that all of the evidence connecting Trent to the murder is missing."

"Missing? What's missing?"

"The murder weapon, with Trent's prints. The interview with the girl stating he was not with her for the crucial hours when the crime was determined to have taken place."

"So now the police have nothing to connect Trent to the murder?"

"No. They still have the fingerprint report and match to Trent, but without the dagger, it's not enough to hold him. A defense lawyer would probably eventually get the case dismissed since the defense cannot examine the original evidence."

Reed didn't let on that according to Beth, Trent actually had handled the weapon. But what the hell did this mean? "I don't understand. Is this good news or bad news?"

"On the surface, it's good for Trent. Underneath, I'm pretty fucking suspicious. And worried."

Reed waited for Kobayashi to explain. He picked up his own cup of tea and sipped. It was cold. He poured more from the pot, but the resulting mixture, while warmer, was slightly bitter. He frowned. "And?"

"I think his attorney can get the case dismissed. The prosecutor has nothing to go on right now."

"Was the evidence signed out by someone else?"

"Not according to the records. I asked. That department can be a little sloppy when they want to be. Like when the Yakuza are involved…."

Reed nodded. He understood what that meant. Things did go missing and held up cases, sometimes, so they had time to find additional evidence. "So Trent might be let out?"

"I don't think it could hurt to have his attorney petition for an inspection of the evidence. If it's genuinely missing, they might let him go. If it's simply misplaced, it might help me figure out who has it and why—by how the prosecutor responds."

"I'll get Hammel to work on the legal side of this. Thanks."

"No problem. As far as I know, the team is still working under the assumption Trent is the murderer. The police have one guy in Kyoto following leads, and I'm writing reports on everything the other two guys find. But everything else I've seen so far is circumstantial. Without the hard evidence—the fingerprints—it's not so cut and dried."

"It just doesn't make any sense."

"I need to watch what happens for another day or two, but I have a theory. Let me gather my own evidence, then I'll know more, one way or another."

"That's it?"

Kobayashi shrugged. "This is the best I can do right now. I have to play this carefully. My name is the last on the check-out sheet for that evidence, so my ass is on the line if someone else is fucking around with it. I don't know if this is a trap for me, or something bigger."

"Then be careful."

Kobayashi nodded and left without another word. The scent of his cologne lingered long after he had gone.

Reed's emotions were in a jumble. If there was no evidence, Trent could get out, but if someone had hidden it, why? Who would gain from that, and what would they gain? Only he, and presumably the US government, wanted to see Trent freed. The real killer and whoever he represented would want Trent locked up as a patsy.

A soft knock sounded on the door, and Hammel let himself in. "Kobayashi was here? What did he have today?"

Reed filled Hammel in on the developments.

"I can't make sense of this. All I can say is, let's get the lawyer, Tanaka, involved. If she can get Trent out of detention, we can send him home."

"I agree. Let's talk to Tanaka and see what she can do."

TUESDAY NIGHT, Trent slept soundly. He'd showered with the body wash Reed had brought and put on a clean shirt and sweat shorts that had also been in the bag. He woke refreshed on Wednesday, more confident that everything would be cleared up soon, despite the negative report his attorney had given him the day before.

As he ate his breakfast, he went over the evidence Tane Tanaka had listed: the fingerprints, the statements from Beth, the restaurant and hotel employees, and the limo driver. Naoko's statement and the list of artworks showing several missing pieces, including the woodblock print Motofuji had given Trent. Who had taken the other things? They hadn't yet turned up. Only the woodblock print had been recovered: they'd found it with Trent's belongings. He hadn't attempted to hide it. That should prove he hadn't stolen it.

Reed would have all of this information, and if he thought Trent needed a different lawyer, then the new one would certainly point out these key facts. Despite his improved mood, he still felt a sadness, an unnameable ache when he thought about Motofuji. He had been kind to Trent, and knowing the man had been brutally murdered moments after Trent left his home was shocking and horrifying.

He hoped Reed would help the cops find the real killer. That person deserved to be locked up for what they had done. Motofuji's violent past had caught up with him, but even so, his murder was a crime. And if the same person had deliberately framed Trent, then he should pay for that too.

Trent had barely pushed his breakfast tray back into the hallway when someone pounded on the cell door and then swung it open, shouting—in Japanese, so Trent had no clue what was going on. He recognized the mean guard's voice before he even entered the cell. Another guard stood in the hall while Meanie grabbed Trent's bag of clothing and tossed items from his little shelf in there: toothbrush, body wash, folded clean clothing.

"What's happening?" Trent asked, despite knowing he'd get no intelligible reply.

The guard nodded toward the hallway and, still holding the bag, herded Trent out of the cell.

Was he getting moved? He hoped it wouldn't be back to one of those four-person cells. He kind of liked his privacy. Sandwiched between the two guards, he shuffled through several locked gates that slid open as the trio approached, clanging shut behind the trailing guard. Other prisoners watched the little procession and a few shouted. Trent had learned a few new words, none of which he'd say in front of his mother, but he nodded to his new acquaintances as he passed.

Finally, they arrived at the same counter where he'd been booked, and a guard returned his watch, wallet, shoelaces, and belt. He was being released! He finally let his excitement bubble to the surface. He hadn't wanted to get his hopes up, but now he was sure. It felt like a huge weight slipped from his shoulders.

He was told to sign some papers—in Japanese—which he did. He didn't have a clue what he'd just signed, but it couldn't be too bad if they were letting him out. They let him change in a cubicle near the booking desk.

He followed the guard out to the hallway outside the detention center, and the guard said something that sounded like the words for "good-bye."

He was free! Trent looked around for Reed or Beth, or his lawyer, or even the original woman from the embassy, but he didn't recognize anyone. Then he realized the one thing he hadn't gotten back was his cell phone. He glanced around for a phone but wondered whether he'd even recognize a Japanese payphone—and if he did, he wouldn't know how to pay.

He sat down in a noisy waiting area, filled with relatives and friends of the recently detained, and waited. If no one showed up within an hour, he'd take a cab back to the hotel. He could find Beth and have a nice steam shower and get in contact with Reed from there.

When it was clear no one was coming for him, Trent made his way outside and spotted a row of cabs. The first one wouldn't take him—no surprise, based on what Beth had said about communication issues with foreigners. The second ignored him and Trent was reconsidering his plans when a cab drove up and honked. The driver waved him in and opened the rear door.

With relief, Trent hopped into the back and settled himself and his bag of clothes into the plush interior. Boy, these Japanese cabs were luxurious compared the ones in LA. Considering what they cost, it was only fitting, he decided.

"Park Hyatt Hotel," Trent said, leaning through the opening in the partition. He hoped the driver understood him.

"Pāku Haiatto, hai!" the driver responded and pulled away with a satisfying squeal of tires.

Trent was out of danger! He hadn't expected Reed to get such quick results, and as they drove through the crowded streets, Trent considered ways to reward Reed for his accomplishment. Maybe Reed would be in the room waiting for him? Would Beth think it too rude if they sent her to the lobby or shopping for a while so they could enjoy a private reunion?

Trent considered the possibilities as the car approached the now-familiar Park Hyatt building. When the car came to a stop, he pulled out his wallet to discover he didn't have enough cash to cover the fare.

He showed the driver the bills he had and pointed up, hoping the guy would understand that he had money inside. Thankfully, the driver nodded and shutoff the engine. He let Trent out of the car, and before Trent made it through the entrance, the driver was half a step behind him.

"Okay, sure, come on up." Trent nodded and smiled. Might as well be polite even if the guy couldn't understand him.

The driver smiled and nodded back, a large grin on his face.

Trent put his plastic key card in the elevator and pushed the button for his floor, and with a soft whoosh, the elevator sped them up in only a few seconds. As Trent neared the door of the room he and Beth had stayed in when they returned from Kyoto, a sinking feeling came over him, knocking out the elated butterfly effect of his anticipated reunion with Reed.

Something yellow fluttered from the doorknob and when he got within ten feet he recognized it: crime scene tape? This one had Japanese characters, but it was still obvious what it meant. What the hell had happened here? Was Beth okay? Was Reed okay? This was very, very bad.

Trent turned just in time to see the driver curling up one hand into a fist. He punched at Trent's jaw, but with the height difference, he barely grazed Trent. He was more surprised than injured by the blow. Trent whirled to avoid a kick, and out of the corner of his eye, he saw someone else coming from the other end of the hall.

"Help? Help!" Trent shouted as he felt the cab driver's heel make contact with his stomach. It knocked the breath out of him, and the rock in his gut started burning. He thought he'd puke up his breakfast. He hoped the guy from the other end of the hall would help before the driver did any real damage. Trent's reflexes kicked in, and he recalled some of the defensive moves he'd learned on his training course. He bobbed and spun on one foot, staying out of the driver's reach.

Finally the other guy reached him, and Trent expected him to help in the attack, but instead he pulled a knife.

Now it dawned on Trent: this guy had been waiting for him to get here. They wanted something Trent had—only he had no idea what it was. He kicked at the knife, surprised that he caught the guy's hand and heard his grunt as the knife thudded on the thick carpet about ten feet away. Its owner ran to retrieve it while Trent turned toward the driver who was wiping blood away from his face. Trent didn't remember hitting him. Then he realized the only weapon he had was his bag. He swung it around and it hit the driver full force against his nose.

The bottle of body wash connected with a satisfying crunch and the driver went down. Trent ran like hell for the staircase and held the door against the other thug. Trent's brain threatened to overload. What could he do now? He glanced over the railing—about fifty floors down if he took the stairs. He looked through the little window in the door: the knife-wielding thug didn't look particularly fit. Trent figured he could outrun the guy. He spotted a fire hose a few feet away and yanked the door open and ran part of the hose through the door handle.

That should stay for a while, Trent hoped and sped down the stairs two at a time. He heard the thug pulling at the door with no success. He'd gotten four flights down when he finally heard the door creak open and Trent exited the stairway and came out into the hotel hallway. He spotted a door with Japanese characters on it instead of a number and ducked in there. It turned out to be a maids' supply closet. He stayed in there for half an hour. Long enough that the thug must be gone, if he'd even figured out which floor Trent had come out onto.

Despite the break, Trent's heart was still pounding in his ears, and he tried to control his breathing. He was a little out of shape with no exercise for the past week and sitting in a jail for half of that time. But he could sort out a new workout regime later. At the moment, he had to find Reed or Beth.

Since he didn't have a cell phone, and he didn't want to flaunt his presence at the hotel front desk, he dug his wallet out of his pocket. Sure enough, he still had the little stack of emergency cards Beth had written for him if he needed to communicate. One of them read "Take me to the American Embassy," with a little hand-drawn map on it.

Trent took the elevator down to the ground floor and looked carefully before he exited the building. He didn't spot the cab that had brought him here from the jail. That didn't mean the driver or his buddy Knife weren't still around. Not much Trent could do to disguise his appearance, so he walked confidently and slowly past the taxi rank and down two blocks, where he ran into a group of teenage girls with brightly colored backpacks and a wardrobe Beth would kill for.

"Are you American?" one of the girls asked.

"Yes."

"I love America!" another girl said. "I'm applying to Columbia for graduate school!"

The incongruity of those two statements wasn't lost on Trent. "Really? You're in college?"

"Yes. We all are. At Keiō University."

"You all speak English?"

They nodded. They didn't look old enough to be college girls, but what did Trent know about girls, much less Japanese girls?

"Can you help me? I'm kind of lost." Trent smiled, hoping his tall Americanness would be intriguing enough for them to help him. He handed one of the girls his Embassy help card. They grouped around him, but as they giggled, Trent spotted a cab driving slowly past them. He caught the driver's eye: the same driver!

Trent could see the frown on the man's face as he took in the scene of the Japanese girls clustered around Trent. The driver continued past and Trent asked the girls if they wanted to practice their English a little before they went to the embassy. He suggested going into a café nearby, and the girls obliged him. He hoped the driver didn't see them enter the store, and he kept an eye out, glancing through the front window while the girls took turns asking him questions: What city did he live in? Did he have a girlfriend? Did he like sushi? He enjoyed making up flirtatious answers until someone asked, "How big is your penis?"

"Oh, time to go. I have to get to the American Embassy."

Not wanting to end their English practice, the girls escorted him to the subway, but Trent steered the conversation to less personal topics.

"*Chikatetsu*," Trent said as they walked down the steps.

All the girls giggled. "You speak such good Japanese, Torento!" one of them said. Keiko? He couldn't remember all their names. "We'll ride with you, okay?"

When they emerged at the correct station, the girls walked him to the front of the embassy, and he thanked them. They waved and watched him go through the front doors.

Once inside he felt his blood pressure coming down and his shoulders loosening up. He didn't think he'd been followed, but even if he'd been spotted coming in here, he knew he was safe. As long as those thugs didn't work for the embassy, no one could get him here. It was as good as being on American soil.

He was on home turf. Now all he had to do was find Reed and Beth. How hard could that be?

ON WEDNESDAY morning, Nora Paul called Trent's attorney while Christopher Hammel and Reed sat in her office.

"I've had some news from the police that they don't have all the evidence they've indicated…."

"Where did you hear that?" The voice came over speakerphone.

"I can't say, but it's from a contact at Tokyo Metro Police. I don't think it matters who told me."

"No, Nora. But what do you want me to do?"

"Petition for a dismissal and release. If it's true, they'll let Trent Copeland out. And if it's not, then we'll know for sure someone's not telling the truth. Maybe the information will help at some point."

"I'll draw up the papers, but if you hear anything new, let me know. I don't want to risk my standing…."

"I understand. I wouldn't want that either. If I didn't have a strong source, I wouldn't suggest this."

"I appreciate your information. I'll let you know when I hear anything."

"Thank you." Nora disconnected. "There. Now will you tell me how you got that information?"

"Sorry, Nora. I can't. But we appreciate your help."

"Sure thing, Christopher." Nora's smile stopped at her mouth and didn't make it to her eyes, which narrowed as she watched Christopher get up and head for the door. "Mr. Archer."

Reed nodded and thanked her. She suspected something from his silent presence. Christopher had introduced him but said no more than that. Didn't Christopher trust her? Reed's head was spinning now. Who could be trusted and who couldn't? This was Tokyo, not Baghdad or Moscow. How could there be so many secrets floating around the embassy here?

REED AND Hammel were eating lunch in Hammel's office and going over a recent report from an undercover Interpol agent who was in one of the middle-level yakuza groups when Nora called Hammel.

"What's up, Nora?"

Reed looked up from the report at the mention of her name, a pricking at the back of his neck warning him she wasn't calling with good news. He knew better than to trust that Kobayashi character. Divided loyalties meant neither side could trust him. But why would he lie? There was nothing in it for him if Trent was in or out. The same yakuza problems would continue. Trent's arrest and conviction wouldn't make Japan any safer.

"Well, find out what the hell is going on down there!" Hammel's raised voice ripped through Reed's thoughts, and he felt an immediate headache settle into the base of his skull. Hammel slammed the phone down, sending further shockwaves through Reed's brain. "You won't believe this."

"Try me.

"They released Trent two hours ago."

"That's great. Do we go down and get him?" Reed's gut began to unclench.

"No. He's gone. They sent him packing with his belongings and a warning not to leave the country—of course that's written in Japanese, but he left the detention center and the police building."

"Where did he go?" Why hadn't he called Reed? He had that cell phone. Maybe he called Beth. Reed grabbed his own cell phone and punched speed dial for Trent's Japanese cell. It went directly to voice mail.

"Let's get over to police HQ and see what they can tell us. Can you put your mustache on in the car?"

Reed had nearly forgotten his disguise! He had the furry thing in his pocket and pulled it out to show Hammel. "Got glue?"

"Yeah." Hammel rang down to the garage for a car and grabbed a bottle of spirit gum from his desk. He dropped it into his pocket as he and Reed raced for the garage.

As the driver negotiated the traffic, Hammel prepared Reed's alter ego. The driver watched them in the rearview mirror. Reed wondered what the man had seen. He wouldn't repeat any of it, or risk losing his job. Once the transformation was finished, Reed punched in Beth's cell number and got her on the second ring.

"Randy!" He marveled that she remembered to use his alias. He was having trouble remembering who he was from minute to minute. "Do you have news?"

"Have you heard from Trent today?"

"Trent? Of course not. He's in jail and can't call, right?" She paused. "Is he out of jail?"

"Yes, that's what we've been told—"

"But you don't sound excited."

"We don't know where he is, and after what happened at the hotel, I'm worried. Someone wants something from one of you. They may think Trent has whatever it is."

"You're scaring me, R-Randy." Her voice trembled.

"Stay inside the embassy until I know what's going on. And if you hear or see Trent, call me immediately." At least Reed wouldn't have to worry about keeping Beth safe too.

"Of course I will."

Reed hung up. He was torn up over not knowing where Trent was or if someone had him. He had been safer in jail than wandering the streets of Tokyo. Someone thought he had an item of value, and Trent didn't know what they wanted. Or did he? Reed hadn't been able to ask him during their quick discussion at the detention center. He'd asked Beth about the print, but maybe Trent knew something he hadn't told her.

"Wait here." Christopher yanked the door open before the driver had come to a full stop. Reed slid out of the backseat, and they moved swiftly into the police HQ. It wouldn't do to run, though he could barely hold himself in check. Running drew attention, and neither Hammel nor Reed's alter ego had any reason to be this worried about any old American accused of a crime.

"Should we get Kobayashi?" Reed asked as they squeezed into an already full elevator.

"No. Need to keep him out of this."

"Okay." Reed understood.

They arrived at the detention center, and Hammel waited in line at the information desk. Reed would have stormed to the front of the line, but Hammel yanked his elbow when he spotted Reed's intention. "We need to do this their way. If you make a scene or fuss, you'll annoy them, and they won't cooperate today or for a month. It will make it harder for us to do our jobs even after you and Trent go home safe and sound."

Reed nodded. He'd never had much patience when it came to Trent, though it had been such a big part of his training. Why did Trent have this effect on him? He made Reed want to break all the rules and damn the consequences. But it would be selfish to risk Hammel's reputation in the process.

When they got to the desk, Hammel spoke in careful Japanese. Reed hadn't realized how proficient he was in the language. The desk officer took them into a room and a nonuniformed man came in. He spoke for a few moments with Hammel and then bowed and left.

"He's the supervisor here. He's checking to see what time Trent was released and under what circumstances. He'll also check whether the surveillance cameras show him leaving the building."

Ten minutes later the man returned and had a brief exchange with Hammel. He bowed to both of them and left.

"Trent left at 10:17 a.m. and got into a taxi. They'll send me a copy of the video at the embassy later. The paperwork releasing Trent was authorized by someone who the supervisor doesn't know. Not the prosecutor and not anyone on the police team. He'll get his superior's permission to send me a copy. For now, there's not much to do. Let's go back—"

"No. You go back. I have to do something. Look somewhere."

"Where would he go?"

"The only place he knows is the Park Hyatt. He doesn't know we moved Beth or that someone was killed in their old room. I want to see if he went there."

"Okay. I'll go with you."

The driver got them to the hotel, despite crazy traffic in the Shinjuku area. It was particularly clogged up near the hotel, and as they neared the building, the cause became clear. Several police cars were parked in the entryway, and dozens of uniformed cops swarmed the building entrance like bees outside a hive.

A familiar face came out of the crowd. Sam Kobayashi.

"Christopher, Randy. You got here awfully quickly."

"Sam, what happened here?"

"Copeland was released from detention this morning. Apparently he came directly here and went up to his room. Another guest found a dead yakuza *shatei*—the lowest rank—cut up and blocking the door to the stairwell. Knife's still in the guy…."

"You think Trent did this?"

"Look, Archer, I know he's your friend, but this time there's about a dozen witnesses who saw Trent go upstairs with a man who's a known yakuza and someone died shortly after. Stabbed to death. Again."

Reed's stomach churned and he thought he might throw up. "No. It's not Trent. He hates blood. He can't even eat a rare steak. I can't see him stabbing someone even for self-defense." Reed hoped he was right. What had Trent learned in Quantico? He'd surprised Reed with his driving skills, but he couldn't have suddenly become a killer. There was another explanation. He just needed to sit down and concentrate. First he needed some air. Reed felt himself getting faint and walked away from Hammel and Kobayashi. He needed to be alone for a few minutes.

The two men let him go, but he could see them staring at him from the front of the hotel. Kobayashi was shaking his head, that big thick forelock flopping back and forth. Reed turned his back to them until he heard Hammel shouting.

"Archer, I have to get back to the embassy. You're coming with me."

"No. Let me check out the crime scene. Maybe there's a clue upstairs or on the video."

"Sam will get copies of that. Come back. There's a package waiting for you."

Someone waiting at the embassy. Trent? Hammel wasn't letting on to Kobayashi that he knew where Trent was, so Reed played up his reluctance to go. "No. I'll meet you back there later."

"They won't let us go inside. No jurisdiction."

"Okay." Reed let himself be persuaded. They got back in the embassy car and sped off, Kobayashi staring after them as they pulled away.

THE RIDE back to the embassy seemed interminable. Reed was ready to jump out of the car even before it entered the underground garage, but Hammel reminded him he wasn't supposed to be seen entering the building. Reed smothered his impatience only because he knew he'd be seeing Trent in less than ten minutes.

He was sitting in Hammel's office when Reed and Christopher arrived. He looked like hell. Reed fought the urge to run up and check him for injuries. He had a large bruise forming on his jaw and was bleeding from a gash in his arm. The sleeve was ripped cleanly away—someone had used a knife, but not Trent. He gave a brave smile when he saw Reed.

"Hi, Ricky." Trent gave a lopsided grin at their old joke.

"You sure got some 'splainin' to do." Reed tried to smile but there was too much truth in that sentence for it not to hurt.

"I was hoping you'd explain what's happening. Two guys tried to jump me when I went to the hotel. And there was crime scene tape on our door. Where's Beth?" All the words came out in a jumble, one long sentence with barely a pause for breath between words.

"She's fine. She's staying in the embassy and perfectly safe; don't worry."

"I want to see her. Let her know I'm okay and—"

"I told her they let you out of detention." Trent looked relieved and Reed continued. "Let's get you patched up first, then we'll go over everything you need to know. Can you wait?" Reed put an arm around Trent's shoulders, careful not to put too much pressure just in case there were other injuries.

"Yeah. You're right. I want to know what's going on."

"Trent, did you meet Christopher Hammel? He's a Bureau liaison here. He's helping me with your case."

"Hi." Trent nodded. Reed could tell from his reticence Trent had been pushed past his limits. Usually he was polite, even chatty, with new people, especially Bureau agents.

"I'll send a nurse to your quarters, Randy. And how about some lunch? Then afterwards we can meet back here and talk about what has to happen next."

Reed helped Trent up from the chair and carried his bag of clothes. Trent leaned his weight against Reed and was unsteady on his feet. "Trent, are you okay?"

"No. Maybe I just need a nap, or a hug, or a cheeseburger. All of the above. I'm not sure." They got to Reed's room and he unlocked the door. Trent went in and sprawled on the bed.

Reed sat at the edge of the bed and brushed Trent's hair out of his eyes. Trent smiled and closed his eyes. Reed kissed his forehead and played his fingers through Trent's hair. The bleeding was just a trickle, and Reed could see the wound wasn't deep, but that didn't mean it hadn't been harrowing for Trent. Reed leaned over and put his cheek against Trent's. He held him close, but carefully. He inhaled, taking in Trent's familiar smell under a layer of fear and sweat. He could feel Trent begin to relax and his heartbeat slow until it beat in time with Reed's. They lay like this until a knock sounded at the door.

"Nurse," a woman's voice said.

"Come in," Reed called and she entered.

"I'm Lt. Driscoll." She wore an Army officer's uniform and carried a medical bag. She was in her thirties, and Reed could tell from her gait she'd had a serious leg injury—perhaps even had a prosthetic leg. She'd probably seen combat. Maybe this posting was a reward for her service. A glance at the ribbons on her uniform confirmed his suspicion.

"Desert Storm?" he asked as she stepped close to the bed and put her bag down.

"Yes." She mentioned her unit's name and number, and Reed told her his. She nodded. "What can I do for him? Anything besides the knife wound?"

"Not sure. He was in police detention for a few days and then got roughed up by some yakuza this morning."

"I can speak, you know." Trent opened his eyes and winced as he tried to sit up. He gave Reed a low-powered glare.

"Why don't I let you do your job and I'll wait outside." Reed stood up and moved toward the door. He wanted Trent to call him back, and when he didn't, he experienced such a strange mixture of pain and pride he didn't know how to describe it. He needed to let Trent deal with things himself. He couldn't take Trent's pain away by holding his hand or stroking his cheek, though Reed wanted to do that so badly it hurt. Trent had to be his own man, even when it might be unpleasant. Reed admired how much Trent had handled on his own.

But Trent was here, safe, if slightly damaged, though nothing that wouldn't heal. And it wouldn't be long before they were alone and could share a private moment to say the things they couldn't say in front of anyone else.

Reed paced the halls of the embassy residence for twenty minutes until Driscoll called to let him know she was finished with Trent. Outside the closed door, she explained, "He's exhausted, a little underfed, and dehydrated. A few days of bed rest would be a good idea. He took seven stitches and he has a bruised rib. I'll get him some mild pain meds, but he probably needs a few good meals, some sleep, and some TLC." She gave him a wicked grin. "I left my number on the nightstand. If anything gets worse, call. If I'm not on duty, another nurse or doc will be. 24/7."

"Thanks, Lieutenant. I never expected Japan would be so dangerous."

"You'd be surprised." She hoisted her bag over her shoulder, gave a little salute, and left.

Reed opened the door quietly in case Trent was sleeping. He didn't stir so Reed sat in the chair opposite the bed and watched him. He wanted to crawl in bed with Trent and plaster himself against Trent's side. He wanted to feel his soft skin and soft lips and his hard maleness, all at once. Trent was so many different people now that Reed almost felt he was being left behind as Trent's world expanded and Reed felt his own narrowing.

"Why are you watching me?" Trent's voice was raspy, throat dry.

"I'm trying to figure out who you are."

"You know who I am." Trent gave a weak smile. "You're the one with the ever-changing alias."

"I know who I thought you were. But apparently since I dropped you off at the airport ten days ago, you've become an international assassin, done a stint in jail, and now you're a knife-wielding menace to Japanese society."

Trent's smile widened. "All that in little more than a week? No wonder I'm so tired."

"You should sleep."

"I hate sleeping alone." Trent's voice dipped into the flirtatious range, and he slid over to make room for Reed on the bed. "Come here and let me know you missed me."

"The nurse said—" Reed stopped himself as he remembered her grin. "The nurse said that was the perfect prescription for you."

"I love modern medicine." Trent pulled Reed close and kissed him. Just a soft, lazy kiss, but it unleashed a tidal wave of emotion and desire. He let his mouth fall open to welcome Trent inside. The kiss lasted longer than Reed expected.

"Mmm. Minty," Reed whispered against Trent's cheek.

"I brushed while the nurse was in here." Trent smiled and shifted as Reed went in for another kiss.

Trent slid his hand under Reed's shirt, fingertips leaving a trail of fire as he pulled the shirt up. Reed trembled at Trent's touch and the cool air on his overheated skin. Then Trent leaned in to take a nipple into his mouth. He teased with the tip of his tongue, and pleasurable waves washed over Reed's entire body, gathering and intensifying at his core. He felt himself harden and reached for Trent's cock.

Trent pushed Reed's hand away. "Not yet. I won't last long."

"And you think I will?" Reed let out a moan as Trent's only answer was to resume sucking the nipple. He kept moaning softly as Trent's fingers made their way back down his torso, leaving another trail of flame before they went to work on Reed's belt and jeans.

The buttons popped open one at a time, Reed's arousal growing with each. He missed Trent's hands on him, the things those long, slim fingers could do. Trent knew every inch of Reed, and despite what he'd been through this week, he focused his waning energy on Reed. It would be so easy to lie back and accept the pleasure. But Reed never took the easy route.

"Let me. I want to take care of you first. Let me do that?" Reed practically gasped the words out because Trent was slowly peeling back his shorts and running a fingertip along Reed's cock. "Oh, God. Mmm." He swallowed whatever words he'd intended to say as his brain ignored his mouth in favor of responding to Trent's hot touch.

"I want you inside me, Reed. Will you do that for me?"

Reed nodded and got Trent's shirt off. In thanks, Trent licked at Reed's nipple again until Reed didn't think he could take any more. He choked on a breath as Trent's hand tightened around the base of his cock. "Trent."

"Mmm?" Trent was working on Reed's other nipple.

"Your pants."

Together they got that job done, though Trent's refusal to let go of Reed's cock and nipple made it a little tricky. Trent shifted again and lifted his leg to give Reed an easier angle and access. Trent worked Reed's pants lower and pushed them down with a skillful foot movement.

"Face-to-face, Reed," Trent whispered.

Reed nodded and realized there was one last thing. "I don't have—"

Trent produced a tube of lube from under the pillow.

"Where did that come from?"

"The fuck fairy." Trent opened the tube as Reed laughed. He watched Trent apply some to himself, grateful he did. Reed didn't think he could survive Trent lubing up his cock. He just hoped Trent had used enough. He didn't want this to be rough, but he'd do whatever Trent wanted. He wished he could watch Trent prepping himself. That always got Reed even hotter—though in this state, he might not survive that either.

"Ready," Trent said and shifted position again.

Reed took hold of Trent's knee and lined himself up. Concentrating on moving slowly and carefully helped rein in the sensations at first, but once he pushed into Trent's tight heat, Reed held his breath. A day ago he hadn't known when he'd have Trent in his arms again, and he hadn't believed it would be so soon. He'd put the thought of making love to Trent out of his mind as he'd raced around Tokyo, trying to get to the bottom of the murder.

And now, they were as close as they could be. Reed slid in all the way and felt Trent tighten around him like a little greeting. A signal. Welcome home. Trent felt like home. Trent *was* home. Reed gathered Trent close, wrapping his arms around him and holding him, neither moving or speaking. He felt Trent's body loosen and relax, tension and fear draining away. Reed would take that and carry it for him.

Trent's large hands cupped Reed's ass, and when he felt the familiar squeeze, he pushed forward with his hips, driving himself as deep as possible. Then deeper. Trent let out a soft moan before giving Reed's ass a more insistent squeeze. Reed slipped out, then back in, shallow little thrusts. Trent's breath came in short bursts, and Reed felt Trent's cock pressing hard against his abs. One bigger thrust and the bed gave a God-almighty squeak. Reed tried again, more gently, but the bed protested anyway.

Trent let out a giggle, ruining the mood entirely. "Sorry."

Reed felt a little trickle of sweat where their chests pressed together. He covered Trent's mouth with his and pulled Trent's body close and resumed thrusting, bed be damned. Trent shuddered and gave a small whimper, and a few seconds later he came, hot and messy all over Reed's chest and abs. He inhaled Trent's essence deeply and concentrated on Trent's body engulfing him. Trent trailed a finger through the creamy puddle and painted Reed's lips with it. Reed captured Trent's hand and sucked the finger into his mouth, enjoying the burst of salt and Trent on his tongue.

He knew that was it. It was too good. Trent here with him, their bodies too tense, their emotions too raw. But it was enough for now. Reed let himself relax, allowing the pleasure and relief to wash over him as he fell into the delicious depths of orgasm. He whispered Trent's name against his throat and was swallowed up by the pleasure.

When the world started up again, Trent still held him tight. "Should we keep moving?"

"Why?"

"In case anyone's listening. You don't want them to think—"

Reed wanted to smack Trent's cocky expression but kissed him silent instead. Then he added a few noisy bounces for good measure, and a few more as Trent laughed into his mouth.

When they'd finished, Reed leaned back so he could get a better look at Trent. He hadn't been able to shave in detention and had a prickly light-brown beard. It didn't suit Trent's face, with its delicate features, and hid his beautiful mouth. But his smile, wide and bright, hadn't changed. Thankfully, Trent found a reason to smile for Reed.

"I think you need a shower," Trent said finally. "And a shave."

"No, you need a shower."

"Let's save tax dollars by conserving water," Trent suggested, and they headed into the bathroom.

WHILE THEY were dressing, post shower, Reed's cell phone chirped. "Yeah, Christopher?"

"How about lunch in my office? Fifteen minutes be enough?" His tone left no doubt about what he assumed was occupying Reed and Trent.

"Sure," Reed replied, though he really wanted a snappy comeback. He just couldn't think of one. He watched Trent pull on a clean shirt over the smooth curves of his muscular torso and arms, wishing there was more time to enjoy the scenery. There was no suitable reply for Hammel because he was correct. He closed the phone and helped Trent tuck in his shirt. Probably not a good idea because slipping his hand down into Trent's jeans made him want to do anything but meet Hammel.

"I guess that call wasn't very important?" Trent asked, staring at Reed's hand still in his pants.

Reed pulled his hand back and shook his head. "Hammel wants to talk with us over lunch."

"Okay." Trent sat on the bed and leaned down to slip on socks and shoes. Reed admired the curve of his back and the way the shirt tightened against his frame. Soon this would be over, and he would have Trent all to himself again. "Ready to go."

As Trent headed for the door, Reed noticed he barely favored his injured arm or rib. Reed hadn't been as careful as he should have with Trent's injuries, and he felt guilt curl through his stomach. But the nurse's visit, sex, and a shower seemed to have Trent almost back to normal, which Reed would never have expected. Trent could handle a lot—he had in Thailand and Italy—but he had never bounced back so quickly. Was this a good thing, Reed wondered as he and Trent made their way to Hammel's office.

Over lunch Hammel and Reed asked Trent for a summary of his recollection of the night of Motofuji's death and the subsequent events.

"Your story matches up with everything else we've heard, though the question of who actually killed him is open to interpretation since there is no witness," Hammel said when Trent had finished. "The forensic evidence was the key to the prosecution's argument. Without it, everything's circumstantial."

"What do you mean 'was'?" Trent asked.

"I thought you knew. We believe you were released because the evidence against you—the most damaging evidence—went missing from the police evidence room."

"Missing? Did they lose it?"

"Unclear," Hammel replied. "There are a lot of possibilities, from someone destroying it to it being held to bring in later, though technically that's illegal."

"Why would someone destroy it? Someone's on my side, knows I'm innocent?"

Reed let Hammel reply, intending to interrupt if he said too much.

"It's complicated. Someone clearly wants you out of jail, but we don't know who or why." Hammel glanced at Reed and didn't say more. Reed was grateful Hammel didn't start on the next topic.

"Trent, you need to leave Japan. For your own safety."

Trent shook his head. “No. I’m not running away from this. I want my name cleared. Is my name cleared?” Trent pointed to the papers he’d signed when he was released from the detention center.

“No.” Hammel spoke. “You’re still the prime suspect, but without that evidence, they won’t prosecute. But you’re not supposed to leave the country without permission.”

“Getting around that won’t be a problem….” Reed glanced at Hammel.

“No.” Trent slapped the table, rattling dishes and silverware. “I still have to finish what I started for the gallery.”

“Trent, how can you think about that now?” Reed shook his head.

“Because I made a commitment to Leah. And it’s half my gallery. I want to do something to earn my percentage. The other collector, Waseda….” Trent’s voice trailed off.

“No. You can’t go back there. He might be involved.” Reed hated laying down the law, but Trent had no idea what kind of danger Waseda now represented.

“I’m just supposed to hang around here? Or go shopping with Beth? Where is Beth?”

Reed had forgotten about her too. “She’s here at the embassy. She’s fine. I’ll call her when we’re done here. But Trent, listen, and please don’t interrupt until I’m done.”

Trent eyed Reed and turned his mouth down before Reed could continue. “All right.”

“Should I go?” Hammel asked.

“It’s your office. We could go.” Reed glanced at Trent.

“No. Say whatever it is.”

“Trent, did you forget someone attacked you at the hotel? That there’s a knife that might have your prints on it? That someone’s clearly framing you for two violent deaths? Don’t you see the danger?”

“*Two* deaths? Who else did I kill?” Trent’s eyes went wide and his voice rose.

“Another yakuza got himself sliced and diced at the hotel. The surveillance cam shows you in the hallway with him.”

"I kicked a guy and ran down the stairs. I didn't stab anyone!" Trent calmed himself and looked at Hammel and then back at Reed. "Yes. I see. Someone let me out of jail so they could kill me or follow me. I get that."

"I want you safe while I find out who and why—and stop them."

"Last time you sent me somewhere safe, I ended up in more danger."

In Italy. Reed remembered well. "Just forget that detail." Reed let out a wry laugh. "Okay, you're right. No babysitter this time. But we think it's best if you get out of Tokyo and hide somewhere in the countryside where no one will think to look for you. With Beth, if she wants to. Otherwise she can go home." Reed wished he'd phrased that differently. He would hate to see Trent's reaction if Beth left him here to deal with the mess and went back to LA. Not that he could blame her. But Trent might be hurt, even if he agreed she should go.

"Okay. I'll go if you take me there and you let me know what you're planning."

"Trent…."

"Reed, that's all I ask. Go with me and then I'll stay there. I promise."

"Fine. Christopher, did you have someplace in mind?"

Christopher pulled a map of the Tokyo area out of his desk and unfolded it on the table. "There's a peninsula southwest of here." He pointed. "It's popular for weekend trips for Tokyoites, beaches, hot springs, views of Mount Fuji. But it's pretty traditional. There are some very expensive old inns, and they don't allow yakuza as guests. It would be my first choice. It's a few hours by car, and the scenery is beautiful. Why not take a few days down there while I handle arrangements here?"

"A few days?" Reed was impatient to track down whoever had framed Trent.

"Yes. Go relax in a hot spring and let my contacts poke around. I can't safely get information much more quickly. I'll have an embassy car drive you—not one of the regular limos, but an SUV. It will just look like an employee driving home in case someone is watching."

Reed glanced at Trent who had an expectant smile on his face. "Hot springs? Traditional inn? Doesn't that sound nice?"

"Yes. It *sounds* nice, but… how traditional?" Reed raised an eyebrow toward Hammel, leaving the rest of the question unspoken.

"The area is pretty gay-friendly. Don't worry. No one will care if you're sharing a room or a bath—that's normal in Japan," Christopher replied.

Trent clapped. "It sounds nice. Reed, you're going to like a traditional inn. We stayed in one in Kyoto. The food...."

"Okay. Okay. Calm down. It's not really a vacation. Just a lull."

"Fine."

Reed shook his head. Trent seemed completely back to normal. "Let's call Beth and tell her the plans." He speed dialed Beth's cell phone and asked her to come to Hammel's office.

She rushed into the office less than five minutes later and threw herself at Trent, wrapping him tightly in her arms. "Oh, God, you have no idea how worried I was about you! I can't believe you made me wait this long to see him!" She turned and directed that last complaint toward Reed and smacked his shoulder. "After the musical hotel rooms and everything. Of course I was worried."

"I'm sorry. We had to sort some things out first," Reed said. He hadn't realized how upset she'd been, but he should have.

"Trent, what happened to you?" Beth's fingertips hovered near the bruise on Trent's cheek. "Did this happen in jail? Did they hurt you?" Her voice dropped low, as if she didn't really want to hear the answer.

"No. Jail was fine. Not fine, but not really scary like American jails. No one got beat up as far as I could tell."

"So what happened to your face?"

"Oh, that happened at the hotel."

"What hotel?" Beth asked.

"It's kind of complicated," Reed answered before Trent could launch into the full story. "Trent and I can explain on the way."

"On the way where?"

"Out of Tokyo. I want Trent away from danger until I can clear up this yakuza connection. He's not allowed to leave Japan until I can find out who killed Motofuji."

"How are you going to do that? Isn't that the cops' job?"

"You see how well they've done so far, haven't you?" Reed let out a loud sigh. "We'll put you two out in Izu. I'll go out while Christopher arranges some meetings for me. He thinks you should be safe there."

"Izu Peninsula? That's very nice." A smile returned to Beth's face. "Did anyone talk to Leah yet? Or Naoko? Are we dropping the real purpose for this trip?"

"I called Leah," Reed replied. "I should update her now that Trent's out of jail, but forget the gallery. I can't have either of you out in the open."

"I still don't understand." Beth glanced at each man in turn.

"I'll explain everything, don't worry."

THE DRIVE to Izu took four hours, and it was dark by the time they arrived at the *ryokan*—a traditional Japanese inn. Trent had never seen anything like the place. It was nestled in a forest of pine trees and looked much like the inn in Kyoto, at least from outside. Inside was something quite unexpected. Small streams flowed through the lobby with miniature red Japanese bridges connecting the sections. Huge goldfish swam among the rocks in the streams.

"Koi," Beth said. "They're good luck."

The owner, a middle-aged woman, resembled the owner of the Kyoto inn: short, dark haired, slim, wearing a pastel-colored kimono and thick white socks. Beth arranged their check-in, and they were shown to their rooms.

Even Reed was impressed with the place. He'd watched Trent's excitement over the dramatic lobby décor impassively, but secretly he'd found the place charming and unique. Their room was spacious, though sparsely furnished. There was a small balcony that looked out toward the sea, or so they were told. It was too dark to see. Just below there was a small lighted area with benches and a Japanese bath built right into a larger stream.

"That stream is hot spring water! Outside baths are best for your health." Beth had translated the owner's comments as she pointed out the bath. Reed noticed the bathers were nude and felt voyeuristic watching them.

The owner showed them the bathing schedule: men's hours, women's hours, and co-ed hours. All clothing optional. "I think we'll stick to the men-only hours," Reed said after the woman had departed. She informed them that dinner would be served in thirty minutes.

"You're going to love this, Reed." Trent was inordinately excited about the meal, and Reed wondered how he had any idea what they would be served.

The dinner was delicious, featuring fresh-caught fish since they were close to the town where deep-sea fishing boats brought their catches. But Reed couldn't enjoy it, knowing he'd be leaving soon and that every minute he delayed the investigation made it that much more difficult to catch the culprits, even without the disadvantage of the language and cultural barriers. Reed didn't have his usual resources, and he couldn't blend in here. But he wanted to make this last day with Trent special, just in case.

THE DRIVE back to Tokyo felt like it took forever. Reed's emotions were torn. He'd had a full day and night with Trent, a chance to relax and see Trent recover from the stress of jail and being charged with murder. It hadn't sunk in until he was away from Tokyo, and Reed realized Hammel's suggestion of getting Trent out of the city had been a good one.

Now Reed was on his way to meet one of Hammel's contacts, a guy called Shindo. The driver would take him to a bar in the eastern section of Tokyo, far out of Shindo's usual environs. He didn't want anyone to see him with Reed, at least not for this first meeting.

Reed wore jeans and a black leather jacket as he entered the bar. There was smoke everywhere. He'd spent so much time at the embassy and in their private room at the Izu ryokan, he'd forgotten how much the Japanese smoked. Smoke and blaring music assaulted his senses, and the blue haze stung his eyes until he got used to it. He sat at a booth near the back, where he could keep an eye on the door and most of the room. He trusted Shindo sight unseen based on Hammel's endorsement, but Reed felt uneasy this far off familiar turf. It had been a long time since he'd worked in Asia, and he didn't have his finger on the pulse of the Tokyo underworld the way he had in Thailand.

A waitress came by and he ordered beer. It was the same word in Japanese, and it kept drinking simple. He kept an eye on the bartender as he popped open the bottle and handed it to the waitress. No chance for anyone to slip something inside between the bar and his table. He still took only a tiny sip, though anyone watching would think he'd sucked back half the bottle. He'd spill the contents under the table later before ordering another beer.

Fifteen minutes after the appointed time, a young Japanese guy entered and headed directly for the bar. He handed a bill to the waitress and one to the bartender before taking a seat at the bar. Drink in hand he turned and surveyed the room, leaning back against the bar like he owned the place. His hair was slightly slicked back and he wore black jeans and a T-shirt with a Japanese name printed across it, probably some fashion designer, Reed surmised, based on what he knew of Japanese fashion, which admittedly wasn't much. The guy wore a gray jacket over the T-shirt.

The sound of billiard balls clacking on the pool table in the corner caught Reed's attention when the loud music paused between songs. The newcomer swaggered over to the table and said something to the men playing. He hovered as they finished their game and then played the winner.

Reed had no doubt this was Shindo. He watched him work the room, acting like the thug he was portraying and making no obvious overture toward Reed. This guy was good. Reed immediately sensed his ability to monitor everything at once. He'd looked over at Reed for a split second before focusing his attention on the pool game, but as Shindo lined up various shots, Reed knew he was also scoping out everyone else in the room. It was well done.

Shindo beat his opponent effortlessly and took the man's money. He shouted, presumably challenging others to a game, but no one dared after seeing him beat the first opponent. Shindo approached one man who waved him away. Then he came up to Reed's table.

"Hey, gaijin, Mista America." He made a shooting motion with the pool cue and Reed shook his head. He had to try hard not to smile. "Money, money, Mista America?" He nodded toward the table, and Reed made a show of reluctantly accepting the challenge.

Reed won the break and sank five balls before ceding control of the table to Shindo. He'd left some difficult shots, and Shindo had trouble with two of them but made both. They exchanged almost no words, just a few taunts in their respective languages. Shindo had only the eight ball remaining and blew the shot, losing to Reed. He blustered and shouted, clearly challenging Reed to another round.

Reed accepted and cleared most of the table. He deliberately missed, leaving Shindo an impossible shot. By now half the men in the room had gathered around, watching the foreigner beating the bigmouthed yakuza. Shindo made that shot but not the next. Control went back and forth. Reed was actually enjoying himself. He won this round and they played another, also a close match. Everyone was watching now, even the bartender.

Reed won mostly on skill. He knew Shindo had deliberately missed one shot. It changed the dynamics in the room when Reed, the silent foreigner, beat the thug no one dared cross. The room erupted in cheers, and several people bought drinks for Reed. He nodded graciously and drank. No one expected to chat with him due to the language barrier, so he could easily slide back into the booth.

Shindo came after him. At this point no one questioned the move. Shindo sat with his back to the room—a major concession for an undercover agent—but this way no one could see him talking to Reed.

They raised glasses and shouted "Kampai" and drank. No one gave them a second glance as the patrons turned their attention back to beer and pool or staring at the television hanging from the ceiling, tuned to a sports channel. Reed paid slight attention to the sumo wrestling as he waited to hear what Shindo had to say.

"Good game," he said in near-perfect English. He leaned forward over the table, which made him seem larger somehow. But up close he was slim, although the tight T-shirt revealed some muscle definition.

"Yes. Good game, and I don't mean the pool." Reed smiled. Shindo raised his glass in a toast, acknowledging the compliment. "We have a lot to talk about. Is this the best place?"

"No. But I thought it was important for you to trust me."

"I do. I'm impressed."

"I'll be at Hammel's office tomorrow morning at nine."

"The embassy? You don't mind being seen there?"

"I can handle it." Shindo smiled. Reed looked at him closely. He had smooth, almost perfect skin. Did he even shave? His hair was jet black and glossy even in the low light. High cheekbones gave him a distinctive look, along with the perfect almond-shaped eyes. But the feature Reed noticed first was his even more perfectly shaped mouth. The lower lip was full and the upper a gorgeous cupid's bow. Looking at Shindo's lips made Reed feel guilty. Was it cheating to imagine another man's lips against his, even if that was never going to happen?

Reed forced himself to look away from Shindo's beautiful mouth. He shifted his gaze to the hands. No, bad choice. Too smooth and slender, the nails perfectly shaped. All ten of them. How did he pose as yakuza with ten fingers? He'd ask tomorrow. Tomorrow in the full light of day and not now when he was a foot away from this beautiful man.

"Nine o'clock," Shindo repeated and looked Reed directly in the eye.

Reed nodded and hoped Shindo hadn't detected even a fraction of what he'd been thinking.

All the way back to the embassy, Reed reminded himself he was doing this for Trent. He loved Trent and Trent trusted him. A bubble of attraction wasn't so bad if no one acted on it. It was the trust that mattered. He'd never betray Trent. He didn't want to, but why did he have such a powerful reaction to meeting Shindo?

18

"JUST BECAUSE Reed stuck us out here doesn't mean we can't be part of the investigation, Beth."

"How?"

"Well, they think it's got some connection to Motofuji's art collection."

"Besides the fact of him being killed with his own jade piece?"

"Yes. We went there to appraise the collection, so whoever wanted to frame me could only know of my visit through that channel, agreed?"

Beth stared at Trent for a moment, then gazed out the window. "Yes, that has to be it. It's not likely the real killer would just happen to choose that day completely randomly. It's too much of a coincidence."

"So the killer, or the person who hired the killer, has to be someone who knew of our visit and our schedule."

"That's just us, Leah, Reed, Naoko, and…." She paused. "I don't think anyone else knew. Oh, Motofuji's staff would have known."

"One of those people could have told someone else. Let's make a list and interview them."

"Interview them? Trent, how would we do that? Besides, aren't the police working on that?"

"The cops think I did it. They're not looking for the real killer."

"But they let you out."

"I think it's temporary, or someone made a mistake. Unless we hand them the real killer, I won't be able to clear my name. Even if I leave. I wouldn't want some warrant for my arrest if I ever come back to Japan.

"Trent, don't be so melodramatic!"

"Am I?" He didn't think his idea was that farfetched.

"Yes."

"Sorry, I guess my imagination runs wild sometimes."

"That's great when you're writing, but not so useful in real life."

"Fine. But we can still contribute."

"What about those interviews?"

"Right, you can call up the suspects and ask some questions. Pretend you're with the police. Or you're a reporter. I don't know. Maybe both—depending on who you're talking to. Who would they say something possibly incriminating to?"

"Oh, I see. Or if they give information inconsistent with someone else, someone we know is telling the truth?" Beth's eyes gleamed.

"Slow down, Nancy Drew." Trent laughed. "That's a good strategy. But we need to make the list."

The final list included Leah, Motofuji, Naoko, Motofuji's housekeeper and driver, Waseda, and anyone else those people had told.

"I think we can take Leah off the list," Beth said, pen poised about the paper.

"She didn't do it, but she might have told someone. We need to ask her."

They e-mailed Leah.

"Can you call Naoko and ask her who else she told?" Trent asked. They were sitting on the balcony overlooking the outdoor tub, Mount Fuji looming in the distance. Trent couldn't enjoy the scenery. He had to find out something to help Reed.

"Why me?"

"She likes you. Talk about clothes or cartoons, and slip the questions in."

"Anime is not cartoons!"

Trent nodded. "Of course not."

Beth grabbed the cell phone and chewed on the end of her pen for a few minutes. "Okay. I'm ready." She dialed. Trent leaned in to listen.

"*Moshi-moshi*," Naoko's voice sounded like she was in the next room.

"Naoko, it's Beth Conti." Trent was grateful she spoke in English.

"Beth-san! How are you? Are you okay? I've been hearing crazy things on the news. About Trent."

"We're fine."

"Where are you? The police had Trent's photo on the news for a couple of days."

"I better not say."

"At the American Embassy?"

"No."

"Oh. Why did you call? Do you need something from me?"

"Uh, yeah." She glanced at Trent and then got up and went inside. He could hear that she'd slipped into Japanese. Probably easier for her to ask the questions that way.

Ten minutes later, she returned. "Okay, she says she didn't tell anyone where she was going, as part of the confidentiality of the appraiser job. Only which city, but not which collection she would be looking at. She had to disclose to her boss at the museum that she was working for Leah's gallery. If the museum had an interest in purchasing any of the items, she would then have to disclose her connection to the sale."

"You believe her?"

"Yes. She's so respected in her field. I think she's careful not to lose that respect."

"Do you think she suspects why you called?"

"No. I told her we wanted the appraisals and inventory. Something about Leah's tax write-offs and supporting the expenses since Motofuji's sale wouldn't take place."

"Good thinking."

"Sometimes I can make shit up as well as you can."

Trent laughed.

Beth finished her calls, except for Waseda.

"The driver and housekeeper have worked for Motofuji for literally decades. They would maintain an oath of secrecy involving him and his activities and wouldn't tell anyone about his business meetings. I think we can cross them off the list."

"Then it has to be Waseda."

"I agree."

WHEN REED walked into Hammel's office the next morning, he found Christopher talking to a Japanese businessman. The visitor wore a dark-blue suit, white shirt, and blue-and-yellow striped tie—the businessman's uniform. The man rose and held out a hand as Reed approached.

The man's hair was thick and soft, shining in the bright fluorescent light. "Good morning, Archer."

Reed stared at him. If it hadn't been for the almond-shaped eyes and the exquisite lips—which he'd dreamed of in that morning half-sleep that bred so many daydreams and fantasies—he would never have recognized Shindo. "Fuck," was all he could say.

Shindo and Hammel laughed.

"I can't believe the transformation."

"That's good. I need to make sure no one knows when I come here. If I'm caught, I'm dead."

Reed couldn't stop staring. This man somehow looked even hotter as a cookie-cutter businessman, though he'd looked pretty fucking fine in black jeans and a tight white T-shirt. *Focus on Trent, Acton!* Reed blinked and looked away.

"Shindo's heard some rumors. He's working in a second-rate yakuza group that runs some real estate companies and blackmails businessmen."

"I have to deal with corporate types, which is why they don't expect me to get the ink. I'd do a lot for this job, but that's too far. I figure I can forget about almost everything else I have to do for this gig, but you can't easily erase a full-body ink."

Reed nodded, wishing Shindo hadn't brought up the image of his smooth, unmarked skin. "How can you help?"

"Rumor has it that Waseda arranged the hit on Motofuji with one of Motofuji's lieutenants who was too impatient for the old man to die and give up power."

"That's great. How do we prove it?"

"That's not going to be easy."

"So, who's looking for easy. I'm just looking for possible. What's it going to take?"

"You know Motofuji collected art and antiquities?"

"Yes." Reed waited for Shindo to tell him something he didn't know.

"And Waseda fancies himself a collector. But he has terrible taste. It's a running joke among his men. They poke fun at the items he has on display in his home and office." Shindo smiled. Damn those lips! "I think the killer took something of great value from Motofuji's collection, something Waseda couldn't turn down. If one of the missing items can be found in Waseda's possession, it may be enough to tie him to the murder."

"That's brilliant." Reed acknowledged Shindo had come up with a feasible and effective strategy.

Hammel nodded and grinned. "I told you, he's your guy."

Why had Hammel phrased it like that? Did the universe really have to throw Shindo at Reed just now? He didn't deserve this temptation, this test.

"What's the plan?"

"I can have someone I know in his organization approach Waseda and ask for a job for me. Once he trusts me, I can get into his house and start looking around. If I can find the proof, Hammel can arrange a warrant through the police. Or Interpol if I spot anything that's stolen."

"Did Motofuji have stolen artwork?"

"No. He was pretty clean for a yakuza boss. He was old school. Conservative. He collected art because he loved it. Or his wife did. She got him started, and after she died, he kept collecting pieces she would have liked."

"And Waseda?"

"He's always looking for the short cut. He would hear of a scheme another gang was doing, and he'd copy it. He's not clever enough to think up any original schemes himself. He bounces around with whatever seems to be the most profitable. He's been the target of a lot of other gangs who want to cut him out of the business permanently. Even the yakuza think he gives the yakuza a bad name." Shindo chuckled.

"I admit that I don't quite understand why there's this concern over yakuza image in the public eye? Or how yakuza even fit in with modern Japanese business. You go to work wearing a suit like this?"

"No. Not like this. I'm not so conservative. I'm in this getup to keep my cover here. I do wear a suit, but more stylish, and no tie. And I'd slick my hair back. The public expect that too."

"That's what I'm talking about. This concern over public image. I find it almost amusing."

"It is to some extent. But yakuza have been part of Japanese society and business for hundreds of years. They've learned along the way how to fit in better."

"Fit in?"

"At first the yakuza were outcasts in society—there was a caste system. Now it still attracts people who aren't accepted, particularly Japanese of Korean or Chinese descent." Shindo shook his head. "That's too complicated to explain…."

"I get it. I spent a lot of time in Hong Kong and Thailand. There's a similar discrimination against other Asian ethnic groups."

"Right. But the yakuza created a space for themselves that wasn't being filled. Some of it's the vices: gambling or prostitution. They also have a protection racket, like the American mafia. But the longer the authorities let them exist, the more the rest of society sees them as acceptable to a certain degree. You want girls—or boys—or something illegal, you go to the yakuza. Someone you know knows how to get it. But the average Japanese doesn't have to come in contact with them."

"How did they get involved in business?"

"If the cops aren't trying to stop you, then there's no need to hide. Having an office means your customers can find you to get what they want. Over time as a group, they got more educated and figured out easier ways to make money, like stock price manipulations. A good stock deal will make millions in a few hours or less, but it takes much longer to get the same profit with gambling."

Reed nodded. "But these murders. How do they fit into the yakuza business?"

"Most gangs have a territory or an area of expertise. As long as there is no overlap, they coexist. There are gang wars. And the usual internal power struggles. When one gang is in disarray—like after Motofuji's death—another can take over their turf."

"But you think more than one gang is involved here?"

"Speculation on the street says Waseda or another gang leader arranged to kill Motofuji in an agreement with someone in his organization. The junior guy takes over while Waseda's group takes a piece of their business or something else he wants. The new leader must think it's worth running a slightly smaller organization than risk not being named the successor."

"And this just goes on with the cops not doing anything?"

"They investigate, but they rarely catch the perp. As long as average Japanese citizens aren't involved, the police can let a lot slide. That's why framing Trent Copeland is so odd. Why choose someone to take the fall? I'll need to ask a lot more questions, which is dangerous, unless I can achieve a trusted position in Waseda's gang."

"You seem awfully confident Waseda will hire you. How realistic is that? It might be months before he trusts you enough to let you into his house."

"I have a fast-track plan. If what I've heard about him is true, it won't be very difficult to catch his eye." Shindo winked.

Reed wasn't sure he'd understood. "Can you elaborate?"

"He likes to visit a certain club a couple of times a week. A host club."

"Hostess bar, sure, isn't that pretty normal?" Reed wasn't sure how this would help Shindo.

"Not hostess bar. *Host* bar. Male hosts...."

"He's into guys?"

"His bodyguards say so. He's married, but his wife lives out in the countryside somewhere. I don't think he visits her much. He makes a big show of buying hostesses out for the night, but he doesn't bring them home. He pays them to tell stories, if anyone asks. He pays even more for the boys he does take home—and for them not to tell stories."

Hammel raised an eyebrow. "What's your plan? Get him to take you home?"

Shindo shook his head. "No, that's not enough. He has to think I'm worth keeping around. I need to think about that a little bit. Figure out the right angle to play him."

"You really want to go that far?" Reed felt uneasy with this plan: it put Shindo in extreme personal danger, as well as potentially forcing him into a sexual relationship with a vicious and ruthless man. Reed wasn't willing to be responsible for that. No one at the Bureau would authorize something like this, knowing from the outset it would be heading in that direction. Agents had made judgment calls along the way when things got sexual, but the Bureau never asked it as part of the strategy.

"Like I said, I can forget just about anything. Even going to bed with Waseda if it means taking him down for good."

"I can't condone that. And I don't know who would even authorize something like that."

“Don’t worry. I’ll talk with my superior at Interpol and work out a suitable—and ethical—plan, okay?”

“Yes. I’ll feel better if I know the plan is legit and there’s support and backup if necessary.”

“Let me get back to you later.”

“Look, Shindo, I want in on the operation,” Reed said as Shindo stood to leave.

Both Hammel and Shindo stared at him like he’d grown six heads.

“Archer, be realistic,” Hammel said, shaking his head. “How—”

“I don’t care how or what. I’m sure Shindo will figure out the specifics, or I’ll go above his head.” Reed wasn’t sure how much pull he’d have with Interpol, but it was worth a shot. He couldn’t sit on the sidelines and leave Trent’s future to someone else, no matter how much he trusted Shindo’s abilities.

Shindo gave Reed a slow, head-to-toe appraisal. “It might work. I’ll need to find out more about his tastes….”

“What about the art angle?” Hammel asked. “Archer heard he’s selling and wants to buy.”

Shindo shook his head. “There’s no angle for me in that. I’m known in the other gang, and not for art. I can’t show up with a buyer out of nowhere. Waseda’s no genius but he can smell bullshit a mile away.”

“Shindo’s right. We have to go in together, without arousing any suspicions.” Reed watched Shindo consider their options.

“Then you better be sure about this. All in,” Shindo told Reed. “Because the only way he’s going to let two total strangers—one a gaijin—into his house is on our knees.”

Hammel pressed his lips together and fidgeted with some papers on his desk. “I—I don’t like this.”

“Fine, Shindo. Get the ball rolling on this with your chain of command. Make the arrangements you need and let me know what you need from me.” Reed felt adrenaline coursing through his veins now he was making active progress to find Motofuji’s real killer. He squeezed his hands into fists and fought to keep them at his sides.

“I’ll call you when it’s arranged.”

They exchanged contact information and procedures, and Shindo gave Reed a reassuring smile and shook his hand before taking his leave. Was it

Reed's imagination that the handshake lasted a beat longer than necessary? And had he imagined the acceleration of his pulse at that touch?

Oh, fuck, this would be a tough operation. Reed wanted to take a shower and wash all thoughts of Shindo out of his brain. He wished he could call Trent. This was all for him, Reed reminded himself.

And how could he tell Trent he'd just signed on to cozy up to a sleazy yakuza boss and a smoking hot Japanese Interpol agent?

NOT TEN minutes after Shindo's departure, Detective Kobayashi and his partner Nishikatsu arrived to speak with Christopher Hammel.

"I don't want Nishikatsu to see you here. You got the mustache?"

"No. I didn't think I'd need it."

"There's a side room. Stay in there. Use the headset on the desk to listen in." Hammel slid a bookcase along the wall, revealing a door with no knob. Hammel pushed it and Reed slipped into the hidden room. He heard Hammel close the door and move the bookcase. He sat at the desk and put on the headphones.

Reed heard someone speaking in Japanese—probably Nishikatsu, since he didn't recognize the voice. Damn. He wasn't going to understand any of this conversation!

"Detective, I'm having some trouble understanding you. Could we do this in English?" Hammel asked. Reed loved working with this guy.

The two Japanese exchanged a few words, then Nishikatsu spoke very slowly. "Where is Torento Cōpurando?"

"I don't know," Hammel replied. Reed wished he could see his face.

"We want to talk to him. Park Hyatt."

"He's not here. Wasn't he in police custody?"

Reed heard Nishikatsu let loose a stream of angry Japanese.

"Hammu-san,"—this was Kobayashi—"he is a witness at the hotel. We would like to talk to him." Reed noticed he altered his pronunciation to sound less fluent than he really was.

More Japanese from Nishikatsu. Apparently Kobayashi was translating. "His release was a clerical error."

"That's unfortunate," Hammel replied. "But we don't require our citizens to inform us of their whereabouts."

"Thank you for your time," Kobayashi said and Reed heard the men leave. It was several minutes before Hammel let him out of the hidden room.

"That was odd," Reed said. "But you handled it perfectly." He'd noticed Hammel hadn't offered to help the police.

"Kobayashi helped us out. He never specifically asked me for anything. If he'd asked me to inform them if we did know where Trent was, then it would be a lot harder to ignore the request. I suspect Nishikatsu didn't realize how little Kobayashi actually said. But I'm glad we got Trent out of Tokyo."

"Do you think they'll issue a warrant for him?"

"They'll probably check with immigration to see if he left the country, or block him from leaving. They can ask hotels to check their guest lists, which is why I registered you as Clark Porter. You didn't put Trent's name on the register, did you?"

"No, and the woman at the desk didn't ask."

"Good. Well, the next step is up to you and Shindo. But I admit, I don't know what the police are doing."

REED GOT a call from Shindo that afternoon to meet at a men's clothing store. The specifics of Shindo's plan were still hazy, but he promised to clue Reed in on the details in person. The shop was in a high-class neighborhood called Aoyama and thankfully located right across from the subway stop.

Reed felt overwhelmed as he strolled into Comme des Garcons. He was not into fashion and this was worse than the shops in Italy. Trent would love it. A young man came up to him as he looked through the first rack, completely out of his element.

"Good, you found it."

Reed stared, speechless. Shindo had transformed himself yet again. His hair was pulled back into a ponytail, exposing his incredible cheekbones but giving him an entirely different appearance than his other two incarnations.

Shindo stared at Reed and shook his head. "We need to get you dressed properly for your role as a host. The women expect something specific."

"Women?"

"Yeah, I know this guy who runs a host bar Waseda likes. I told him I want to meet Waseda—he thinks it's just to get into the gang. I mentioned my good-looking gaijin friend. He'll let both of us work there tonight. And he won't be suspicious when we set up the meet with Waseda."

Shindo pulled jackets and pants off racks and had Reed try on various combinations while he scrutinized Reed's appearance. It almost felt like shopping with Trent, who liked to buy clothes for Reed. Reed hated clothes shopping. He'd wear the same comfortable jeans and button-down shirt until they fell apart, if he could. He didn't even care which shirt, so Trent liked to have some input into his wardrobe. At first it had pissed Reed off; then he began to enjoy it because Trent enjoyed it so much.

Like Trent, Shindo either had something particular in mind, or he liked checking Reed out in a variety of clothes. "Tighter pants. You need to show off your body more. And a smaller size shirt. Same reason." He sent Reed back with another armful of clothing. He ended up with a charcoal gray suit with pinstripes—not too narrow and not too wide; Shindo's standard was exacting—and a white shirt, which he was supposed to have nearly halfway unbuttoned.

Reed did one more catwalk pass, and Shindo approved the outfit. "You're not the typical host. They usually have longer hair. But you're a foreigner. You'll be popular."

"I don't want to be popular."

"You have to look like a challenge to him. He needs to win you away from the girls."

"I get it." Reed just didn't like it. But he'd insisted on being part of the action, and he'd follow Shindo's orders.

"Now go to the hotel at the corner and get some sleep. I'll come get you at midnight."

"Midnight?"

"These places open late. Okay, eleven. You'll need some practice." He handed Reed some cash and a key to a hotel room he'd already rented. "Grab some food along this street somewhere before your nap, then we'll eat together later."

REED GRABBED the Japanese version of fast food: tempura vegetables on rice. The place looked just like McDonald's, except for the menu, and the food was surprisingly tasty. He napped during the afternoon and evening and got up in time to shower and dress for his role.

Shindo knocked on the door, and when Reed let him in, he realized they were dressed nearly identically. Shindo didn't have his hair slicked back and it flopped into his eyes. He kept pushing the bangs back behind his right ear as he spoke.

"Do I meet with your approval?" Reed did a little spin. "I didn't know if I was supposed to shave."

Shindo reached out and ran his fingers along Reed's cheek and jaw, then he smiled. "No. Good that you didn't. A little stubble is good. Japanese guys need a week to get the same stubble you can get in twenty-four hours." He grinned. "It will set you apart."

Reed tried not to read anything into Shindo's grin or the way he'd stroked Reed's face, as if he enjoyed the feel of his stubble. But Reed found himself repeating Shindo's motions and touching his own jaw. He consciously had to pull his hand away from his face.

Once they left the hotel, Reed was amazed how the street had changed from day to night. It was off the main road, but there were lots of people walking around under a sea of neon signs so bright it made his eyes hurt. Loud music blared from most open doorways, and touts stood outside, trying to lure customers in. Tall blonde women stood in doorways handing small cards to passersby.

"Kabukichō is the center of a lot of late-night activity. Some legal, a lot not. We're going to a legal club, but it's owned by Waseda's gang."

"Shit, why didn't you tell me that? Are we ready to go in there?"

"Yeah. It's fine. If we don't get his attention tonight, we keep trying. Trust me, this will work."

They went around the corner and up a narrow stairway. "This doesn't look very fancy. What kind of women come here?"

"It's the employee entrance. The ladies go up in the elevator. They'd break their heels on these stairs."

"Sure." Reed had no clue about high heels. When they got inside, he changed his mind about the place. It had plush red carpet and about a dozen tables scattered around the edges of the room. The center of the room was a dance floor, complete with disco ball. The lights were low, but Reed could see a few booths and tables were occupied. Each had one or two women and two or three men. As his eyes adjusted to the light, he realized the women were older, possibly bored, lonely housewives who came here while their husbands sat at hostess bars or went drinking with work colleagues.

A middle-aged man came up to greet Shindo. He had slicked hair—jet black, which didn't look entirely natural on a man of his age—and a glossy suit with wide lapels, and he had a cigarette in one hand, which he waved dangerously as he spoke.

"My friend, Pee-su," Shindo introduced Reed. "Pee-su, this is Goto-san."

Reed tried not to laugh as Shindo dumbed down his English pronunciation. They decided he should call himself Pierce, because the women who came here would associate the name with Pierce Brosnan, a popular star here in Japan. He just hadn't expected it to sound like "piss" when Shindo said it with a thick Japanese accent.

"Harō, Pee-su!" Goto shook his hand in both of his, the cigarette still floating around menacingly.

The men exchanged a few words in Japanese and Goto went into a back room.

"You're hired."

"Just like that?"

"It's a yakuza club. Did you think they wanted your resume and a valid work visa?"

Reed loosened up as he chuckled. "No. I'm just so out of my element. I wish we'd come here before we were going to meet Waseda."

Shindo smacked him on the back. "Relax. You won't make anything if you can't relax. They'll suspect you of something."

Reed knew Shindo was right. "Okay. What do we do?"

"We just sit with ladies and chat, but mostly you listen. And you get them to buy you drinks. Tonight Champagne is your favorite. Make sure to tell them that. You get paid by the number of bottles you sell, plus tips. The women pay a time charge for the table, about a hundred dollars, but the real profit is on the drinks."

It was no different from the Thai bars. Except there the customers paid for extras or upstairs time. "Are there extras?"

"Yes." Shindo gave him a sly smile. "I didn't think you wanted anything like that. I guess you fooled me."

Reed didn't know whether to be offended or flattered by the comment. "I don't. I just need to know what they're expecting."

"That's usually for regular customers. No one will ask the first time they meet you. They have to trust you first. I'll handle the situation if it comes up."

"You will?"

"We'll work as a team tonight. Ladies who can't speak English will have me translate."

"Okay. And Waseda?"

"He'll come in to check out how the place is running. He'll want to see you—Goto's probably on the phone with him now boasting about the new gaijin host. And we'll play it by ear. But he doesn't speak much English, so you'll make sure he brings me along."

Reed nodded. "Okay, let's get this party started." Why couldn't Waseda be the *pachinko* king?

A tall, slim Japanese man was the room host, seating the ladies and then bringing over their personal hosts. He took Reed and Shindo—"Peter" for tonight because Japanese women liked Western names—to their first customers, two thirty-something women who looked like they'd come from a dance club. They wore glittery sleeveless tops and had their hair up. They giggled when he and Shindo sat down.

"I'm Pierce," Reed said. Was he supposed to shake hands? He watched Shindo.

"It's Pierce's birthday."

The women squealed. Champagne was ordered and they poured drinks for the women and then each other. They drank slowly while the women drank quickly. Soon one of the women ordered a second bottle. The women asked Reed a few questions in English, about where was from and if he liked Japan. Shindo nodded and smiled a lot. The girl next to Reed kept putting her hand on his arm and after the second bottle of Champagne the hand moved to his thigh. He ignored it, but if she moved it again, he'd put a stop to it. After about an hour, the room host came by and escorted the ladies toward the door.

"That was weird," Reed said as he gulped water in the back. "Why'd they leave?"

"Their time was up. They could have another hour, but they didn't take it."

"Oh." Reed felt slightly offended. He hadn't minded talking to the women. The host came over and handed each of them a few bills. Twenty-five thousand yen. "What's this?"

"That's your earnings from the first table. This place pays after each one. Some places pay at the end of the night, or only once a week."

Reed calculated the equivalent in dollars, nearly three hundred. Just for chatting for an hour and drinking Champagne? How much would they pay for a fuck? No wonder this business was popular, lucrative both for the hosts and the club owner. It was like printing cash.

"Good place to launder cash too," Shindo whispered, apparently having read Reed's thoughts.

"I might never leave. Lot safer than my day job."

Shindo laughed. "We're on again." They were led to another table and repeated the whole process.

By the third table, Reed was getting impatient. Where was Waseda? He glanced around the room, hoping to catch a glimpse of the man. He'd had three birthday toasts. This customer had a wandering hand, and it was getting old trying to remove it from his upper thigh—and once from the waistband of his pants. Shindo had laughed his ass off as Reed felt his face burning.

The room host came by to tell her the time was up, and when she wanted another hour, she was told Pierce was booked for the rest of the night. The room host had a good eye for when a customer got out of hand. Reed marveled at how smoothly this system operated.

By customer number four, Reed sipped at a fake martini. Just plain water with an olive. Only the customers were supposed to get drunk, not the hosts. Reed chatted as he spotted the room host pointing at their table. Next to him stood an older, stocky man with the trademark punch perm that had once been a popular hairstyle with the yakuza. The man nodded and turned his attention elsewhere.

Shindo locked gazes with Reed and nodded. "That's him," Shindo mouthed.

But Waseda didn't come over to meet Reed or Shindo. It was only after the fifth customer of the night was escorted to the cashier that Reed spotted Waseda watching him from across the room. Reed acted as if he hadn't seen him.

That was their last table. They got paid, and Shindo suggested they stop for a drink.

"It's 5:00 a.m. and you want a drink?"

"No. I want to talk to you away from here."

They walked two blocks and took an elevator to the tenth floor. This bar was half-full but still noisy and smoky. Reed was disoriented by the fact that the bar was on the tenth floor and barely thought to wonder why the place was so busy at five in the morning.

They sat at a booth and Shindo ordered. The waiter brought them beer and breakfast—scrambled eggs with bacon and toast. Reed hadn't realized how hungry he was and quickly devoured his. The beer tasted surprisingly good with breakfast, and he reminded himself never again to drink beer with breakfast.

"Okay, Shindo, that was a fucking trip!" Once nourished, Reed felt an odd excitement about the evening, despite not earning more than a couple of passing glances from Waseda. He pulled the wad of cash out of his inner jacket pocket and counted. "More than a thousand bucks!"

"Really?" Shindo counted his. "About eight hundred. You, my man, have a real future as a host!"

"Fuck you." Reed sipped his beer and laughed. "Hey, that one that kept trying to get in my pants, what was she saying? You didn't translate."

"She heard Americans have big dicks, and she wanted to find out," Shindo said with a completely straight face. Then he burst into laughter, which Reed joined in. When their laughed died out, Reed got serious again.

"Waseda… he didn't talk to us."

"I know. Remember, Japan is different from the States. We don't rush into everything, need instant gratification—except that one woman. We watch and wait. We make sure before making a move. We don't have to have the answer immediately. And we don't trust people who rush into things. For a guy like Waseda, he didn't get where he is by taking big risks. He takes calculated risks, has to know the probabilities and the payoffs before making a move."

"Just be patient?"

"Yes."

Shindo walked Reed back to the dive hotel and Reed fell into bed and slept until the sun was high in the sky. He showered, then wandered down the street for food. While he ate, he turned over the events of the previous night in his mind. What a strange world these people inhabited, men getting paid to talk to women and pour their drinks, or dance with them. The street was packed with similar bars and clubs—even up to the top floors of the buildings Reed thought housed offices.

Were those men preying on the female customers? Taking their money for so little work? What drove those women to frequent these bars? How empty were their lives that they wanted to drop a few hundred dollars for a drink and a chat with a man who did nothing more than listen and give them undivided attention? It was one step away from prostitution, but if both parties were happy, did that make it okay?

Reed couldn't imagine doing that night after night. But he felt exhilarated at the thought of repeating the experience again tonight. He wanted to meet Waseda, but from what Shindo said, it could take weeks before they gained his trust.

Shindo. Reed couldn't deny he'd had fun playacting with Shindo. They had a similar sense of humor, despite the small language gap. And Shindo had a smile that really could light up a room, bathe the recipient in a warm golden glow. Reed smiled thinking about Shindo's lips. The women the night before had enjoyed that smile and tipped him well.

I'm just missing Trent, Reed told himself. He pulled his cell phone out of his pocket and was about to dial, and then he decided not to. Shindo had gotten him that hotel room for a purpose. While he was acting the part of a host, he had to stay away from Trent, Hammel, the embassy. Waseda might have him followed or intercept his cell calls. Anything was possible. He had to act like a host. He put the phone away. It wasn't even his phone. That was back at the embassy. It had photos of Trent, of the two of them together. Reed had only his memories until they could get into Waseda's house.

Hammel had other agents working other avenues, seeking information. But most signs pointed to Waseda. He just needed enough proof to convince the police to arrest and prosecute the real killer.

"I SWEAR I'll turn into the world's largest prune if I spend one more minute in hot water."

"Stand in line. I've already got that title." Trent let out a sigh and wrapped the hotel robe around himself as he and Beth shuffled back from co-ed soak time at the bath in the middle of the stream. The novelty had long since worn off. At least Trent had mastered the art of walking in the wooden clogs the inn provided for guests to use outside of the building.

Back in their room, Beth checked her e-mail.

"Leah replied," she shouted to Trent.

"What did she say?" He stood behind her and hovered as she crouched over the laptop.

"She didn't reveal Motofuji's name as a client to anyone."

"Well, we already know it's Waseda, and Reed and Hammel are already looking into him."

"But, wait." Beth paused. "I'm still reading."

"Read out loud."

"I got Naoko's spreadsheets and your photos. We really don't need that much evidence for the taxes, but thanks. Out of curiosity I took a look at Naoko's preliminary appraisals. It's really too bad we won't be liquidating the collection. It probably doesn't matter, but several pieces seem to be missing from Naoko's spreadsheets even though you have photographs of the items. They are in photos 7, 12, 15 and 16. Gorgeous pieces. Naoko's specialty, so this was strange. Well, who cares now. Be safe and keep me posted on developments."

Beth turned toward Trent. "Hmm. I wonder what's in those photos. Can you pull them up?" he asked. He pulled a chair up to the desk and sat next to Beth so he could see the screen.

"One is the print he gave you. We knew he wasn't selling that." Beth opened Naoko's spreadsheet. "It's not on the sheet."

"There are a few entries where she noted 'preliminary estimate' or 'further research needed.' So why wouldn't she have a similar note for the other items? She's even got the jade dagger listed as 'not for sale.'"

"Understatement," Trent said.

"Yeah, that's for sure." Beth flipped through the images and opened the files for the other three pieces. "Did you make notes on these, Trent?"

"I made notes of everything we photographed." He pulled the pad from his messenger bag. "Number seven was the woodblock print; the others are pottery bowls. I don't have anything about twelve, but fifteen and sixteen I noted being a pair of matched bowls from the Heian period." He glanced at the image on the screen. "I remember those bowls because of the glaze. It shimmered like gold. Motofuji said they were almost a thousand years old. They are really beautiful. Is that Naoko's specialty?"

"I thought she said it was Jōmon period, which was considerably earlier and much different style, less refined techniques. I think twelve is from that period. It's certainly ugly compared to the other two. If I had a choice, I'd rather study Heian artifacts."

Trent looked at the exquisite workmanship in the photos. "Me too." He recalled the glass cases in Naoko's office. He hadn't paid enough attention then to determine which period of pottery she had displayed in her office.

"Bowl twelve is ugly. Why would someone steal that?" Beth asked.

"Maybe it's more valuable than it looks. Or someone wants it for another reason. It could be a clue…" The prospect of another mystery got Trent's blood pumping.

"So someone's wrong or someone's lying." Beth sat back in her chair. "Leah hired Naoko for her expertise, so I don't think she's wrong. But why would Naoko tell us something completely different?"

"Did you talk about art with her at all in Japanese?"

"No."

"So she thinks you're just an interpreter and that you wouldn't know your Heian from your Heisei, right?"

"Look at you, Trent, you did learn something about Japanese history." Beth leaned over and gave him a kiss on the cheek.

"How do you think I write books about things I know nothing about? Research." Actually, he couldn't remember when Heisei was, but thought it was fairly recent. "But speaking of history, it just hit me. Motofuji's collection was mainly old Asian stuff, right?"

"Not the most elegant description, but yes. Why?"

"And Waseda's collection was more recent, Western paintings, Western sculpture…."

Beth shook her head. "Japanese collectors have different interests."

"Yes, of course. But why would Leah hire Naoko to appraise Waseda's collection too, when it's clearly not her area of expertise?"

Beth nodded. "Right. Good question. Naoko should have engaged another expert."

"Now we have two questions: Why would Naoko insist on handling the Waseda collection herself—"

"And why did she leave those items off her list?" Beth finished his thought.

"I have a couple of theories." Trent looked Beth in the eye. "And I don't like either of them."

19

THAT NIGHT, Shindo came by the hotel a little earlier and they ate dinner at a noisy Japanese-style pub. The menu had photographs of all the dishes and Shindo chose three and ordered beers.

"Are the portions that big?" Reed asked as Shindo poured beer into his glass. He reciprocated before taking a drink.

"Not really. It's Japanese style. In this kind of place, we order a few things to start and then more as we want. See what you like or what looks good on the other tables."

"Okay." Reed had eaten plenty of Japanese food in LA, but now he realized those restaurants didn't have many Japanese patrons, just the staff. He was learning a whole new side of the country from Shindo.

Reed chose the next two dishes, and they drank another bottle of beer before Shindo turned the conversation to their work.

"I heard that four pieces are missing from Motofuji's art collection after the police compared the contents of the home to the appraiser's inventory. One woodblock print, a Jōmon bowl, and two valuable Heian bowls, a matched set."

"The police have the print, it was a gift to Trent. He has a letter stating that fact, signed by Motofuji. Or stamped with his seal."

"*Hanko*."

"Right." Reed didn't care what it was called. "So if we can find the other pieces at Waseda's…."

"Yes. We should look specifically for them."

"If we get in there."

"*When* we get in there. Have some faith." Shindo raised his glass in a toast. Reed drank but he didn't feel very optimistic. At least Shindo's team was working other angles, gathering intel. It made Reed feel less guilty about sitting around drinking with bored Japanese women when he really wanted to beat the crap out of Waseda until he confessed.

"Let's go." Shindo stood up, put a pile of cash on the table, and headed for the doorway—hung with several strips of thick fabric with Japanese writing.

The host club was busier than the previous night and the women were particularly chatty, requiring more of Reed's attention than he expected. After the third table was escorted out, he and Shindo went in the back for a short break in the staff room, which reeked of men's cologne and hair products. The room host came up to them and spoke to Shindo, but his gaze was on Reed. The man gave a small shrug and returned to his station near the door, greeting and seating new guests.

"We're requested in the back room for a special guest," Shindo informed him. "And they want us to wear ties."

"Ties?"

"We just follow directions." He pulled two silk striped ties from the wall and handed one to Reed. They used the mirrors to put on the ties and check their appearance, then headed out. A man Reed hadn't seen escorted them to a private room in the back. They'd had one invitation from a customer for a private hour before—Reed didn't know exactly what that entailed, but he'd declined. Now it seemed they didn't have a choice, but he considered that a good sign.

The man knocked twice on the door, and Reed noticed part of his little finger was missing. A very good sign. After a shout from inside, the man opened the door and they entered.

Reed tried to hide his exhilaration when he saw Waseda sitting at the table. Another man, wearing a stern expression, stood just behind him. From his bulk and demeanor, he must be a trusted personal bodyguard.

"Good evening," Shindo said in English, then he greeted Waseda in Japanese. Reed said, "Good evening," and they sat only when Waseda motioned for them to do so.

"Good evening," Waseda said in heavily accented English. "I'm Haruo."

"I'm Pierce," Reed said, "and this is Peter."

"Do you want drinks? Whisky?"

"Thank you," Shindo said and Reed nodded. Waseda growled at the bodyguard, who went to the door and repeated the growled order to the next underling. A few minutes later, one of the waiters brought glasses, ice, and a bottle of Glenlivet thirty-year-old whisky. Thank God it wasn't the sickly sweet Champagne the club's female customers preferred. Waseda poured for his guests, and Reed poured for Waseda, giving him slightly more than he'd received.

"Thank you," Waseda said with a smile. "You know our customs?" He was pleased that Reed knew how to serve him.

Reed waited. He had no proof, just suspicions, but he knew this guy was involved in Motofuji's death and the cause of Trent's misery. It took every ounce of willpower not to attack him, and Reed's anger coiled in his muscles, ready to strike. His heart rate accelerated, but on the surface, no one would know. It would be foolish to do anything with the bodyguard in the room.

"Kampai," Reed said, controlling his voice and using the same fake-pleasant tones he'd learned to use with the women. The three of them sipped their whisky, but no one spoke. Waseda looked Reed up and down and did the same with Shindo. Reed lowered his gaze, waiting. He had to play this role if he hoped to get Waseda to trust them and take them home with him.

Waseda asked Reed the typical questions he'd heard from nearly every customer, and he answered them, speaking slowly and not using complicated words or speech patterns. Shindo translated a few times. The whole time, Waseda's gaze traveled over Reed's body, and Reed resisted the urge to flinch or recoil under the obvious scrutiny.

After the second round of drinks was poured, Waseda told his bodyguard to leave. *Now we're getting somewhere*. Reed prayed he and Shindo appealed to Waseda's taste. He shifted in his seat a little. Shindo had told him to act uncomfortable and not too eager to please. Waseda wanted to feel like he was getting Reed to do something he didn't want to do, liked having some power over people.

"You like the job here, Pee-su, host job?"

"Yes. It's fine. Easy work." He smiled. "The ladies like me." Out of the corner of his eye Reed saw Shindo's grin.

"You want to make money, that's why you came to Japan?"

Reed wobbled his head. "Well, yeah."

"I have another job you might like. Help at a party at my house."

"When?"

"Tomorrow."

"I'm working here…." Reed lifted the glass to take a sip, and Waseda smacked the glass back down to the table, shocking Reed with his quick temper.

"I own this place. I'll tell you where and when you're working."

"Oh." Reed feigned fear, but he didn't have to act too much. Waseda's flash of aggression had left him off balance. He'd played this whole game too casually and hadn't realized this man's cartoonish exterior belied his true nature.

"You want to work for me or find new job?"

"Where is the party?" Reed gave a nervous smile as whisky dripped onto his lap.

"The host will give you the address. You and Peter. Be there at ten. Wear ties." Waseda stood up. He pulled a handkerchief from his breast pocket and wiped at Reed's lap, mopping up the whisky and feeling him up at the same time. Reed stared at the man's hand and didn't respond. Then Waseda left.

It took Reed a minute to catch his breath.

"Jesus. I thought you were going to piss yourself. Very convincing."

"Thanks." Reed gave a weak smile. The mix of adrenaline and fear still raced through his veins, and his head spun a little. He felt unprepared, and he hoped Shindo hadn't noticed.

"Well, we're in. We better get back outside and see if we have new customers at our table." Before they got to the room host's podium, the manager came up to them and handed each an envelope and said something in Japanese.

"We're done for the night. He said we should be good tomorrow and make Waseda happy."

"Let's get out of here. I really need a drink now."

They went to the breakfast bar, where they ordered more whisky and breakfast burritos. Reed would never figure out Japanese food preferences. He peeked into his pay envelope and counted the bills. "Two hundred thousand." About two thousand dollars.

Shindo frowned. "I only got half that. Asshole."

Reed wasn't sure if the insult was directed at him or Waseda. He laughed. "I guess he likes me."

"Or he likes what he found when he cleaned up that whisky."

"Fucking perv."

"That's what we're counting on, remember?"

Reed knocked back the rest of his whisky and groaned. He dreaded finding out what their duties at the "party" would be.

THE NEXT night they were picked up at the host bar by a limo and driven to Waseda's. They'd discussed the layout of the house and the location of the art collection, based on information from Trent and Beth's visit and copies of the city planning permits Waseda had gotten when he did renovations to his house. Shindo had contacts all over the place, continually surprising and impressing Reed.

"I DON'T think there's another explanation, Trent."

"I just can't believe it could have been Naoko. She was so nice. And you said she's highly respected."

Beth nodded. "I really liked her. We bonded. I can't believe I bonded with a killer."

"Maybe a killer. Almost definitely a thief."

"Look, she lied about her area of specialty to us, and she didn't put those bowls on the list. From the little we could find on the Internet, they're of enormous historical importance, as well as being beautiful. Plus they're worth a fortune. They're missing from the police inventory too. She has to have them."

"Would someone kill for bowls?"

"Crazy art collectors kill for all sorts of reasons. Didn't you see *The Da Vinci Code*? The art collector was behind everything!"

"He didn't kill for the art, he killed for the religious secret!"

"That's not how I see it."

"Beth, we don't have time for a Siskel and Ebert moment right now. We need to decide what to do with this information."

"Call Reed."

"He told me not to." Trent hoped he didn't sound like a kid in time-out. "It's dangerous for us to contact him if he's in the middle of something."

"Okay. Then the next best person is Hammel at the embassy. Agreed?"

"Yes. Let's call him." Trent reached for the phone, then stopped. "What about the ugly bowl? Maybe Naoko only took the pretty bowls, and the killer took the ugly one because it's a clue, or it's important for another reason."

"Two thieves?" Beth turned down the corners of her mouth. "Too complicated."

"But then Naoko isn't the killer. Isn't that better?"

Beth shrugged. "Yes, but…"

"Let's just call Hammel and tell him what we learned. He can figure out what it all means."

Despite Trent's expectations, Hammel didn't brush off their theory. Trent had too many memories of Reed questioning his logic and assumptions.

"That's certainly a lead. I'll report what you've discovered to the authorities. If they find the pieces in her possession, or some proof she took them, then the police will have a strong motive on her part."

"Great. Keep us posted." Trent hung up, then stared at the phone. "I should have asked him if we could come back yet."

"I'm bored too. But until they have Naoko—assuming she *is* the killer—you're possibly still wanted by the police."

"Hammel didn't say that."

"He probably doesn't want to upset you."

THREE HOURS later Hammel called Beth's cell.

"The police are executing search warrants for Naoko's office, home, and a storage unit she rents on the outskirts of the city. That last location alone looks suspicious. She's at work today, and they're keeping her under surveillance while they search her property. I'll let you know when there's more news."

"That's great. Thanks." Trent couldn't help feeling relieved at Hammel's news. "That's it, then. We figured it out. We'll be heroes and not fugitives!"

"Speak for yourself, Trent. I'm not a fugitive."

"Let's head back to Tokyo. When's the next train?"

Beth consulted the train timetable app on her phone. "The connections aren't very good now. Why don't we wait for the morning? Hammel might have news for us, or Reed might call back."

"Okay. First thing in the morning. Let's get all packed up tonight."

They selected clothes for the next day and packed everything else in the suitcase. Beth sat on it, but she couldn't get it to close.

"You bought those souvenirs and they're taking up too much room."

"I'm sorry. It's compulsively Japanese. I can't go away without buying *omiyage*. I told you. I have to bring some gifts back from here or I'll never hear the end of it from my mother."

"Fine. But you have to figure out something you can leave. Most of this is your stuff." Trent was glad he wasn't the one who'd overpacked this time, because usually he was.

Beth pulled everything out of the suitcase. The last thing she pulled out was one of the tubes from Motofuji. "Trent, what's in here?"

"Oh, I forgot about it. It's the frame for the woodblock print he gave me."

"What's so special about a frame? Can't you just buy another one back home?"

Trent grabbed the tube away from her. "I don't know. It's a gift. And considering what happened…."

"Yeah, it's kind of ghoulish to keep it."

"I think it would be disrespectful to throw it away. I liked him."

"He was a gangster."

"He was nice to me. And to you. People can change."

"At least look at it to see if it's worth taking home, or get rid of the tube."

"Okay." Trent popped the end off the tube and pulled out the pieces of wood. He spread them out on the tatami floor to examine them. "It doesn't look special, but I'm not an expert. Maybe it's valuable. I want to keep it." He tried to reassemble it, locking the corners together. The fourth corner wouldn't connect.

"Look, it's broken. Let's leave it here."

Trent wasn't about to give up. He examined the two pieces. "There's something stuck in the slot, that's why they won't fit together." He saw a piece of black plastic and pulled. Then he set it down on the floor.

"That's a flash drive."

"I think it's a clue. Good thing we didn't throw this away, like someone suggested."

Beth looked down at her knees for a moment then grabbed the drive from Trent. "Let's see what's on it." She leapt for the desk.

"Hang on, what if it's got a virus?"

"What do you suggest, turning it in and hoping someone eventually tells us what's on it? Aren't you dying to know?"

Trent took the drive and turned it over in his hand. It could be a clue, or it could be something very dangerous. He inhaled for a count of five and exhaled for five. Then he pushed the drive into the laptop.

Beth grabbed for the mouse and looked at the file directory. "It's some images and video files." She looked at Trent. "Maybe it's just porn."

"Well, I want to see what kind of porn an eighty-year-old gangster would hide in a frame, don't you?"

20

WASEDA INVITED them to sit on the couch—one of those plush sectional things that could be arranged in various configurations. Waseda's was an L-shape. An open bottle of whisky sat on the low table in front of the couch with several glasses and a bucket of ice. One glass with a splash of amber already sat on the table. Shindo immediately poured a generous amount into Waseda's glass, then plopped chunks of ice into two glasses and splashed in some whisky for himself and Reed. He passed the drinks around and they raised them in a toast, Waseda encouraging them to drain their glasses.

When he reached to pour more, Shindo did so, and again Reed noticed that while he gave Waseda another long pour, he put the smallest amount possible in their glasses. The extra ice made it look like more.

"Waseda-san," Reed began.

"No. Call me Haruo." Waseda's gaze burned into Reed's, and Reed had to look away. It was frightening.

"Haruo." Reed gave a shy smile. "Do you have any vodka?"

"Vodka?" Waseda glanced at the whisky bottle, then back at Reed—or at his body. "I have vodka if you want." He hoisted himself off the couch and shuffled to a bar on the opposite side of the room. He opened the cabinet and started shouting names of vodkas, but with the accent, Reed couldn't understand a single one.

"Berubedēru," Shindo whispered, using the Japanized pronunciation for Belvedere.

Why couldn't he have said something easier to pronounce? "Beru-be-dēru," Reed repeated, hoping he got the syllables correct.

"Okay!" Waseda brought the bottle, and Shindo poured—tiny little portions masked by the ice.

A huge plasma TV hung on one wall and Waseda turned it on, flipping through channels as if this would impress his guests. They pretended to be impressed. He stopped flipping on a porn channel.

Reed and Shindo had been sitting on the long side of the L, with Waseda on the other.

"Come closer." Waseda patted the spot in the corner. "Pee-su, here. Pee-ta, there." He pointed to a spot next to Reed.

He asked Reed questions about how he liked Japan, and Japanese food, moving closer to Reed with each question. Suddenly he reached out and started to loosen Reed's tie. Reed flinched at the unexpected motion.

"You look hot. Relax," Waseda said. He wore a shirt with a few buttons undone and no jacket. Shindo and Reed wore suits and ties as requested, and now Reed understood. He frowned at Waseda, playing the straight guy like Shindo had told him, and Waseda let go of the knot, trailing his hand down the length of the tie. It might have been a turn-on if it had been anyone else.

Reed knew this was coming, that it was part of Waseda's intention, and it played into Shindo's expectations. They needed to be sufficiently friendly to gain his trust enough to get them access to the house, but not too friendly. The question was where to draw the line with this man. He was cordial and smiling, but Reed hadn't forgotten the flash of anger and aggression the night before. If the rumors were true, this guy had had people killed for disobeying him. How much would he expect of Reed?

Waseda said something in Japanese, and Shindo nodded. "He wants me to help you relax." Shindo smiled. He kicked off his slippers and got on the couch, walking on hands and knees toward Reed, who had no clue what he'd do next.

Shindo stopped about a foot away and licked his lower lip. Reed tried to look away. Then Shindo reached out and tugged at the knot of Reed's tie. Then he tugged again as it loosened. Reed gulped air to calm himself. Out of the corner of his eye, he saw Waseda watching and grinning. Shindo yanked the tie once more so the knot hung about four inches from Reed's throat. Reed clenched his jaw. He wasn't supposed to be enjoying this. He didn't need to act when Waseda reached out and undid the top button, then two more.

"Relaxing?" he asked.

Reed nodded quickly. Waseda's touch had canceled out the effect of Shindo's. Reed gave Waseda a wary glance, and it wasn't all playacting. Waseda smiled and slid a hand inside Reed's shirt, pinching at a nipple. Then he grunted something at Shindo and slid back from Reed a foot or two.

"I like to watch." Waseda's gaze raked over Reed as Shindo reached for another button. Reed put out his hands to stop him, but Shindo kept going. Waseda laughed. When Shindo moved to put a hand on Reed's chest, he knocked it away roughly. "Pee-su-kun, you will let him. You will like it. I'm paying you." Waseda's tone held a warning, and Reed thrust his head back against the couch, resigning himself to acceding to Waseda's wishes.

Waseda unzipped his own pants and pushed his shorts down, taking hold of his dick. He yanked a couple of times and muttered in Japanese. "He said the pill didn't start working yet," Shindo translated. Reed glanced at Waseda. He'd seen bigger worms used for fishing bait, but he didn't speak. Waseda added something in English.

"What? I didn't understand," Reed said.

"He knows American guys have big cocks," Shindo translated. He emphasized the word "cocks," and Reed swallowed. "He wants to see you get hard."

Reed stared at Waseda through narrowed eyes, amazed at the man's apparent pleasure in forcing Reed to do things. Shindo was correct, Waseda liked power. Just the thought of it seemed to get Waseda excited—or it could have been the Viagra kicking in.

THE IMAGES on Motofuji's flash drive showed a series of paintings by European artists. They were dark and grainy, even for digital. The video showed the same paintings. It became clear the person shooting the video was hiding the camera because his fingers occasionally obscured the lens. Muffled voices spoke in Japanese.

They watched the video twice, but neither Trent nor Beth understood what it meant or why Motofuji wanted Trent to have it. "Can you tell what they're saying?"

"No. The audio's terrible. Maybe with headphones."

Trent went through the messenger bag until he found his and handed them to Beth.

"Hang on. One of those paintings looks familiar."

"Trent, they're by Rembrandt and Vermeer. They all sort of look familiar. Are you saying you actually saw these exact paintings before?"

"I think so. I just can't remember where."

A scrap of memory fluttered just out of reach. He'd looked at so many art books and videos before the trip—he hadn't just been watching yakuza movies. But something else jogged his memory. A glimpse of a frame through an open door….

"I know where I saw it. At Waseda's."

"Oh. No. You must be confused. We already looked at the list from his place. He had some French impressionists, one Naoko said was a copy—not a forgery, though I don't know what the difference is."

"It's about whether the artist—"

"Trent, let me rephrase that: I don't care what the difference is. But I don't remember a Rembrandt."

"I do. I peeked into the room he skipped when he was showing us his collection. And I think I saw that one of the woman sitting down. I remember the collar."

"Half Rembrandt's stuff has those. It was the fashion."

"Humor me? Do an image search on Google of that one."

"It's so grainy…."

"Then move over. I'll do it."

"I'm searching. I'm searching." The results page came up. "Oh my fucking God," Beth said. Trent smiled. She almost never dropped F-bombs. "If you're right about where this was shot…."

"Listen to the audio."

Beth put in the ear buds and listened. Trent waited, tapping his hand on the desk.

"I can't hear with that racket."

"Sorry."

She made notes in Japanese as she listened. Trent hadn't seen her write it before. He was impressed.

"One of the voices could be Waseda's—he has a specific accent—and he's debating whether he should sell them. Who might want to buy them. I can't make out any names."

"Do you think they're real?" Trent's pulse skyrocketed.

"I don't know. But I think we need to tell someone about this."

"Reed," they said together.

Trent didn't care about the risk in calling Reed now. Trent left a message on Reed's cell saying he'd found something important, but not what. He just hoped Reed would check the messages soon. "Let's call Hammel too."

But Hammel's assistant said he was unreachable. Trent didn't feel comfortable leaving a message about something like this.

"Okay. We'll wait until we hear back. If no one contacts us by morning, we should still go back to Tokyo. Agreed?" Trent asked.

"Yes."

"There's one other option," Trent said. He was on edge and tired of playing phone tag. "There's the cop who's working with the FBI. Kobayashi. He would know how to get in touch with Hammel."

"You think we should tell him what we found?"

"I didn't meet him, but I know Reed trusts him."

"If you think so." Beth found the number of the Tokyo Police and asked for Kobayashi. When she was put through she spoke in Japanese and made notes on a piece of paper.

"Well?" Trent asked when she hung up.

"I told him we found the flash drive hidden in the frame and that he needed to see what was on there. He suggested we meet him tomorrow morning and hand the drive over, for our safety. Then he'll take us to the embassy."

"Okay. But if we hear from Reed or Hammel in the meantime, we let them decide."

"I agree."

Beth looked more relaxed now that a plan had been made, though Trent felt uneasy about how much information she'd given Kobayashi. But Reed had said Kobayashi was gathering information to pass to Hammel, so he brushed the worries away.

"You'll need to repack the suitcase." Trent grinned and Beth threw a shoe at him.

Trent unrolled his futon and watched Beth pack from under the warm quilt. "Oh, I can't wait to talk to Reed about this. He'll be so surprised." With so many thoughts racing around his brain, he'd have trouble sleeping. "I wonder what Reed's doing now."

REED PUT his hand on his cock and rubbed himself through the fabric of his pants. Shindo's proximity helped, but Reed's guilt over what he was doing balanced Shindo's effect, and he couldn't get completely hard. Shindo leaned close and whispered in the ear Waseda couldn't see. "*I* know not all American cocks are huge. Maybe I should have checked before we got here."

"It's bigger than his," Reed whispered back. Shindo laughed and licked the lobe of Reed's ear. Then he leaned down and repeated the action on Reed's nipple. The effect was embarrassingly rapid and Reed felt his pants becoming tight. Shindo sucked the nipple and Reed couldn't help the groan that slipped through his lips.

Waseda laughed and grunted a little as he started jerking himself off. Reed didn't want to watch, and he hoped like hell he wouldn't be expected to help. Waseda gave Shindo another order. He'd lost his ability to speak English, apparently.

"Loosen my tie and I'm going to undo your pants. He wants to see your cock." Shindo smiled, and a mischievous twinkle lit his eyes. Reed tried not to return the smile. "Act like you're not enjoying it," Shindo added in a whisper.

"Who says I'd have to act?"

"You don't fool me. You are enjoying at least some of this."

"I'm just a good actor." Reed reached out and yanked at Shindo's tie.

"Yes, you're good." Shindo unbuckled Reed's belt and slipped it off him, drawing out the motion in an overtly sexual way. Waseda grunted his approval. Shindo went to work on the button and zipper as Reed made a show of trying to stop him. Shindo tugged the trousers down Reed's hips. The head of Reed's cock stuck out over the waistband of his shorts. The sight of it seemed to impress Waseda.

"*Dekai*," he growled.

"Huge," Shindo translated.

Reed tried not to notice how Shindo's lips looked as he mouthed the word, but he couldn't take his gaze away from the full beautiful lips and the "o" shape as he said "huge." Reed tried to ignore how close Shindo was, and how good he smelled, and the way his fingertips got him even more aroused as they peeled back his shorts.

"He wants you to come. You can do it yourself, or I can do it."

Reed grabbed his dick and glanced over at Waseda. The man was slowly stroking himself, gaze fixed on Reed's cock. Reed hadn't done this for an audience before and he wanted to get it over quickly.

"Slower," Shindo said. He still hovered over Reed, hands on Reed's hips.

"You know I'm practically married…."

"I know about Trent. And you knew this would be part of the job. The only way to get in here fast. But it doesn't mean you can't enjoy it."

Shindo peeled Reed's shirt toward his shoulders and tweaked a nipple. Then he moved in and pressed his lips to Reed's, surprising him. He tasted of vodka and whisky and his lips were soft even though the kiss was rough. His tongue was like silk as it explored Reed's mouth. Reed tried to break the kiss, but Shindo held his jaw in place.

Finally, Shindo pulled away, yanking his own tie off completely and pulling his shirt over his head. "He wants you to come on my chest. You close?"

Reed nodded.

"Slow down a little."

"Don't kiss me again." Reed meant it.

Waseda laughed, still working away at his cock. It no longer resembled bait but Reed didn't want to get any closer to it unless absolutely necessary. He closed his eyes and thought about Trent. How Trent's kisses tasted and how his mouth felt on Reed's cock.

"Now," Waseda said.

Shindo sat back on his heels in front of Reed.

Reed stared at Shindo's chest, smooth as tan silk, with dark areoles and tight budded nipples. His torso was muscular with a respectable six-pack. Not the slender, almost feminine, body Reed had seen on other Asian men. Shindo's pecs were well developed and emphasized his nipples. Reed wondered what they might taste like. The simple thought shifted his focus from the conscious motion of stroking himself to the heat and tension building at the base of his balls. He let himself feel and receive the pleasure, not from his own actions, but from the sensuousness of watching Shindo strip down, the beauty of his body, and the image of Shindo's hands or mouth on Reed's cock instead of his own hands.

He felt the balance tip and let any semblance of control slip away. The pleasure crashed through him and he came in thick ropes across Shindo's chest, leaving a creamy trail from nipple to belly button. Reed lay back panting as he heard Waseda's orgasm, a series of low grunts and growls.

Reed's embarrassment and humiliation weren't artificial. As soon as he'd finished, he hated himself for putting on this show, for enjoying Shindo's body and kisses. He hoped this ridiculous plan would work and free Trent. But how the hell was Reed ever going to tell him about this? He didn't want to lie to Trent—not ever again—but would Trent hate Reed as much as he hated himself right now?

Waseda pulled his shirt off and cleaned himself up, his heavy belly sagging and hiding his dick. "Easy money, huh? Feel good and make money."

Reed looked away and started doing up his pants.

"Not yet. Drink more." Waseda poured drinks for everyone and knocked his back, then walked down the hall, presumably to the bathroom.

Reed grabbed a napkin from the table and handed it to Shindo. He didn't want to see his come all over his chest, but Shindo put the napkin back down. Reed forced himself to look at Shindo's face. "What about you? Should I…?" Reed left the sentence unfinished. He felt guilty that he didn't want to pleasure Shindo unless absolutely necessary.

"Don't worry. He wants me to fuck him."

Reed stared at Shindo. "What?"

"He said you're too big and you'd kill him." Shindo laughed. "It's a compliment."

"You okay with that?"

"I don't want to, but I will." Shindo's voice betrayed no emotion; he was back to being a typical Japanese. "He'll probably fall asleep after, then we can look around."

"Fuck. I'm sorry."

"I knew this might happen going in. Better me than you, right?"

Reed shrugged. He felt even worse now. He'd jacked off on this guy, mentally cheated on Trent, and now poor Shindo would have to fuck the yakuza scum to help Reed.

"He wants another show from you while I'm fucking him. If you need it, there's a bottle of Viagra on the bar. Or I'd be happy to fluff you for your close-up." Shindo grinned, back to his previous joking mood. "I give great head." He swiped his tongue across his lower lip.

"I'll bet. I'm not sure I could survive that."

"Thanks. I'll take that as a compliment."

Reed popped the Viagra as Waseda came back into the room. He was completely naked now. Reed didn't envy Shindo's situation right now. He'd even help fluff Shindo if necessary.

"Come to bedroom." Waseda pointed down the hall.

Reed pulled his trousers back up around his hips and followed Shindo down the hall.

Inside the bedroom, Waseda lay in bed. A box of condoms and some lube sat on the bedside table. The bed was huge, easily room for all three. Reed's stomach churned.

Waseda told Reed to sit in a chair in front of the bed and undress Shindo. From Waseda's position he could see both men's faces. Shindo stepped close to Reed. He still wore his trousers. Reed's semen was drying in flaky white streaks on his chest. Reed reached for Shindo's belt, wanting to look away, but forcing himself to keep playing the game—for Shindo's sake. He unbuttoned the waistband and ran his hand along the outside, feeling the firm ridge of Shindo's dick. Waseda grunted; he liked watching Reed touch Shindo.

Reed unzipped the pants and let them fall. Shindo stepped back and kicked them away. He stood there in pale-blue boxer briefs that hugged his shape so well Reed could already tell Shindo wasn't circumcised. He hooked his thumbs in the waistband and inched the shorts slowly down Shindo's slim hips. He felt the same mixture of excitement and revulsion, but excitement won out when Shindo tangled his fingers through Reed's hair. *Bastard*!

Reed yanked the shorts down and Shindo's cock sprang out, half-hard. His hair was straight and silky, not curly, and his foreskin and shaft were dusky, as if an artist had traced his outlines with charcoals. Shindo stroked himself, his cock lengthening but not thickening. Reed tried not to look at it even though it was inches from his face.

"Suck him, Pee-su."

"No." Reed shook his head.

Reed didn't move. Waseda reached over and opened a drawer. He pulled out a gun and pointed it at Shindo. "I'm paying for a party. Fuck his face!"

Shindo looked down, apology clear in his expression as he pulled Reed's head back by his hair.

Then the phone rang. Waseda grabbed it and bellowed. Reed couldn't understand a word, but he almost felt sorry for the person at the other end. As Waseda grew increasingly agitated, he started waving the gun around. Reed looked at Shindo's cock two inches from his face and decided sucking it was better than a bullet anywhere in his body, but he was grateful for the interruption.

Waseda barked at the person on the other end of the phone for a few minutes and slammed it down on the bedside table. "Get dressed. Party's over." He gestured toward the door with the gun before he realized he still had it and put it on the table. "The car will take you home," he added in a more civilized tone.

They scrambled into their clothes and retrieved their shoes by the front door and raced for the car, shirts unbuttoned. The back door opened to let them in, but the driver didn't pull away. One of the guards lumbered up to the car and knocked on the back window. Shindo pushed the button to lower it and the guard handed him two envelopes; Reed recognized the pay envelopes as Shindo raised the window and the car took off.

Back in Reed's hotel room, they opened the envelopes. Reed had been given nearly three thousand dollars and Shindo two thousand. He frowned. "Lousy gaijin!" He glared at Reed. But Shindo's envelope also had a note.

"Come back tomorrow night for another party." Shindo translated as he showed Reed the note. It was handwritten, and even though Reed couldn't read Japanese he could tell the characters were unevenly formed; Waseda probably hadn't had much education.

"I'm not sure how much more party I can handle," Reed said. "We should have just drugged him tonight."

"I did. I put something in his drinks. It didn't seem to affect him at all."

"Well, double it tomorrow. We need to look around, and don't take this personally, but I don't want there to be any fucking tomorrow."

"Ditto."

Reed laughed at Shindo's command of English.

"On the other hand," Shindo said as he moved a hand across his crotch, adjusting his dick. "I think that Viagra is really working."

"You can take care of it yourself, at your place. Go home and I'll see you tomorrow. Let's meet for lunch and plan."

"You sure? Looks like you've got the same problem." Shindo pointed toward Reed's obvious erection.

"I'm sure. But thanks."

Shindo stood up and headed for the door.

“Shindo, what was that emergency phone call about? Not that I’m ungrateful for it.”

“Something about them finding a package and needing a frame. Could have been some yakuza slang or code. I didn’t understand it.”

“Strange. See you tomorrow.”

“Trent’s a lucky guy.”

Reed locked the door behind Shindo and turned on the shower. He undressed and stepped into the warm spray. “I’m the lucky one,” Reed said out loud. He worked off the effects of the Viagra while imagining Trent’s hands on him instead of his own.

He tumbled into bed, still damp from the shower, and sank into a peaceful, relaxed state.

21

WHEN HE woke the sun was already high in the sky and light streamed through the open curtains.

A hazy memory from the night before struggled to penetrate his consciousness. Reed pushed it away, not wanting to recall details of the humiliating evening. At least it hadn't made things irretrievably weird between him and Shindo. Thank God for that timely phone call.

Until the meaning of the call hit him.

The package and the frame. Trent had a tube with pieces of a frame for the woodblock print from Motofuji. Reed had glanced at it and dismissed it as unimportant. Was there some connection after all?

What if Waseda had found Trent?

Reed dressed and raced out of the room. He wandered down the street until he came to an electronics store. Even in this part of town, they were nearly as thick as Starbucks in Seattle.

He bought a prepaid phone and dialed Beth's cell phone. He got a recorded message in Japanese that sounded like the one announcing the user is out of range. Why had they sent Trent into the boonies? Then he tried the number for the ryokan in Shuzenji where Trent and Beth were staying. He'd memorized the number so he didn't have to risk someone finding it written in any of his belongings. The woman who answered didn't understand him when he asked for the Americans, so he apologized in Japanese and hung up. He'd have Shindo call when they met for lunch, only about an hour from now. But Reed was too agitated to relax.

He called the embassy, but Hammel was unreachable—out following a lead, according to his assistant, another agent. Reed didn't leave a message. He wandered the streets in the bright sunshine. It was almost too bright for him. He'd been part of the strange nighttime world on the edges of the Tokyo underworld for less than a week, and already the sun felt unfamiliar. He knew thousands of people slept all day and worked through the darkness, providing legal and illegal entertainment in this city—and all over Japan. All over the world. Luckily, Reed could go back to a more normal existence when this particular job was over. Most of the others didn't have that option.

BY THE next morning, neither Reed nor Hammel had called back, so Trent and Beth followed the plan to meet Kobayashi. They arrived at the prearranged station, a few stops before Shinjuku. Kobayashi said it would be easier to meet there. After Trent's few experiences with the mazes inside Japanese train stations, he was fine with the plan. They took the exit Kobayashi had told them to, and they found the black SUV parked across the street.

"You ready to do this, Trent?" Beth asked before they stepped into the sunshine. "You're absolutely sure you trust this guy?"

"Reed does, so I'll trust him too." Trent took a deep breath. "Yeah, let's do this. If something feels wrong, we don't have to give him the flash drive."

"I'll let you decide."

"At the worst case, Christopher Hammel will know where we are. Besides, if he's gone after Naoko, then we have nothing to worry about."

"I don't know. The paintings are American property. I'd feel better if the embassy is involved, and not just the Tokyo police. After what happened to you, do you trust the cops?"

Trent took a breath. He *didn't* trust the police. He was only willing to trust this one guy because Reed had vouched for him. "Maybe you're right. Let's just go directly to the embassy." He glanced at Beth and she nodded. They turned to go back into the station when Trent heard his name. A Japanese man stood between them and the entrance. "Cōpurando-san and Conchi-san. I'm Kobayashi."

He was wearing a Yankees baseball cap, and Trent thought he might have been one of the cops working the Motofuji case after he got arrested. "Oh… hi," Trent said, recalling this guy hadn't been very nice to him. "Sorry, but we think we should take the evidence to the embassy."

Kobayashi said something in Japanese.

"He says it's evidence of illegal activity in Japan, so the police should have it too. He'll drive us to the embassy where we can make a copy," Beth translated, her voice wavering.

"That's okay. We'll take the train." Trent tried to push past him.

"Please help me too," Kobayashi said in English, then added something in Japanese.

"He says he'll get a big promotion if he helps uncover this," Beth said.

Trent noticed Beth's furrowed brow. Whatever had worried her, she couldn't risk telling him in front of Kobayashi. They'd just hold on to the drive until they got to the embassy. "Okay." Trent nodded and they followed Kobayashi to the SUV.

REED MET Shindo for lunch at a ramen shop not far from his hotel. They sat at the counter and were served huge bowls of noodles with vegetables and sliced pork floating on top. Reed slurped his noodles for a few minutes before speaking. He still felt uneasy with Shindo after the intimacies of the night before.

"Look, Reed, it's just work. Just a job. I know that."

Reed turned to look at Shindo. "I felt uncomfortable. I want to talk about that before we consider going back there."

"Fine. Remember he thinks you're a straight guy getting forced into this. Your reactions reinforced his belief. He thinks I'm from another gang and will do anything to get into his gang. I had to push you to play with my character. He believes we're both in it for money."

Reed looked into his bowl and poked a piece of pork with his chopsticks. He didn't have much appetite. "You're right. I shouldn't have taken any of it personally."

"You're okay? We might have to do more tonight. Wouldn't you rather do it with me than with Waseda? I hear he sometimes likes things rough. I don't want either of us to have to take that risk."

Reed nodded. He managed a weak smile. "Yeah." He ate a few bites of lunch and rested his chopsticks on the edge of the bowl.

"Something else is wrong. This isn't just about last night, is it?"

"I think something's wrong out in Izu. I can't get in touch with Beth and the ryokan people don't speak English."

"Want me to call?"

Reed nodded.

"Finish your lunch. You'll need your energy and wits later. We might not have time for dinner." Reed's appetite improved a little but he couldn't finish the huge portion. He was amazed at how much Shindo could eat. Reed glanced around and noticed a slim woman slurping away at her noodles. A few minutes later she left and the chef took her bowl and dumped out the contents. There was only some broth left.

Out on the street, Shindo used Reed's burner phone. As soon as he finished, he pulled the card out and stomped it under his boot, then threw the pieces in different trash cans.

"What?" Reed had a bad feeling.

"They left this morning. Packed their bags and took off back to Tokyo."

"Shit."

"Now what?"

TRENT AND Beth sat in the back of the SUV after stashing the suitcase in the cargo area. Kobayashi closed the back door and climbed into the driver's seat. Trent thought that was a good sign. He hadn't arrested Trent. Maybe this would work out okay. Kobayashi started the engine and turned. "Tell me what you saw on the flash drive."

"Some photos of paintings that might be forgeries. Maybe stolen. We don't know which. But we thought it was important." Trent didn't want to reveal his suspicions just yet.

Kobayashi responded in Japanese. "Good idea," Beth translated. "Give the drive to him, J.T."

It was their prearranged code if Beth caught something in Japanese that worried her. Trent looked at her and pulled the flash drive out of his jacket pocket, then handed it to Kobayashi.

"Thank you. We'll go to embassy and give them copies."

"Okay, thanks for giving us a ride," Trent said.

They drove through the now-familiar Tokyo traffic, stopping at nearly every light. Trent didn't recognize any of the locations, and from the way Beth was watching the few street signs, neither did she.

"J.T., Japanese don't talk about promotions that way," Beth whispered.

"He's American too. Dual citizenship, Reed said."

"Then why does he prefer to speak Japanese? Something's fishy."

The police radio crackled and occasionally bursts of discussion came through.

"Let's find a crowded corner and run for it. Squeeze, okay?" Trent whispered.

Beth nodded. She reached her hand across the space between them and they locked pinkies.

Kobayashi didn't try to make conversation, and Trent tried not to look at Beth, hoping to appear trusting and relaxed.

At the next loud burst of activity on the police radio, Kobayashi grabbed the mic and started speaking. He got angry and pulled his cap off and smacked it on the steering wheel.

Beth squeezed Trent's finger as he noticed Kobayashi stare at her in the rearview mirror. Without the cap Trent spotted the three moles forming a triangle on Kobayashi's cheek. They both swung open the doors while the SUV was still in motion and ran for the corner through a crowd of people.

"He answered a call from Kobayashi, identifying himself as Nishikatsu!" Beth shouted as they bumped their way through angry pedestrians. "Train station."

Trent looked back and saw the SUV had stopped and Kobayashi—fake Kobayashi—was making his own way through the crowd. Beth grabbed Trent's hand and pulled him along. She was much shorter, so he could only go as fast as she could. He wouldn't leave her behind. She raced down the steps into the station, teetering on her heels. At the bottom she pulled them off and ran for the entry gates, shouting in Japanese.

People moved out of their way and Beth hopped over the entry gate. Trent followed. He took a moment to glance back and saw Fake Kobayashi still after them, flashing a police badge. Most people just stopped and let them pass, but Trent worried someone might try to apprehend them, or at least him: the suspicious foreigner. They raced along the platform as a train was coming and instead of hopping on, Beth suddenly swerved and pulled Trent toward a stairway down to another platform. They were going the wrong way in a sea of people trying to go upstairs.

Trent's heart pounded and he squeezed Beth's hand. She squeezed back and kept going. They went to the end of the platform and there was no way up or down from there, just a brick wall. A train was at the platform and Trent heard the bell for the closing doors just as he saw Fake Kobayashi coming at them. He stopped, grinning as he must have seen them up against the wall. Trent jammed his arm between the doors of the train and felt the pain as they closed on him, but a second later they reopened and he and Beth hopped on. The doors closed again before Fake Kobayashi could get on.

They saw him watching them as the train moved out of the station.

Then the pain in Trent's arm reminded him of how they'd escaped.

"Are you okay?" Beth examined his arm, panting as she stood in stocking feet, still holding on to her shoes.

Trent didn't want to look. He'd felt a sharp pain and thought he might be bleeding. He'd rather not know. "Yeah, I'm fine."

"Liar," Beth said and put her arms around him. They stayed like that for a while until they both caught their breath.

Finally Trent looked and there was no blood. The shirt was dark from the rubber tubing on the edges of the door and his arm hurt like hell. But they were okay, and for now they'd eluded the cop pretending to be Kobayashi.

They got off at a busy station—Trent didn't know which one—but they looked around and no one was following them off the train. Finally, Beth put her shoes back on. "He wasn't Kobayashi," she said when they exited the station and sat down in a coffee shop to recover. "He called himself Nishikatsu on the radio."

"It's a good thing I gave him the wrong flash drive," Trent smiled. "I hope he likes the first draft of my last book."

"Me too." Beth stared at the laptop of a girl at the next table. "Trent, there's a picture of you on the Internet."

"What?"

"Let's get out of here, but don't run or you'll draw attention to yourself."

Trent glanced around. It seemed everyone was looking at him. He felt even more self-conscious than usual here in Japan. Two giggling girls in school uniforms kept their eyes on him as he passed. "I don't want to go back to jail, Beth."

"I have an idea." She took his hand and led him to a department store. "Let's get you a wig."

"What? No."

"Trust me." Beth consulted a store map near an escalator and they ascended slowly. Trent looked around at everyone, feeling as if he were ten feet tall. "Sit here." Beth settled him on a couch near the women's restroom. She came back ten minutes later with a bag and motioned for him to follow her inside the bathroom.

Reluctantly, he did and was surprised to see a room with plush couches and chairs and a set of mirrors along one wall with seats like at a hair salon.

"Sit down." Beth motioned to one of the vanity chairs and pulled the wig out from the bag and placed it on Trent's head.

He stared back at himself under short, straight black hair. "Do you think I look Japanese now?"

"Of course not. But you don't stand out so much anymore. There are plenty of tall Japanese men now, and people will need to get very close before they can be certain you're not Japanese. Well, except for your clothes. But we don't have time for a total makeover now."

"What should we do?"

"Call Reed again, and Hammel at the embassy." Beth slipped a hand into her purse. "Oh no, I dropped my phone when we were running. Let's just go directly to the embassy. You'll be safe there as an American."

"Because now I look so American." Trent tried to smile but his stomach cramped with uncertainty. They still had the real flash drive, but now he didn't know who to trust. Who had sent Nishikatsu after them? And why? Where was Reed?

"Okay, let's go to the embassy."

They took a taxi this time, not wanting to risk Trent being seen on the subway. Beth paid and they stepped out of the taxi across the street from the embassy. Despite the ugliness of the building, Trent couldn't remember ever being so happy to arrive anywhere. Ever. Even if Hammel wasn't available, they would be safe here until they could meet with someone they trusted.

Ten feet from safety. They crossed the street, now just five feet from the gate guarded by a tall, handsome Marine in his distinctive uniform—tan shirt and blue pants. Trent relaxed and threw the officer a smile. Two feet. Only two feet.

Then he felt an arm on his. "Torento Cōpurando, you're under arrest."

Trent whirled to see Nishikatsu. Beth walloped him with her purse. The Marine didn't flinch or move to stop Nishikatsu. "Do something," Beth shouted at the guard.

"I'm sorry, ma'am. I can't. He's still on Japanese territory until he gets inside our gates."

"Trent!"

"Why am I under arrest?"

"I think you already know." Nishikatsu cuffed Trent's hands behind his back. Trent tried to run, but Nishikatsu was prepared and even Trent's extra height and weight couldn't unbalance him. Another man appeared almost out of nowhere and gripped Trent's arm tightly—right where the train door had closed on him. He crumpled to the ground in pain, and Beth started toward him, mouth and eyes wide.

"Beth, go inside and tell someone," he managed to shout. The other man yanked Trent up.

"I am." She turned to the guard. "Let me in. I'm American."

Trent watched Beth talk with the guard as Nishikatsu and his larger, meaner friend dragged him to the SUV and threw him in back. He heard the locks click shut on the rear doors. Nishikatsu wasn't going to let him get away again.

WASEDA'S DRIVER picked up Reed and Shindo and drove them to the house for another private party. They didn't speak at all in the car. They knew they had to get the proof tonight or there wouldn't be another chance. Waseda had accelerated his demands on them in a way Shindo hadn't anticipated. If he kept them around longer it was going to be in a sexual capacity that neither was willing to accept.

"Something spooked him last night and he got angry, violent. That phone call only delayed whatever he planned. And I think we'll be in danger," Shindo had suggested when they were waiting for the car. Reed agreed.

There were half a dozen limos outside the house, and music could be heard from the street, but not blaring. Apparently, even yakuza had to be polite to their neighbors.

Reed and Shindo were given cursory pat downs at the gate and again at the front door. About fifteen people stood or sat around the living room, holding drinks or cigarettes. Reed smelled pot mixed with the cigarette smoke. The plasma TV showed a soccer game no one was watching. The male guests looked like younger versions of Waseda, and the women were scrawny, young club girls, but Reed spotted two bosomy blondes draped over short, middle-aged, balding men.

Money could get you whatever you wanted. It was what got Reed and Shindo here—or Waseda's hope they wanted money as much as he wanted them here.

But Waseda was nowhere in sight. Reed and Shindo got highball glasses and filled them with ice and water. They needed to keep their heads tonight. They wandered around getting their bearings in the house and noting entrances and possible exit routes. Neither could risk bringing a weapon, and Reed felt naked without one. As they moved through the rooms, he kept an eye out for anything that might work as a weapon should the need arise. They had to stay together; then they could overpower one or two men.

"The bodyguards are armed, did you notice?" Reed asked as they fixed their hair in a bathroom mirror.

"Yeah. But they're big and bulky. Can't move fast. They're using side holsters, so you have to move in close and fast to disarm them."

A Japanese girl came up and started flirting with Reed, using the three or four sentences of English she knew. He flirted back. There was a lull in the music, and Reed heard Waseda shouting at the other end of the house. Not a good sign. He exchanged glances with Shindo.

The girl was playing with Reed's necktie and pulled him over to an area where some other girls were dancing. She danced close, rubbing herself along his body, and one of the other girls joined in.

Waseda came into the room, and the casual chatter quieted down. Reed saw him glance at each of the guests until Waseda's gaze found him, one club girl plastered against his chest. Waseda's smile turned to a stone mask. Not anger. Reed thought this was much worse. He stepped away from the girl. Waseda walked toward him and reached for Reed's tie and yanked him close, slipping one arm around Reed's waist.

He was never going to wear a tie again. Ever. He felt like a pet being walked around on a leash.

"You want to dance, Pee-su?"

"Yes."

Waseda smiled and started swinging his arms and hips. Reed might have laughed if it wasn't so damn serious. There were too many goals to juggle. Too many people to keep an eye on, and too many ways this could still get ballsed up before they found the stolen pieces from Motofuji's collection.

Reed let Waseda bump and grind against him and pretended to enjoy it. The club girls sneered at him now. He didn't blame them. He was just another whore vying for the same attention, and they didn't like the competition or their odds. Reed hoped Shindo was off exploring the back rooms while he kept Waseda occupied.

Waseda put a hand on Reed's ass and pulled him close. He smelled like garlic and sweat and too much expensive cologne. Reed felt something hard digging against his hip. Had Waseda already popped his Viagra?

Then the hard thing twitched. Or rather, it vibrated. It was Waseda's phone. He yanked it out of his pocket and pressed himself up against Reed again. Someone was agitated on the other end. Waseda stopped dancing and growled into the phone.

"Wait here. Find Pee-ta. I come back soon." He headed for the back of the house.

Reed caught sight of Shindo coming from the hallway Waseda had just gone toward.

"I looked around a little, trying to find the bathroom." Shindo started dancing, moving close to Reed so he could be heard over the music and chatter.

"And?"

"Two doors are locked. One toward the back of the house and one on the opposite side of the courtyard." Shindo swung Reed around so he could see through the floor-to-ceiling glass doors that opened onto a courtyard in the center of the house. There was a room with similar glass walls opposite the living room.

"Glass walls. He wouldn't have anything important hidden in there."

"I agree. Probably so he can spy on whoever's in there from here."

"What about the other room?"

"I tried to pick the lock, but a goon came by. I'll try later. Or you try. Whoever has a chance. Where's Waseda?"

"He got another phone call and left. Something's up. Maybe we need to get in there sooner rather than later."

There was a commotion at the other side of the house. Shindo and Reed had their arms around each other and were dancing close. The club girls ignored them and so did the other men. Apparently everyone knew to keep their hands off Waseda's pets.

Reed noticed a light go on in the opposite room. A man shoved someone in there—a very tall Japanese guy—and Reed saw Waseda standing in the room, arms folded across his chest. Waseda and the other man were shouting and gesturing at the tall man, then Waseda punched him. The tall man slumped a little and fell back onto the bed.

That could be foreplay for Waseda. Better that guy than Reed or Shindo. Reed was tempted to keep watching, but then the light went out in the glass-walled room.

Waseda came back and smiled when he saw Reed and Shindo dancing together. He wormed his way between them and started groping.

"Did you take your little pill yet?" Shindo asked.

"Nooo," Waseda said, grinning—well, leering. "Now?"

"Yes." Reed pulled a pill from his pocket and Waseda swallowed it.

"Let me watch you two dance. Too hot. No ties. No shirts."

Shindo blew a kiss at Reed, and this time Reed could laugh. The blue pill was in fact a strong sedative, and Waseda should be out in ten to fifteen minutes; for all intents and purposes he'd appear to be passed out drunk. Some of the guests were getting frisky and were wandering off to other parts of the house.

"What about the guards?" Reed asked as he pretended to kiss Shindo's ear and neck.

"Just two inside. I gave them pills, after promising them blowjobs."

"From you?"

"No, from you."

Reed laughed. *Fifteen minutes, then we can get what we came for.* Not enough time for Waseda to do any damage.

WHEN NISHIKATSU threw Trent in the SUV, he was only a little worried. He and Beth had figured the man must be working for Waseda. Who else would care so much about the flash drive? Beth would get inside the embassy and tell whoever she could find where they'd taken him. If she was wrong, the only other possibility was to go to police HQ. At least that was what they'd planned for.

When the buildings thinned out, Trent knew they weren't going to the police department. He had no idea where Waseda's house was in relation to the embassy, but he hoped they hadn't completely miscalculated.

They were in a residential area. Then they turned a corner. It was dark, so Trent couldn't be sure it was Waseda's house. He heard music and saw cars and limos parked out front and in the driveway. Well, what would they do to him in the middle of a party? Beth and Hammel might get here before anything painful happened. He had another flash drive on him if that was what they wanted. It was the real one. Beth had yet another copy, so if Trent had to give his up, it wasn't a complete washout. Maybe they'd let him go after they got the drive. He could say he didn't really know what he'd seen….

Hopefully they'd buy that.

They tossed him in a bedroom. Then Waseda came in and let Nishikatsu punch him a couple of times. They yelled at him in broken English. All he understood was "flash drive."

"It's in the car." That should get them to leave him alone for a little while so he could catch his breath and figure out how to keep stalling them until help arrived. His jaw ached. Nishikatsu was much shorter, but he had some strength. It was only the difference in height that mitigated the punches.

Trent struggled to sit up and caught a glimpse of himself in a mirror and got a minor shock. His wig hadn't fallen off. He wanted to laugh but he knew that would piss off his captors. He didn't need to do that.

Waseda shouted and Nishikatsu left, probably to search for the flash drive. Waseda grumbled and turned off the light and slammed the door shut. Trent heard a lock click into place.

As soon as the door shut, he got up and searched for something to pick the lock on the cuffs. They were the old-fashioned metal kind and easier to get out of than the newfangled plastic ones. He'd learned how to do it at Quantico with hairpins, metal nail files, and the like. He hoped this was a woman's bedroom. He went into the adjoining bathroom and located a hair clip and worked it into the cuffs. They sprang open in less than a minute. Trent rubbed his wrists and arms to get the circulation going again. Unfortunately, the lock on the door couldn't be picked from inside.

As he moved back away from the door he noticed the room across the courtyard. It was brightly illuminated compared to his dark room and he could see the party his arrival had interrupted. People dancing, drinking, watching a huge TV.

He scanned the crowd and noticed two figures away from the main group and close to the opposite window. Two men dancing. One of them looked kind of like Reed. Trent missed him so much he was imagining the resemblance. But the dark hair and the general body shape reminded him of Reed.

Trent wished he'd been able to get in touch with him. Maybe Beth had found him and Reed was on his way here now. He watched the men again, the westerner and a good-looking Japanese guy. They moved apart and were unbuttoning each other's shirts. The Japanese guy pulled off his tie and bound the other man's wrists then peeled his shirt back.

Concentrate! He didn't have time to be watching this, even though it was sexy as hell. He should try to get out of here before someone came back. There was a chair that looked heavy enough to break the window. If he did it now, it would draw attention to his escape. He'd wait till he needed to go. Unable to resist, he glanced back at the men.

The Japanese guy kissed the other man's chest, and the westerner arched his back, pushing into the kiss, his body sinuous and supple, head thrown back in obvious ecstasy. What kind of party was this? If he was lucky, they'd concentrate on the sex and forget about him.

Trent had seen someone move just like that before.

It *was* Reed!

What was he doing here, and why was he half-naked and dancing with someone else? Before Trent realized it, he'd thrown the chair through the window. It shattered, spraying glass across the courtyard. Everyone in the party room turned toward the noise.

Trent raced across the courtyard and knocked the screen door open.

People gaped at him. One woman laughed and fell down.

Reed just stood there, half-undressed, arms around another man.

Then Trent spotted Waseda on the couch watching them, eyes half closed. He had a gun in his hand and it was pointed at Reed.

22

"TRENT?" REED pulled away from Shindo and glanced toward Waseda. He'd slumped a little, already under the effects of the sedative, but his eyes were open. "What are you doing here?" And why was he wearing a black wig? Take away the guns and the thugs guarding the doors and this could be mistaken for a Wonderland party. Only Reed hadn't taken any mind-altering substances.

"Dance!" Waseda waved the gun around, and Reed remembered the situation. "You too!" He pointed the gun at Trent, whose expression Reed couldn't discern and he wasn't sure he wanted to. Waseda shouted at Trent in Japanese.

"Trent, come here!" Reed reached for Trent's arm and pulled him close.

Trent pushed him away. "What are you doing? Who was that guy?"

Reed glanced around and noticed Shindo was gone. Now he and Trent were alone with Waseda. The partiers on the other side of the room didn't even look in his direction.

"I'll explain, just come close, at least till he falls asleep." Reed pulled Trent in again and started working on his buttons. "The guy's U/C, got us in here to find evidence that Waseda did the hit, but our plan didn't go quite as expected."

"Which part?" Trent's tone was skeptical and his mouth was a thin tight line.

"Having to put on a show. And how much sedative we'd have to give him." Reed stared at Trent realizing he didn't look worried or frightened, just annoyed. "Why are you here? You were supposed to stay safe."

"We figured out who did it. Not Waseda. Naoko, the appraiser. She stole some ancient bowls."

"We know about the bowls. We thought we'd find them here. Shindo's searching the locked room now." Reed hoped that's where Shino was. Either in the room, or calling for backup.

"I figured something else out, about what Waseda's really hiding in there. I couldn't get a hold of Hammel and called the cops instead. They… it's a long story, but they brought me here because I have proof that Waseda was behind—"

"Pierce, the situation's changed. He doesn't have the bowls." Shindo came up behind Trent and whispered to Reed. "You'll never guess wh—"

The side door burst open at that point, and a woman entered. She had long, straight black hair and wore a green-and-white checked skirt and a white top with enough ruffles to make a pirate jealous. She shouted in Japanese, but all Reed could understand was Waseda's name.

Reed spotted Waseda, finally asleep but with the gun still gripped in his fingers. The woman had seen him too and was heading in their direction. She paused and pulled one of Waseda's samurai swords off the wall, unsheathing it as she advanced on them. The people in the front part of the room screamed and ran out the door.

"It's Naoko Maeda," Shindo said.

She was on Waseda before they could stop her. The sword whispered through the air as she whirled it and caught Waseda in the throat. Blood spurted. Reed stepped back. He didn't know how to deal with a crazy sword-wielding person. Before anyone could move, she'd slashed at the nearest person, Shindo, and he went down, a bloody line blooming along his arm and chest where the sword had sliced.

Reed pushed Trent away and tried to grab the woman from behind as she paused over Shindo. He managed to knock the sword out of her hands and it clanked to the floor. He reached around to pin her arms, only then noticing the small dagger she held in the other hand. She shouted and sliced at Reed, then put the blade to his throat.

The razor-sharp edge stung and Reed felt blood trickle down his neck. He glanced over to see Trent kneeling over Shindo, trying to stop the bleeding. Trent jumped to his feet, but Naoko tightened her grip on the dagger.

"Don't come closer."

A commotion at the door distracted Reed and Naoko kept the dagger tight against Reed's skin. Several uniformed police entered and fanned out near the door. They shouted to one another and presumably at Naoko. She shouted back. The cops stopped.

She maneuvered Reed closer to the couch and retrieved the sword where it had fallen.

"She wants you as a hostage so she can get away." Shindo's voice was a bubbly whisper. "Her shoes."

Naoko sliced again at Shindo with the sword, never easing up on the dagger at Reed's throat. She'd clearly had training with these weapons. Reed wished he'd watched those samurai movies with Trent.

Where was Trent? Reed looked around but he was gone. Good. He was out of danger. There was another heated exchange between Naoko and the cops. Reed looked at Shindo, hoping for a translation, but Shindo was unconscious—or dead. Grief snaked through Reed's gut. What had he said about shoes? He glanced down. Naoko was wearing fancy red heels with little sparkly pink bows. Not what he'd expect from a psycho sword-wielding killer.

Heels? They'd made her taller, but they were also a weakness. Reed moved slightly knowing she'd follow him with the dagger hand, and when she did he quickly pushed at her shoulder to unbalance her, hoping the heels would destabilize her.

Then he heard three shots ring out.

TRENT WATCHED Naoko slump, screaming, roaring in pain or anger. She dropped the dagger and the sword. He'd hit her arm, rather than risk her back—the bullets could hit Reed—but all three had hit the target. The gunshots rang through his head—he'd never fired without ear protectors, and the sound had been deafening. He hadn't thought about it, just squeezed the trigger, his instinct to protect Reed stronger than his fears or self-doubts.

He rushed forward, gun still pointed at Naoko until he was certain she was disarmed, then dropped the gun and moved toward Reed. Blood trickled down his throat and bare chest, bright blotches of red on his opened shirt. He put his arms out for Trent and they fell together, holding on tightly.

The blaring in Trent's head hadn't abated; he could see Reed's mouth moving but couldn't hear the words. Hands grabbed him from behind, but Reed didn't let go. Then Reed was pulled away—the cops surrounded them and took control of the scene. Reed and Trent were cuffed and taken to a room in the back of the house.

Trent heard sirens coming closer—his hearing was returning to normal. Police, paramedics, more police. No one spoke to them, but a guard stood at the door.

"You okay?" Reed asked. He was cuffed to a chair and Trent was on the bed, hands cuffed behind his back.

"I am now. Aren't they going to get the paramedics in here for you?"

"It looks worse than it is. I'm fine."

"I know when you're lying."

Reed grinned, but Trent saw from the tension in his mouth, the unfocused eyes, that he was in pain. Trent hadn't caught his breath yet. He wasn't sure he'd ever calm down from the tension, the adrenaline pushing him on when his brain wouldn't function. He'd never expected he'd need to remember the gun drills they'd learned, but now he was grateful he'd had that opportunity. If he hadn't… Reed might be…. Trent didn't want to think about what might have happened. Even if he had to go back to jail for a crime he really had committed, he would be okay. He didn't regret shooting Naoko. She was a killer, and she had to be stopped.

"Trent?"

Reed's voice cut through his thoughts. "Yeah?"

"Thanks." The gratitude and relief in Reed's voice was too much, and Trent blinked away tears welling up, stinging his eyes. He looked away so Reed wouldn't see him breaking down. "I love you, Trent."

Trent glanced over and saw tears on Reed's cheeks too.

REED TRIED to find a comfortable position on an uncomfortable chair. It was one of those ugly modern pieces, all sleek blond wood and no cushion. It was also heavy. One wrist was cuffed to a horizontal slat comprising the seat, so he sat with his hand between his thighs. Any other time it might have been humorous. Not tonight.

He watched Trent on the bed, a series of emotions playing out on his face and in his body language. From fear to relief and eventually landing on uncertainty as they waited to find out what was going on. Somehow, Trent seemed to know more than Reed did about what had happened, or at least had some idea how Waseda fit into the whole Naoko-Motofuji picture. Every time he tried to ask, their police guard yelled at them or stood between them, attempting to keep them from speaking to each other.

From the sounds, paramedics had taken Shindo and Naoko away. Police still stomped past their little prison on a regular basis, carrying objects that could only be paintings or other framed items. The guard stepped into the hall and Reed whispered to Trent.

"Doing okay?"

"Now what?" Trent asked.

"They might officially arrest us. But Hammel will sort it out. I don't know how long it will take."

"I feel like we've been arrested already."

"They might be waiting for someone who speaks English to read us our rights."

"They don't do that in Japan." Trent shook his head.

Reed had momentarily forgotten Trent had been through the process before.

The guard glanced into the room and Reed stayed silent. He watched the man straighten his posture and salute, and then he stepped away from the door. In walked Kobayashi and Christopher Hammel.

"Jesus, that took long enough." Reed didn't know what to ask first so he paused, hoping they would get the cuffs off and then start filling him and Trent in.

"Trent, you okay?" Hammel asked. Trent nodded but no one would believe that. "You met Kobayashi?"

"You're Kobayashi? I called you, but…."

"I know. Your call was intercepted by someone else on the team. I'm sorry. Let's get you out of the cuffs and back to the embassy." Kobayashi unlocked Trent's cuffs. Reed was glad they'd started with him. Then Kobayashi stepped toward Reed and stared at his predicament. "I should get a picture of this." He pulled his phone out of his pocket and Reed swore at him with the most useful Japanese Shindo had taught him. Kobayashi laughed and unlocked the cuffs.

Reed leapt up and pulled Trent into a hug. "You okay?" He brushed Trent's hair out of his eyes and slid his hands along Trent's arms and chest, checking for injuries. Trent flinched when Reed touched his left bicep. "What happened?"

"It's nothing. You're the one who needs a doctor." Trent traced a finger along Reed's throat. He'd forgotten his injury, putting the sting out of his thoughts, but now the pain came back.

Hammel rushed up and examined Reed's neck. "Are the medics still here?"

Kobayashi spoke to the guard. "No, gone."

"If we're going back to the embassy, Lt. Driscoll could check us out," Reed said.

"Let's get you out of here before anyone decides they want to take you to HQ," Kobayashi said. "Put your hands together like you're still cuffed when we walk through the house."

Reed glanced around as they walked out, spotting puddles of blood on and near the couch—Waseda's body was gone. It looked like a herd of cattle had stormed through. Police were still bringing wrapped paintings and loading them into an unmarked truck, the operation overseen by a uniformed cop—highly ranked, based on his stripes—and two men Reed recognized from the embassy. He was dying to ask Hammel what they'd found—and about Shindo—but he wouldn't ask about him in front of Trent, or Kobayashi. He might still be trying to maintain his cover.

The ride to the embassy was silent. Reed held Trent's hand in the back of the embassy SUV. No one spoke until they were in Hammel's office. Lt. Driscoll was waiting with her medical bag and cleaned the wound.

"Won't need stitches. Not that deep. But you might have a scar. If you're really concerned, I could put in some tiny stitches."

"No. I'm fine." Reed had so many scars, a little line across his neck was nothing. But she'd never seen his back.

She handed Reed a packet of pain pills and gave Trent a quick exam. "You'll be okay with some rest and a few good meals. Both of you. These will help you sleep." She gave Trent a small pill bottle. "This can help, but it's not enough. Do you want to talk to someone about what happened tonight? You're still in a mild state of shock, and it may get worse. I'm here, or I can find someone else. I know what you've been through and how it will affect you, eventually. Feel free to call me."

She put a hand on Trent's shoulder and looked into his eyes.

"I'm okay right now, but I'll call you later, if I need that."

"Okay." She squeezed his shoulder again and looked at Reed. He nodded; then she left.

Hammel and Kobayashi came in, and Hammel locked the door.

"Where's Beth?" Trent asked before anyone else could speak. "Is she here? Is she okay?"

"She's fine. I called her while you were being examined. She got your message to me, but we didn't get to Waseda's until the excitement was over."

"What's going to happen to Trent?" He was Reed's number one concern.

"You'll need to give a report—Kobayashi can take your statement here—and they'll rule the shooting self-defense. We'll keep both of you here, on American ground. Don't worry."

"What about the Motofuji murder?" Reed wanted to make sure Trent was officially off the hook for that, too.

"There's enough evidence that it was Naoko Maeda. She's in surgery, but she'll live. Hopefully, she'll make a statement and explain the whole sequence of events. But what the authorities have so far is enough to get the charges against Trent dropped. Right, Sam?"

Kobayashi nodded, but didn't add anything.

"Naoko? Not Waseda?" Reed wanted to know the details. "I don't understand."

"Trent, you want to explain?" Hammel smiled.

"Leah, Beth, and I discovered that some pieces were missing from Motofuji's collection. We saw them but they weren't in the police inventory. Only Naoko could have taken them."

"Or the murderer. Why did you suspect her?"

"The missing pieces are exactly the type of pottery she specializes in, but she hardly remarked on them at Motofuji's. She also didn't have an alibi for the time of the murder. She wasn't with Beth at the hotel, so she could have been up at Motofuji's house."

"The cops never questioned the hotel staff about Naoko's movements that night, only Trent and Beth. Turns out Naoko left and came back after Trent. It was on surveillance cameras. The hotel doesn't use magnetic key cards, or they might have discovered her absence sooner," Kobayashi added.

Reed was impressed. Even stuck out in the hot springs resort, Trent hadn't given up working on the case, and his logic was impeccable. "And where does Waseda fit in?"

"Trent…." Hammel glanced at Trent.

Reed looked at Trent again. Trent was smiling, but he had that expression he wore when he didn't want to be the center of attention. "What else did you figure out, Trent?"

"Motofuji gave me the frame for the wood block print. I didn't think anything about it at the time, but Beth didn't want to make room for some pieces of wood in the suitcase. When we looked at it carefully, we found a hidden flash drive. In the frame, which is kind of funny. I don't know if it's the same phrase in Japanese…." He glanced at Kobayashi.

"No, we use a different word, but Motofuji spoke English better than anyone thought."

Trent turned toward Reed. He could see the excitement sparkling in his eyes. "So when we looked at the drive, there were some pictures and a video—"

"Get to the punch line already, Trent!" Reed couldn't wait for Trent to weave a tale. No wonder his books were always so damn long. Reed skimmed the middle when he read them.

"The drive contained images of some paintings. Rembrandt and Vermeer. Nothing I knew by sight or name, but I thought I'd seen one of them at Waseda's the day they arrested me. In his secret room. He left it unlocked." Trent wasn't about to be rushed.

"You're killing me," Reed said.

"And we looked up the paintings, and it turns out they were stolen from the Gardner Museum in Boston. The ones that have been missing since 1990."

"Seriously?" Reed had been one of the dozens of agents who'd put in time on that case over the years. Everyone in the Art Squad had rotated through, hoping fresh eyes would result in fresh leads. And Trent had figured it out?

"I didn't get to see them, but Kobayashi—well, a guy pretending to be you—wanted the flash drive, and he tried to kidnap me and Beth. And then he arrested me when I tried to get back here."

"When did this happen?" Reed had been in another world off with Shindo and Waseda. Out of touch with Trent and Hammel.

"Tonight, or last night. I'm not sure what day it is now." Trent glanced at Hammel.

"Beth and the front gate guard told another official what happened, but I'd gone with the surveillance team following Naoko and didn't get the message in time to get to Trent at Waseda's."

"But I'm still not sure how Waseda and Naoko are connected, and why she killed him." Reed glanced to Kobayashi and Hammel, then Trent.

Trent shrugged.

"We still don't know that. You said she was shouting when she arrived, but no one who understood her has given a statement yet. The police are questioning everyone they found at Waseda's, but it seems most of his guests fled as soon as she showed up, and certainly after they heard sirens," Kobayashi said. "As soon as we hear, we'll let you know."

"The embassy is taking possession of the paintings. They'll be appraised—by someone we can trust—to see if they are the genuine stolen artwork or simply copies. Waseda didn't have everything that was taken, but we may get some new leads, based on Waseda's known associates. He's no stranger to the black market in art," Hammel said.

"This is incredible." Reed had no other words. His brain was overloading on information, and he had so many things to say to Trent. Trent, who had saved his life.

"I think you two should get some rest. There will be a mountain of paperwork tomorrow. It'll be a few days before we have more answers." Hammel stood up.

Reed reached for Trent's hand. He couldn't wait to be alone with him. "Let's go."

"Wait. I want to talk to Beth. She must be worried sick. And I have to thank her for—"

"Tomorrow. Get some rest first."

Trent pulled his hand from Reed's, surprising him. But it made him love Trent even more because he wouldn't rest until he knew his friend was okay. Trent was a good person. Reed could wait.

But Beth was sitting in the anteroom when Trent opened the door. She threw her arms around him. "Are you okay? I heard Waseda is dead. You look okay, but…."

Trent hugged Beth close, almost picking her up so her toes nearly left the floor. "I'm okay. Just tired, and kind of dizzy."

"Go to sleep. It can wait. I wanted to make sure you were okay. I was so afraid because I couldn't find Christopher right away." She hung on tightly.

"Okay. We'll call you in the morning."

Beth let go of Trent and turned to Reed. She squeezed him half to death too.

Hammel was still in his office, making notes on a pad. Reed stepped a few feet inside. “How’s Shindo?” He wished he’d asked sooner.

“In the hospital. Had some internal damage, lost plenty of blood, but he’ll pull through.”

Relief flooded through Reed’s body. He remembered Trent trying to stop the bleeding, even after finding him and Shindo together at that crazy party. “I didn’t want to ask in front of Kobayashi….”

“Or Trent?” Hammel was awfully perceptive. “Kobayashi doesn’t know him by name, even though he knows he’s out there, but probably a good call.”

“Do you think I could visit him? Is he still undercover?”

“I’ll see what I can do. I’m not sure how Interpol is handling his cover. Your statements tomorrow will help make that decision.”

“Okay.” Reed walked out. Beth and Trent stood silently, arms around each other again.

Trent turned and locked gazes with Reed. *What had he heard, and what did he know?* Reed would have to discuss the topic. Tomorrow.

23

BACK IN Reed's room at the embassy, they undressed and climbed into bed. Reed switched off the lamp and realized Trent was asleep before he had a chance to say—or do—anything to him. That was good. Sleep would help. Reed popped one of the pills from the nurse too. He rarely took meds, but he knew Trent would need him tomorrow, and he had to get enough sleep to be there when Trent did crash. Naoko hadn't died, but when the adrenaline and shock wore off Trent would feel guilt over what he'd done. Retelling the events for the reports would likely trigger something. Trent's course at Quantico hadn't covered this aspect. There would be nightmares and self-doubt and possibly depression or PTSD. Reed would watch for the signs and help Trent.

ANSWERING QUESTIONS took up most of the following day. They had to give statements to the embassy staff, FBI, Japanese authorities, Interpol, and CIA. Trent and Reed were questioned separately with breaks for lunch and time to catch their breath between sessions. Reed had more questions to answer, since he was with the Bureau, even if his presence was semiofficial here. He also had to speak with White, who was back in LA and not happy with Reed jumping into a Japanese-Interpol operation.

When he'd finished pulling White's shoe out of his ass, he found Trent sitting outside of Hammel's office.

"You finished now?" Trent asked. He looked as exhausted as Reed felt.

"Yeah. It's almost dinnertime. You hungry yet?"

"No."

Reed frowned. Trent was always hungry. This wasn't a good sign. "Want to talk? To me or the LT? Someone else?"

"No. I'm okay." Trent's tone was unconvincing. Reed didn't know what to do or say.

"Hammel said you're cleared of all charges. Nothing to worry about. We can go home whenever you want."

"You should go see him."

Reed didn't need to ask who Trent meant. He looked at his shoes. Why did he feel this ache in his gut when he thought about Shindo? And why had he avoided mentioning him to Trent? "I don't know."

"Hammel says he's awake. Go visit him. I'll hang with Beth. It's okay." Trent grinned, but Reed knew it wasn't a real smile. It was the same smile Trent gave when he said good-bye to Reed at the airport when he left on a mission. Like he might never see Reed again, and he'd resigned himself to massive disappointment. Reed's throat closed up, and he waited for it to loosen before he tried to breathe again. Finally, it did, but the oppressive weight on his chest didn't go away.

"I want to see how he's doing," Reed said. It was the truth. "I would like to go see him."

"GOOD." TRENT was glad Reed had been honest. If Reed pretended not to want to see Shindo, Trent would always wonder. But he had to let Reed go. He had no idea what sort of bond had formed between them, but until Reed let it go—or let Trent go—it would never be resolved. "We can eat later."

"Come with me. You should meet him. I know he'd want to meet you." Reed held his hand out to Trent.

"Meet me?" Trent remained seated. "He knows about me?"

Reed nodded and sat down next to Trent. "He knows all about… us."

"Really?" The darkness floating around Trent's heart began to float away. Why had he imagined the worst? It wasn't as bad as that. He wouldn't lose Reed to Shindo. But Reed's emotions were still hard to discern. There was something between them, but he'd leave it. Maybe Reed would bring it up. If not, Trent could always ask. Later.

They took a taxi to the hospital, though it wasn't far from the embassy. Shindo's room wasn't guarded, which meant he must still be undercover. Only cops or people in custody had guards on hospital rooms.

Shindo looked pale, his long silky hair spread out on the pillow. Trent waited in the doorway as Reed went into the room and watched Shindo's face light up when he saw Reed. Reed picked up Shindo's hand and squeezed it. For much longer than Trent expected. Reed sat at the edge of the bed for a moment, and then Shindo glanced toward Trent at the door. Reed waved him in and pulled up two chairs near the bed.

"Trent! I hear you're the hero. Saved both our lives." Shindo grinned, showing off even white teeth. His eyes crinkled up and Trent couldn't help staring at him.

"Not really. I'm glad you're okay. I didn't really know what to do."

"Well, it was the right thing, apparently."

Trent hadn't really looked at Shindo close up until now. He had smooth skin and high cheekbones. Even under the crisscross of bandages on his torso, it was clear he had a nice body. But it was his lips that Trent couldn't stop staring at. He knew Shindo had kissed Reed with those lips, full and perfect. Trent drew his tongue across his own bottom lip. Was it as plump and attractive as Shindo's?

Reed hadn't kissed him—not on the mouth—since they'd been in Izu. They hadn't kissed the night before or that morning. Wasn't Trent good enough for Reed anymore?

"Trent?"

"What?" He'd missed whatever Reed had been saying.

"Oh, Trent, you should have seen Reed pretending to like the ladies at the host club. Kissing their hands and pouring drinks."

"Host club?" What was that?

Shindo explained briefly, and Trent couldn't help laughing at the idea of Reed playing a ladies' man in order to attract a yakuza boss into falling for him. It was a ridiculous plan to get into Waseda's house. But Trent understood Reed had done it for him. And that made all the difference, didn't it? He hadn't gone looking for Shindo, or chosen Shindo. He'd only used him as part of the plan.

It sounded so much better that way.

24

BETH FLEW home the next day. Her agent had arranged a meeting with a small-time producer who needed someone to adapt a book into a screenplay. It was the kind of thing Beth did well, and it might get her noticed for future work. She insisted Trent and Reed shouldn't go with her to the airport, and the embassy car drove her.

"Did you hear anything about the paintings, yet?" Trent asked Reed. They were at a sushi bar touted as the best in Tokyo, according to Christopher Hammel.

Reed shook his head. "They need to be examined and authenticated. It's going to take time, especially because the Japanese and US governments are arguing over jurisdictional issues." Reed took a bite of fish. "This is the freshest sashimi I've ever eaten. It just melts in your mouth."

Trent nodded and picked at his food. He wished he could enjoy it, but he had no appetite.

"There will be a reward if even one of the paintings is genuine. Even if they're forgeries, finding the artist will be a lead and we may find them yet. Either way, you're looking at some reward money."

"Beth gets half," Trent said to his plate. He was tired of Reed staring at him, waiting for him to implode or melt down.

"You have some incredible luck."

"Luck?" Trent hadn't been lucky, either here or in Thailand, and the reward money wouldn't erase the harrowing memories.

"That wasn't the right word. I hunt these things down for a living and you manage to stumble across them on a regular basis."

"Stumble?" Trent almost laughed. He managed a smile and noticed Reed finally smiling too. "I connected a lot of dots." Following the trail had put him in danger. Maybe he did deserve a reward. He picked up a piece of *o-toro* and popped it into his mouth. It was incredible. He'd had fish practically off the boat in Izu, but this came a close second. He finished his portion and reached for some of Reed's.

Reed grasped Trent's hand across the table and squeezed. "Where do you want to stop on the way home? Anywhere you want. I've got a free pass for two from the Bureau and a week's leave." Reed still used military words for everything: leave, missions, duty.

"Nowhere. Just home." Trent needed to get out of Japan. Back home they would just be themselves again. While they were here, the whole last week hung over every thought and movement. They'd gotten their own room at a hotel, but Trent still felt like they were under the microscope. And they had barely touched each other since the events at Waseda's.

"How about Hong Kong? They have great shopping. You can get some clothes handmade. A nice suit? Some pretty silk shirts?" Reed put his hand over Trent's and squeezed.

Trent remembered Reed and Shindo wearing suits at Waseda's party. They looked good in suits. He remembered them undressing each other. He also remembered Waseda's gun pointing at them, but somehow it always faded away in favor of Shindo's mouth on Reed's body. "No suits. I never need a suit."

"You'd look good in one. We should go somewhere we need to dress up."

"Maybe."

"Or Hawaii? A few days on a beach like powdered sugar? Surfing? Scuba diving?"

"I don't dive."

"Snorkeling, or you could do a diving course. Would you like that?"

"Okay." Trent wished he could snap out of this funk. He read some ulterior meaning into everything Reed said. He knew Reed wanted to cheer him up. He wasn't ready for cheer just yet.

"How about if I surprise you?"

"Okay."

BACK IN their room, Reed reached for Trent when they'd settled into bed. He kissed Trent's neck, then his jaw, but Trent rolled away. They hadn't kissed or made love, but not because Reed hadn't wanted to. Trent wasn't ready. Reed slipped up behind him, not pressing against his back, but close enough to stroke his shoulder and back. Reed had tried not to push Trent, but something was very wrong here.

"Trent? Maybe we should talk."

"Okay."

Trent said okay to everything lately. He never did that. He always had an opinion, about everything. Even when he agreed with Reed, he still had something to say.

"You thinking about Naoko?" Reed decided to start here. Trent hadn't broken down yet, probably because he was still hung up on something to do with Shindo. Reed wasn't ready to go there because, frankly, he was still a little hung up on Shindo. He'd wait until he figured it out.

"Not really."

"Well, I've been thinking about her. It's all so confusing, don't you think?"

Trent rolled over to face Reed. "No. I can't figure out why she killed Motofuji, but all the evidence points to her. Didn't she confess?"

"Yes, but I can't understand why she'd work for Waseda when she didn't have to."

"Her father worked for him, and I guess she felt some loyalty, or he had something else on her. But maybe she just did it because she wanted expensive art pieces she could never buy."

Reed nodded. He knew this, but he wanted to get Trent talking, working through motivations and consequences. "But murder?"

"Waseda knew Motofuji had the flash drive, and he needed to get it back or risk Motofuji blackmailing him to take over part of his empire. He also benefited if Motofuji was dead. So he told her to get the drive and keep whatever she wanted from Motofuji's collection. It makes sense. I don't think she had to kill Motofuji, though."

"But he'd already given you the flash drive, so she killed him for not telling her where it was or because he was still a threat to Waseda. You're lucky Motofuji didn't crack, or she could have killed you, Trent."

"I hadn't thought of that. She's going to spend the rest of her life in jail. And she lost her arm." Trent's voice went low and soft on that last sentence.

"Does that bother you?" Reed hadn't yet asked the question so directly. He waited, afraid to breathe until he knew if he'd pushed Trent too far. It had to happen eventually.

Trent didn't answer right away. He focused his gaze on something behind Reed. "Not really. I didn't like shooting her, but she'd just killed a guy, and I didn't want you to be next. She slashed up Shindo, too. Plus she'd tortured Motofuji." He paused. "No, I don't feel bad for saving your life." Trent's voice was steady, unwavering. He rolled over again.

Reed stared at Trent's back as a chill swept over his body. Maybe Trent truly felt no guilt, and he wouldn't have nightmares or a breakdown. Trent was strong, confident. But he wasn't the same man Reed had fallen in love with. He was harder, tougher. Reed had shot and killed people for less than Naoko had done. He wouldn't think twice about it before or after. Was Trent simply being rational, or had he turned into someone else?

The possibility frightened Reed. It was his fault Trent was in that situation.

But there was hope that Trent hadn't lost his softer, sweeter side. He was still hurt over Shindo. He still had normal emotions and feelings.

Reed had to content himself with that for the time being.

THE NEXT morning they left for the airport. Trent didn't even ask where they were going. Reed hoped he'd made the right decision on his choice of stopovers. They'd spend a few days before continuing on to LA. If Trent wanted to stay in the hotel, Reed could explore on his own.

Reed had the tickets and Trent followed him to check-in and security. He deliberately sat at a different gate so Trent wouldn't see their destination. But Trent had his face in a Japanese men's fashion magazine and barely spoke as they waited to board. Reed would have been happy to see him thinking about clothes, but Trent flipped pages without really seeing anything.

Their flight was called, and Reed put his arm through Trent's as they walked to the next gate.

"Air France flight 275 for Paris, boarding now" was announced in English, following a Japanese announcement.

“Paris? We’re going to Paris? That’s not on the way to LA.”

“Who cares. It’s springtime. It’s going to be beautiful.”

“Paris? Really?” Trent actually smiled. “And romantic.”

“Yes, it’s romantic. That’s why I picked it.” Reed watched Trent’s face for any emotion.

“Thank you, Reed.” Trent wrapped his arms around Reed until the woman behind them—French, not Japanese—started coughing and clearing her throat.

“Sorry,” Reed said, and they handed their boarding passes in and walked toward the plane.

TRENT SLEPT for part of the journey, thanks to a few glasses of Champagne after departure. Reed could get used to Executive class, but it was best not to. They’d have some great food and wine in Paris, and he had at least two weeks off when they got home.

They checked into their hotel, midpriced but still luxurious enough to please Trent, and wandered down the street to find a bistro for dinner. It was cool and just beginning to get dark. Ahead of them, the Eiffel Tower’s lights glittered in the twilight. After a fine meal, Reed suggested a jazz bar or a stroll through the gardens near the Louvre.

“I’m tired. It’s been a long day, with the flight. Tomorrow night?” Trent said. He’d been almost himself at dinner, not quite as chatty, but not as dark as he’d been in Tokyo. It was a definite improvement.

“Sure. Maybe a little walk around the neighborhood before the hotel?”

“Okay.”

This time Trent didn’t sound like a Stepford wife. Reed let out a small sigh of relief.

“LOOK AT this view, Trent.” Reed was on the balcony, which had a spectacular view of the Eiffel Tower with the whole of Paris spread out in between.

“It’s beautiful.”

“So are you.” Reed pulled Trent close and pushed his hair back over one ear.

"Am I?"

Reed planted a soft kiss on Trent's lips. "Of course. You know I think so. Don't I tell you enough?"

"I guess you could always say things like that more." Trent smiled. He didn't pull away this time. "But…."

"But what? Trent, you have to tell me what's wrong. I've been patient, but at least talk to me."

Trent chewed on his bottom lip and wouldn't meet Reed's gaze.

Reed put hand on Trent's upper arms. "Trent?"

"I wonder if you're thinking of him. Of Shindo."

"Why would you wonder that?" Reed needed to know. He *had* thought of Shindo, but it had nothing to do with Trent.

"He's so beautiful. Silky hair and beautiful eyes. His lips…."

Reed didn't know what to say.

"You're attracted to him, aren't you? I saw you two together."

"That guy had a gun on us, Trent. We did what he wanted until he fell asleep."

"I saw the gun. But you looked so comfortable, so good together. Like there was no gun. Like you enjoyed it."

"I did enjoy it. I liked kissing him and touching his hair. Are you happy?" Reed hated himself for saying it, but he'd been lying to himself about it, too. He couldn't move forward until he told the truth.

"Do you want to be with him instead of me?"

"Of course not, Trent. I love you. I've made a life with you that works, most of the time. And I wouldn't throw that away, or give you up, for a few kisses. We played a role for a job. Sometimes it goes farther than we expect, but all we did was kiss. But we'd never have even touched if it hadn't been for the role. To help you."

"I forgot that part." Trent looked away. "I'm sorry. I was worried because you seemed so attracted to him."

"Haven't you seen someone else you're attracted to? I can't be the only guy in the world who turns you on. Young Pierce Brosnan? Matt Bomer? The guy at the gym with the tattoo on his—"

"Okay, I get your point. Yes, I'm attracted to other guys."

"And what if one of them wanted to fool around. Would you?"

"Of course not."

"What if you had to kiss one of them to help me out? Would you kiss him and undress him? To help me?"

"Undress?" Trent grinned. "Could it be Matt?"

"Yes. You have my permission to fool around with Matt Bomer to help me out."

"When you put it that way, maybe I overreacted a little."

"It's okay to have a reaction. Just let's talk about it so I don't have to try and figure out what you're thinking."

"Reed, I think you just turned into a character in one of my books. Wanting me to talk about my feelings."

"Oh, fuck." Reed laughed for the first time in weeks. He pulled Trent in close and this time they kissed for a very long time. Reed slid his hands under Trent's shirt and felt the muscles flow under the smooth skin. Trent slipped off Reed's jacket and unbuttoned his shirt, kissing along the line where Naoko had broken the skin. Trent's lips felt perfect. His kisses left trails of fire, and when Trent undid his belt and slipped his hand into Reed's pants, Reed pushed Trent's back against the balcony door and pressed his thigh against his body.

"Reed, let's go inside."

"Good idea!" Reed turned to see someone on the next balcony, an older woman and her husband.

"Oh, sorry." Reed tugged Trent's hand, and they fell into bed laughing.

"I'm not," Trent said. Then he peeled away the rest of Reed's clothes and his own.

"Aren't you brazen tonight. You're full of surprises. I like it. Keep going."

Trent looked away with an impish grin on his face. "I have to confess something to you."

"You can confess anything you want to me right now," Reed said. Trent had one hand on Reed's cock and leaned down to suck at a nipple until Reed worried he might come in Trent's hand.

"I see why you were attracted to Shindo." Another hard suck. Reed shuddered. "Because before I realized it was you, I watched from the room across the courtyard. I would have kept watching if I hadn't recognized you. Because I thought the two of you together were really, really hot." Trent's voice was low and sounded like silk. Had he meant that? Listening to him say it had been pretty fucking hot too.

Trent applied his mouth once again to Reed's nipple. The heat in his core radiated and intensified, and he shuddered before relinquishing all control and letting himself come, riding the waves as Trent squeezed his shaft, prolonging the pleasure. Trent knew just what Reed liked. Shindo's touch, his kiss, had been exciting and taboo, but Trent was all Reed wanted or needed.

He shifted so he lay next to Trent and kissed him long and deep, floating on a cloud of familiar taste and scent and touch. Trent's arms tightened around him and Trent's cock—big enough to frighten most Japanese—pressed insistently along his abs.

"Thank you."

"For what?"

"For admitting watching me with Shindo was hot." Reed hoped he hadn't misunderstood Trent's remark.

"It's nothing compared to watching me with Matt."

"Am I supposed to want to watch?"

"Of course."

"I suppose that would be pretty hot."

"I guess I'm not the only one who's a little jaded." Trent grinned, then rolled Reed onto his stomach and reached for the lube on the night table.

Reed decided he could get used to this new version of Trent after all.

PRECIOUS GEMS: BOOK ONE

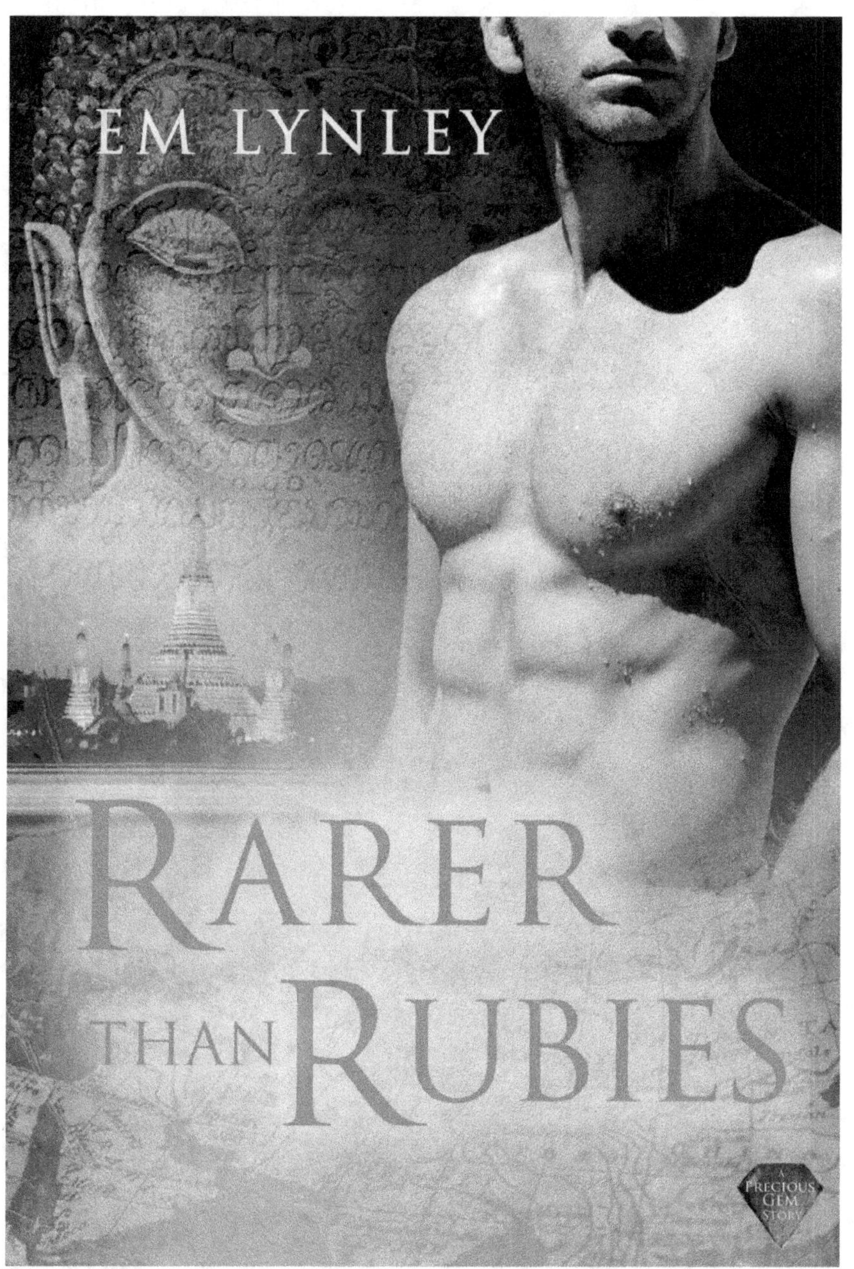

http://www.dreamspinnerpress.com

PRECIOUS GEMS: BOOK TWO

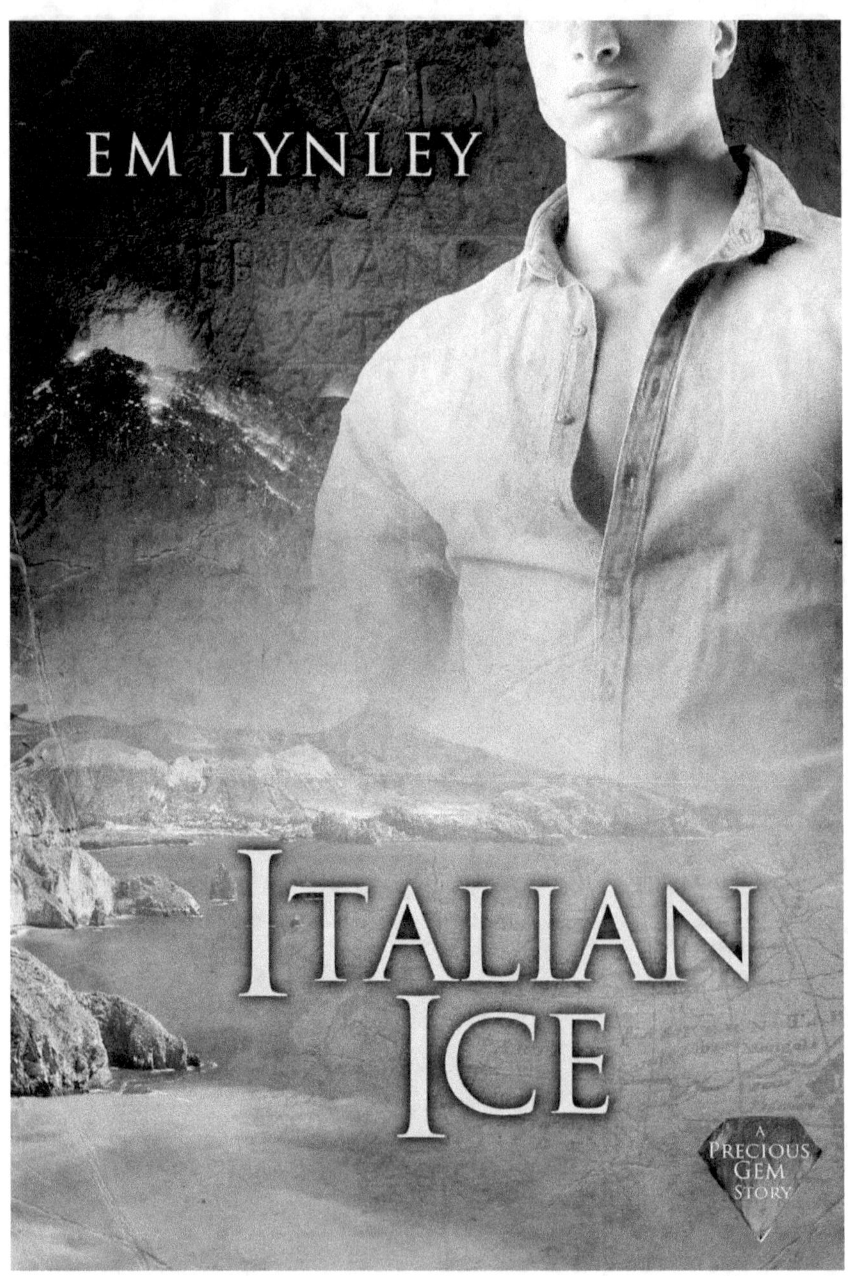

http://www.dreamspinnerpress.com

EM LYNLEY has worked finance, the wine industry, and high-tech, though she'd rather be writing hot man-on-man romance. She spent ten years as an economist and financial analyst, including a year as a White House Staff Economist, but only because all the intern positions were filled. Tired of boring herself and others with dry business reports and articles, her creative muse is back and naughtier than ever. She has lived and worked in London, Tokyo, and Washington, DC, but the San Francisco Bay Area is home for now.

Visit her website at http://www.emlynley.com,
her blog at http://emlynley.livejournal.com,
her Twitter page at http://twitter.com/emlynley,
and her Facebook at http://www.facebook.com/emlynley.

Also by EM Lynley

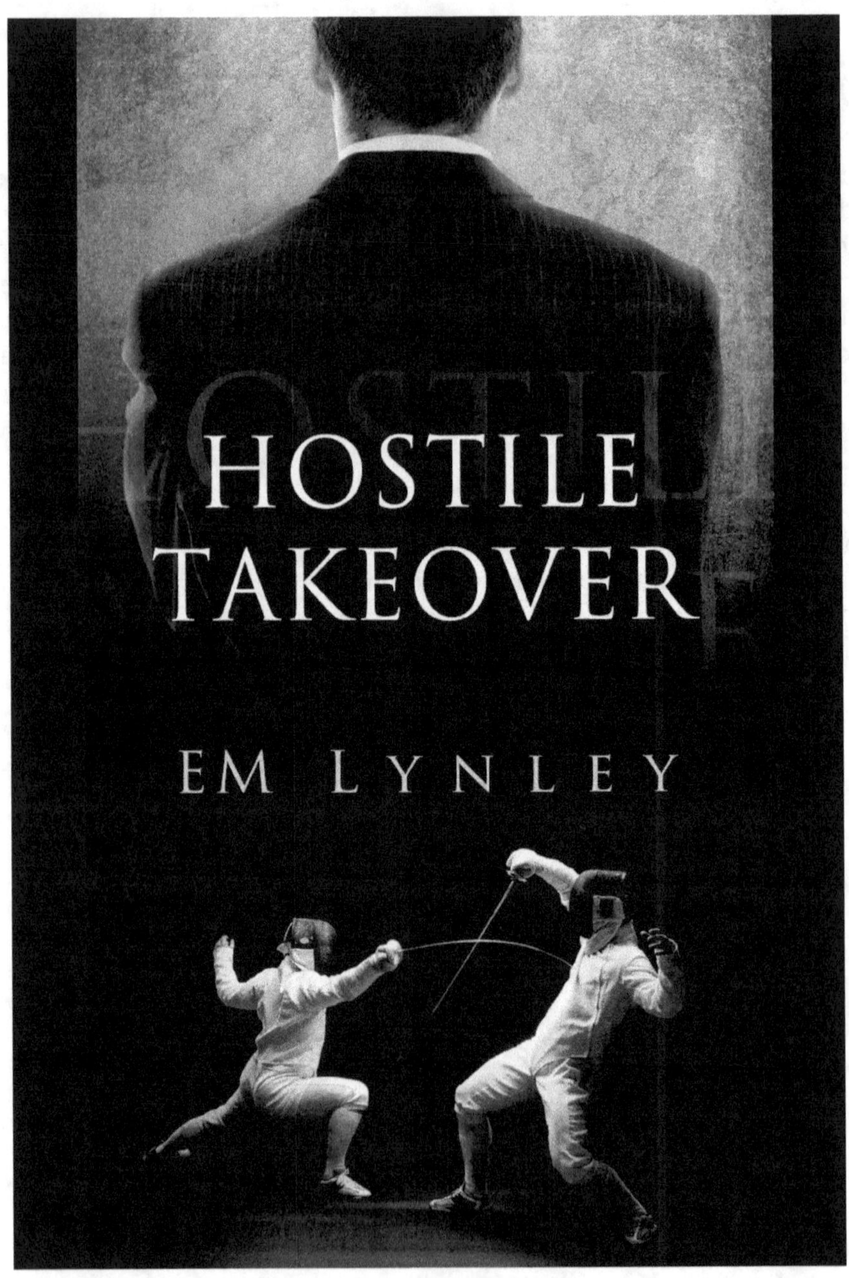

Also by EM LYNLEY

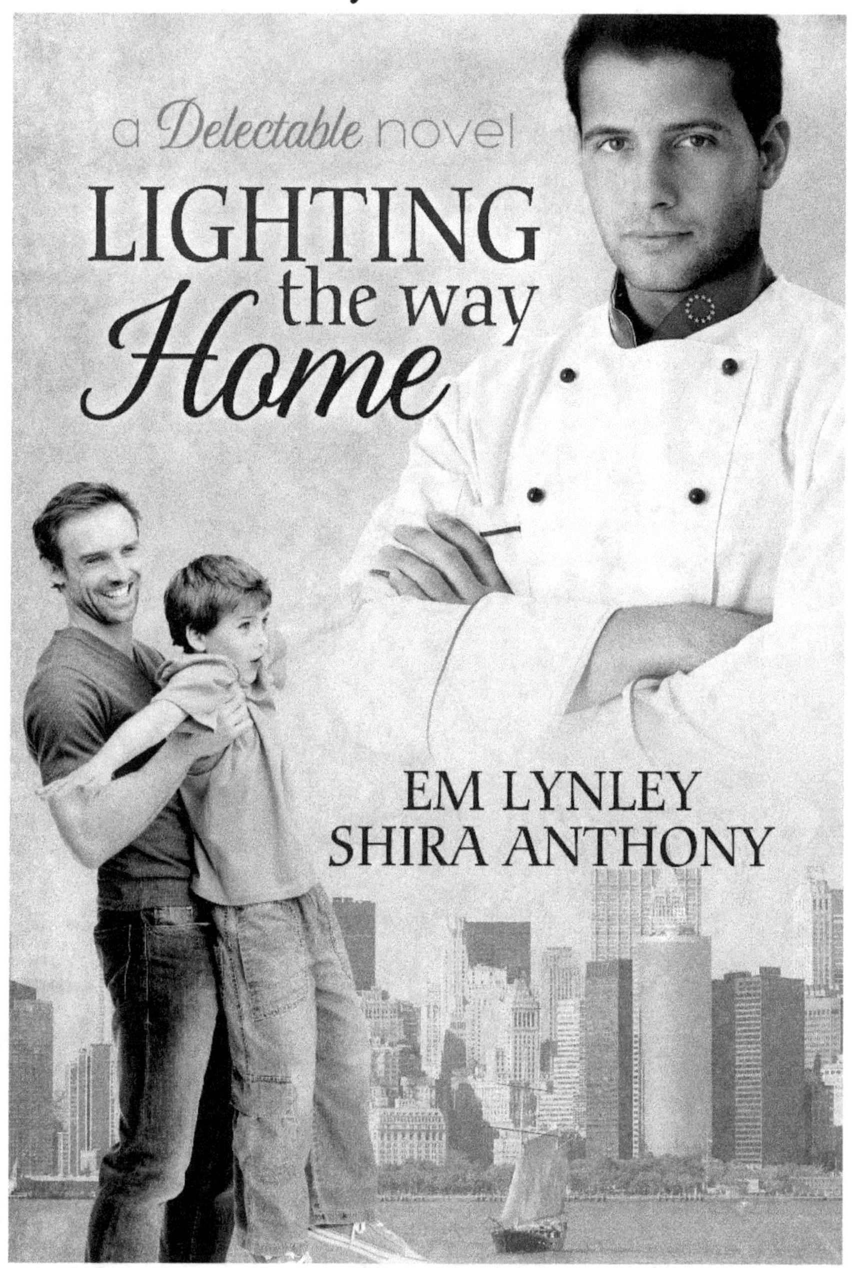

http://www.dreamspinnerpress.com

Also by EM LYNLEY

http://www.dreamspinnerpress.com

Also by EM LYNLEY

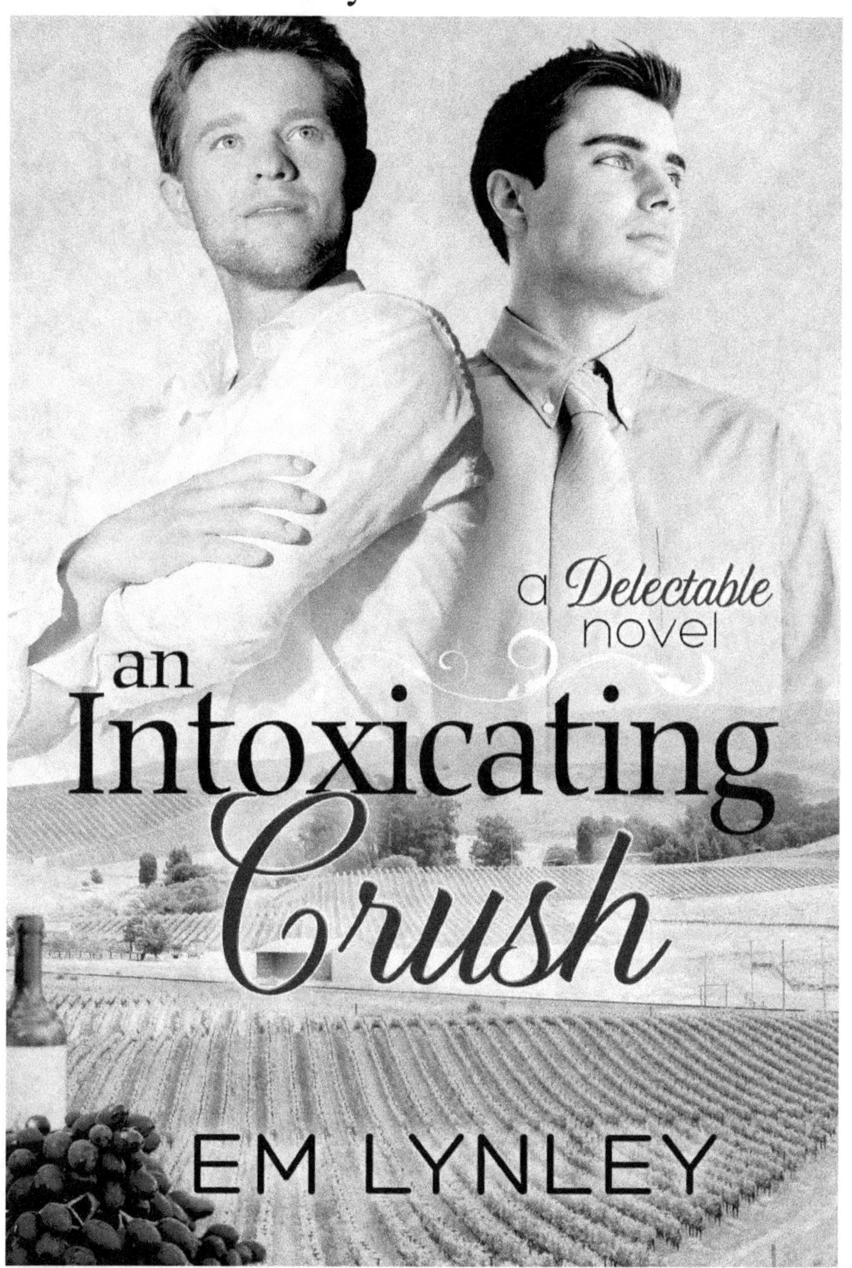

http://www.dreamspinnerpress.com

Also by EM LYNLEY

http://www.dreamspinnerpress.com

Also by DREAMSPINNER PRESS

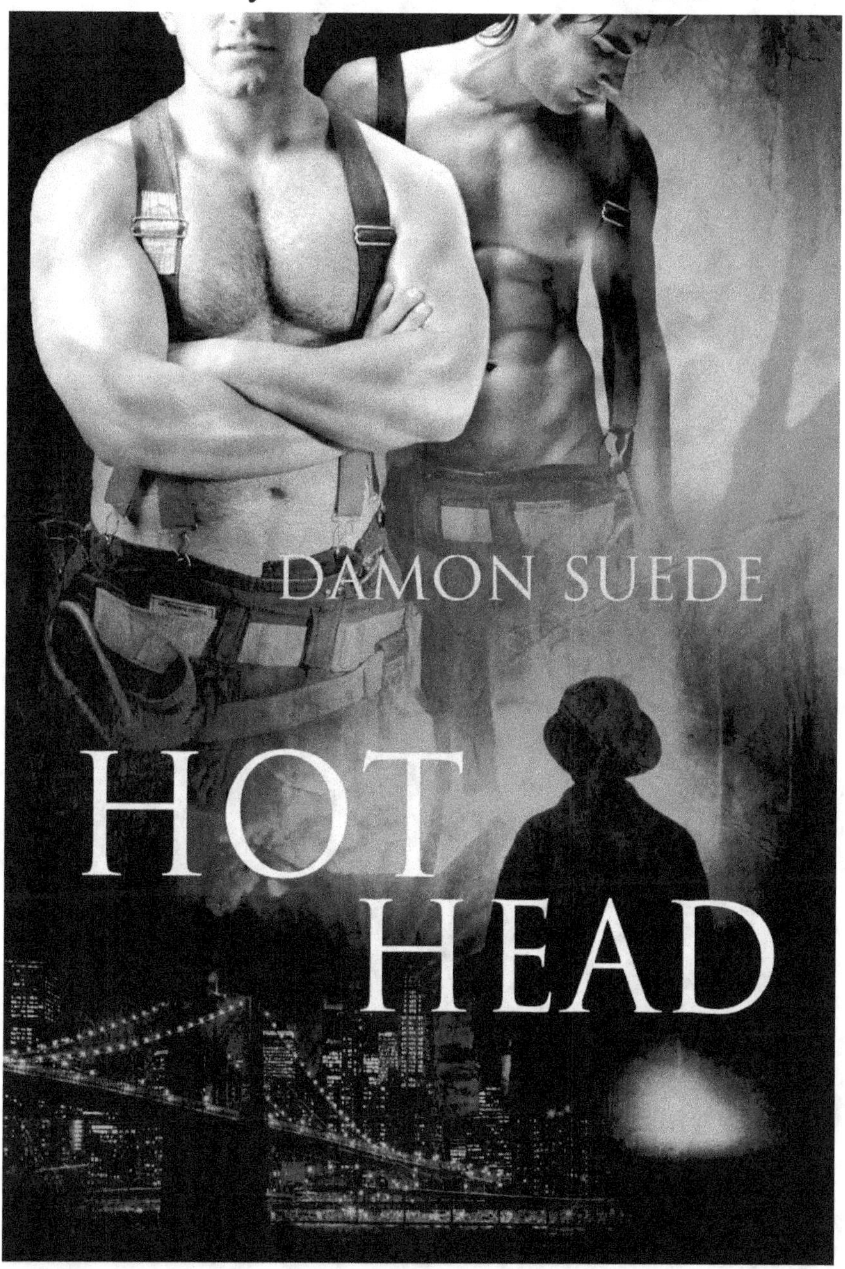

http://www.dreamspinnerpress.com

Also by DREAMSPINNER PRESS

http://www.dreamspinnerpress.com

Dreamspinner Press
For more of the best M/M romance, visit
Dreamspinner Press
www.dreamspinnerpress.com

www.ingramcontent.com/pod-product-compliance
Lightning Source LLC
Chambersburg PA
CBHW051638260626
47170CB00004B/1224

9781627982023